GIRL SEVEN

HANNA JAMESON published her first novel, *Something You Are*, when she was just twenty-one. It was nominated for a CWA Dagger. She has lived in Australia, travelled Europe, Japan and the USA with bands such as the Manic Street Preachers and Kasabian, and worked for three years in the NHS. She is currently studying American History & Literature at the University of Sussex.

HANNA JAMESON

GIRL SEVEN

HEAD
of ZEUS

First published in the UK in 2014 by Head of Zeus Ltd.

Copyright © Hanna Jameson, 2014

9 7 5 3 1 2 4 6 8

A CIP catalogue record for this book is available
from the British Library.

ISBN (HB) 9781781851449
ISBN (TPB) 9781781851432
ISBN (E) 9781781851463

Printed in Germany.

Head of Zeus Ltd
Clerkenwell House
45–47 Clerkenwell Green
London EC1R 0HT

WWW.HEADOFZEUS.COM

GIRL SEVEN

Because once you've got one scar on your face or your heart, it's only a matter of time before someone gives you another – and another – until a day doesn't go by when you aren't being bashed senseless, nor a town that you haven't been run out of, and you get to be such a goddamn mess that finally it doesn't feel right unless you're getting the Christ beaten out of you – and within a year of that first damning fall, those first down-borne fists, your first run-out, you wind up with flies buzzing around your eyes, back at the same place, the same town, deader than when you left, bobbing around in the swill – a dirty deadbeat whore in a roadside ditch. But a little part of you doesn't die. A little part of you lives on. And you make an orphan of that corrupt and contemptible part, dumping it right smack in the lap of the ones who first robbed you of your sweetness, for it is the wicked fruit of their crimes, it is their blood, their sin, it belongs there, this child of blood, this spawn of sin. . .

Nick Cave, *And the Ass Saw the Angel*

Prologue

I could almost see my block of flats from his window, less than two streets away.

Outside the grey cloud melted into grey buildings. Inside I was wrapped in grey sheets with my legs wrapped around Jensen McNamara's head. I couldn't stand him, but he was passably attractive and there was nothing else to do. Everyone here was fucking, being fucked over, getting fucked, on drink, on drugs, on a daily basis.

He was a talker, that was for sure.

'I fucking knew you wanted it. . . You know, right from that moment you were scaring those kids away and you caught my eyes through the window and you knew I was watching you but you didn't find it weird, did you? Most girls would find it weird, get scared by a guy looking at them like that, but not you. . .'

When a guy has his tongue between your legs there's really only one acceptable response.

'Mm.'

It could almost be mistaken for pleasure and I thought I'd heard the end of it. What the fuck else did he expect me to say?

'Go on, talk dirty to me!' he said.

I wondered if I could gag him. It could always be passed off as erotic.

'Talk dirty to me, go on, I bet you can. I bet you can be a right nasty little bitch. . .'

It was funny listening to him for a while but I lost heart not long after that. Even my naturally tanned skin was starting to look grey, like the walls. Everything looked as though it might have been white once, before the flecks of dirt started spreading. I looked down and saw white streaks where some bodily fluid had cut through the grime on the inside of my right thigh.

I couldn't do this, not again, not now, not with this fucking running commentary. . .

'You can stop now,' I said to the ceiling.

'What, babe?'

'I said you can stop now, it's fine.' I swung my legs away from him and over the side of the bed, pulling down the edges of my skirt. 'I'm not in the mood actually.'

'What. . . babe?'

I gave him an exasperated look and stood up.

His hurt pride followed me all the way downstairs and through the doors into the humid air hanging over the estate outside. I walked back towards my tower block with my shoulders hunched and head up. Constantly dodging missiles thrown from the roof taught you to walk with your eyes to the sky.

I'd told my family I'd be back by now. I felt some mild guilt that I hadn't said goodbye to any of them, hadn't looked at whatever my little sister had wanted me to look at as I'd left. . . But then, she was five. How interesting was anything a five-year-old wanted to show you going to be anyway? It was hardly going to be salacious gossip about other people in the building or classified government documents.

I entered the stairwell and broken syringes crunched under my feet. No one touched the handrails now. Too many people had gripped it only to catch their hands on concealed needles.

A gang of kids passed me on the way down, reeking of something faecal.

'Oi, Jap, you got any fags?'

I was half Japanese and half English and couldn't be mistaken for either nationality, but the nickname had caught on months ago.

'No.' I didn't make eye contact.

'Think there's been a fight upstairs, a big one.'

I looked around at them, eyes narrowed. There were three of them, bony and feral with a spattering of red marks down their arms. Even though they only looked thirteen I was barely taller than them.

'Yeah?' I raised my eyebrows.

They shifted.

'Couple of blokes went up, big geezers, like. They had blades like this,' said the eldest, holding his hands in the air a foot apart. 'I thought they were the filth for a second but then there was banging and shouting and all sorts. Someone's got carved up big time. Look.'

The kid pointed and I followed his finger to the blood on the floor. It wasn't an unusual sight. It was fresh though; wet enough to catch the light.

My mind was with my parents and my sister as I carried on up the stairs.

'I wouldn't go up there. There might still be someone waiting.'

Nausea clouded my head, like I already knew.

I ignored them, avoiding the blood on the floor, trying not to think of the blood on the floor and my parents and my sister and *blades like this*. . .

Fifth floor and I stopped.

I didn't want to go further.

I could see my front door, in pieces.

The bile rising in my throat and all I could think of was my parents and my sister and the blood and *blades like this*.

I could have turned around then, called for help downstairs and spared myself, but I didn't. My heart pounded into the silence, thumping on the inside of my skull as I moved forwards to ease myself through the wreckage of the door.

More blood on the carpet and my entire body shook.

Blood on the walls blurred as my eyes filled with tears.

I smelt copper and my eyes refocused on an arm, on the floor, an arm and a body, red matted hair and a five-year-old skull cleaved in two.

Bile hit the carpet with the blood: mine. My knees gave way; choking and shaking, hands over my eyes so hard that my cheekbones bruised but I could still see it, still see it and I would never stop seeing it.

I was out of the flat, scrabbling backwards through the blood as it covered my legs. There was blood on my hands, my hands over my eyes and blood on my face. On my feet, hanging on to the wall, on to the banister, forgetting the needles, and then down the stairs, so fast I was barely touching them. . .

I crashed through the doors on the bottom floor, back out on to the warm concrete. The three kids I had seen on the stairs were loitering, eyes wide and poised to run.

'You!' I pointed with a bloodied hand.

They ran.

I ran.

I was faster.

The nearest boy choked as I yanked him backwards by the hood of his jacket, hitting the tarmac with a strangled yelp and a dry slap before I dragged him up and threw him into the wall.

'YOU SAW THEM!'

He was thrashing, kicking, almost hanging in mid-air with my hands too tight around his throat.

'YOU SAW THEM! YOU FUCKING SAW THEM!'

He was screaming, almost louder than me.

The other kids hung back, terrified. 'Fucking leave him alone! Leave off, what're you doing?'

I punched him, just to stop the noise, just because he was there. All I could see was the blood, and the arm, and the red matted hair and the five-year-old skull cleaved in two.

I let him go and he sank to the ground, cowering and holding his nose, red outlines around his throat and blood trickling through his fingers. The two other kids came forwards, slinking past me to pick him up and pull him away out of harm's reach.

'Crazy bitch. . .'

None of the blood was my own. It was all from my flat, my carpet, my parents and the five-year-old skull cleaved in two. I caught my reflection in a parked red Peugeot and couldn't recognize it.

Behind me was grey brick and in front of me blinding sky.

I could hear one of the kids on a phone, calling someone. Their voices were a meaningless hum in my ears, ringing with screams and later with sirens. I wanted it to stop, this relentless sound. I wanted to back into a corner and drown in silence.

The blood was still wet.

I didn't go back in, but when the police cars arrived it still hadn't dried. I sat on the kerb ignoring their questions, trying not to remember, trying to unsee it, but the blood was still on my hands, on my face, on my bare legs, and it wasn't mine.

I had been less than two streets away and the blood was still wet.

Chapter One

Almost three years later and it didn't feel as though that much had changed. Not really. Everyone was still being fucked. It was just in a slightly nicer and more expensive setting. The Underground club was a place that seemed to form itself around me, like a demanding and dysfunctional family that kept my thoughts and actions occupied day to day, night to night.

I was drifting back and forth across the club floor, ferrying drinks in the dark purple light, when one of the Irish girls stopped me. Onstage behind us, another girl was singing in French. Even after a year of working here I still didn't register many names or personalities; they all looked the same to me, sounded the same, apart from their various nationalities.

But I hadn't started working here to make friends.

'Mark Chester wants you serving his table tonight,' Irish said, winking at me. She winked all the time, to the point where I'd started to think she had a Tourette's-like condition.

I scanned the club, recognizing the name but not a face. 'What, he asked for me? Why?'

'He probably asked Noel for a rec. He doesn't play for our team, if you know what I mean, but he likes to talk. I'm well jealous actually; he's so clever and intellectual, like, you're going to have such a good night!'

'So, Noel recommended me for my conversation? Right.' I could barely contain my sarcasm. 'Which one is he?'

'He's the tall hot one over there. Looks like a model, but a kinda weird one. . . That one!'

Irish put her cocktails on a tray and pushed her mermaid-like blonde hair behind her shoulders. Her name might have been Elise, but I didn't have a clue really. 'He'll either have whiskey or gin and tonic usually. Go ask him.'

She slapped me on the ass as she left.

I ducked into the dressing room behind the stage for a moment to check my outfit. Even if Mark Chester was gay, my primary function here was to be ornamental. My outfit was a black and white bandage-style playsuit and heels; there wasn't enough of it to risk falling into disarray. My eyeliner was a little smudged around my heavily lidded eyes. All make-up looked awkward on me. My features were too large and exaggerated for such a tiny face and my plain black hair had never been long enough to sweep back like Irish.

Plain, as Mum had always said. But men had always liked it. Go figure.

I wondered exactly how my employer and manager, Noel Braben, had come to recommend me. It was common knowledge that he had hired me for his own personal preferences and not for any of my attributes as an employee. It was a running joke of his that for someone working in customer service I was one of the most caustic people he had ever met.

I left the dressing room and its suffocating cloud of perfumes and made my way over to Mark Chester's table, where he was sitting with two other men. Even seated you could tell how tall he was, and he already had a drink.

'Hi, I'm Seven,' I said, smiling, but not too much. 'Can I get you anything?'

'You're Seven?' Mark stood up and shook my hand, an unusual gesture in a place like this. 'How charming; sit down. I've had more than enough to drink tonight already. Do you want anything for yourself?'

'No, thank you.' I did as I was told and sat down beside him. 'How did you ask for me by name? Did Noel suggest me or something?'

'Yeah, Noel told me – I hope you don't mind.'

'No, I don't mind, it's just. . . Sorry, what did he say about me?'

'Well, I was going to be here tonight shadowing a couple of business pals and, as you probably well know, I'd get bored if I didn't find a decent conversationalist.'

'Yeah, I was told I wouldn't be your type.' I shrugged, fixing the half-smile on my face.

'I like my women how I like my coffee.'

'With a massive cock, right?'

He started laughing. 'Well, I was going to say. . . Ha! Yeah, right!'

'How long have you known Noel then?' I asked, looking up at the exposed copper piping snaking its way across the ceiling.

'Oh, years. We chat a lot. . . If you didn't mind, there was actually something particular I wanted to talk to you about.'

'It's a nickname,' I said, pre-empting the inevitable question about my name. 'I got it when I was young. I had an OCD thing.'

I met his eyes. They were an intense green and he had tattoos on the backs of his hands and fingers, from what I could see of them.

He folded his hands across each other, masking some of the tattoos I was trying to examine out of the corner of my eye. 'That wasn't what I was going to ask.'

'Oh. Well, I'll do my best,' I said, worried that he wanted to discuss something I'd be woefully undereducated to handle. 'But I'm not exactly a *University Challenge* contestant with questions. I can do art, martial arts, bit of geography, languages, but I was never that into hard-core subjects, you know. If you're after politics or history or something like that go for, uh. . . Abigail, over there. She's at UCL.'

He seemed amused by me. At least I had made some kind of impression.

'It wasn't so much about stuff like that,' he said, lowering his voice a little. 'Forgive me if I'm crossing a line or if this makes you feel uncomfortable, but I wanted to talk to you about your parents.'

For a moment there was only background noise, electro-guitar music, the clink of glasses and masculine chatter.

Mark had sat forwards with his hands linked on his knees, ignoring his other companions, who seemed happy to chat between themselves.

It was the last thing I'd expected him to say.

I thought about it every day but not at work. The images had never come to me here, when my mind was taken over by mundane repetitive tasks. I'd never thought about the skull cleaved in two and the fifth floor and the front door hanging askew on its hinges. . .

'Um, sorry, what?' I said, hoping I'd misheard. Maybe he'd said *patients*? Or *patents*?

'Your parents,' he repeated. 'Noel mentioned them to me. Don't blame him, he probably never expected me to talk to you. I promise this isn't a joke or morbid curiosity or anything trivial like that. I'm genuinely very interested in your life. Do you know what I do for a living? Did anyone tell you?'

I shook my head.

'I solve problems,' he said, with a glance over my shoulder. 'I solve problems, when problems are people. You understand?'

I understood what he was saying, in a literal sense, but not why. I couldn't recall ever being so wrong-footed by a statement. Noel called me a born smart-arse; it was rarity for me to be unable to muster a response. Maybe I should have been angry at Noel, but in my shock the thought didn't occur to me.

'So you're a private detective or something?' I said.

'I'm. . . more than that. I can track people down, make people disappear, make people suffer. I can make people do most things.'

'So you're a killer?'

'Well, at least make it sound professional. I'm a very professional killer.' He smiled. 'If you don't want to talk to me, I'd completely understand and won't be offended at all. But at the moment, you're the person I find *easily* the most fascinating in this room. And I'd like to make you an offer.'

I watched Irish or Elise or whatever her name was standing across the club, with her hand draped over a man's shoulders.

The girl onstage was still singing.

'I'm sorry,' I said, blood rushing to my face. 'I'm sorry, I don't think I want to talk to you.'

11

'That's fine, my love.' He nodded. His smile seemed genuine. He reached into the pocket of his skinny jeans and handed me a card with a number and no name printed on it. 'If you change your mind.'

'Excuse me,' I said, already standing up.

I crossed the club floor heading for the dressing room, but then changed direction and slipped out into the concrete stairwell instead. There wouldn't be anyone there. My legs were unsteady and I was lightheaded, on the verge of throwing up.

I leant my forehead against the wall next to the fire escape and swallowed, thinking, *You will not cry.* Almost three years and I hadn't yet cried. Everyone thought it was weird. Noel thought it was weird. I didn't think it was weird; I'd just resigned myself to an inevitable nervous breakdown in my early thirties, when it would all come out, having been given time to rot.

I shut my eyes and tried to steady my breathing. The sharp edges of the business card were hurting my palm.

You will not cry.

You will not cry.

You will not cry.

After a while, when I'd forced myself to meditate for a moment and clear my head, I left the stairwell and asked around to see if Noel was at the club tonight. But he wasn't. He wasn't going to be there until early the next morning.

Without anyone to vent my fury on, I told them all I was feeling ill and went home early. I avoided looking back in the direction of Mark Chester's table, but I took the professional killer's business card with the number and no name.

*

I didn't sleep that night, which allowed plenty of time for the rage to build by the time I left for the Underground again at ten in the morning. The air had a bite to it: cold and bitter for this time of year. Some skinhead was already shouting at his young girlfriend outside a Starbucks. I fantasized about putting him in an armlock and breaking his wrist.

I let myself into the club through the staff entrance and found Daisy, the bleached-blonde barmaid, already counting the float into the till.

'All right, Bitch-face,' I called. 'You're early. Is Noel upstairs?'

Daisy looked up at me and smiled. 'Hey, Fuck-rabbit.' Even in the colder days of summer she didn't wear much. In fact, even during winter I couldn't recall seeing her wearing anything that covered her legs, nipples and midriff simultaneously. 'So are you. Yeah, he's upstairs. Do I need to put on the old headphones and whack-up some Tool?'

'Maybe, but not for the reason you're thinking.'

'Yeah, whatever.' She gave me an animated thumbs-up.

Daisy was the only one here whom I distinguished from the other girls. In a way, she *was* distinguished from the other girls. She didn't entertain and perform and fuck and get fucked like the rest of us. Rumour was, her boyfriend had got her the bar job to stop her from getting bored. Her boyfriend was a hitman called Nic Caruana.

A professional killer, I thought, like Mark.

I left her and headed upstairs to Noel's office.

It was silent on the second floor. He never worked to music. He was remarkably sensitive to sound and couldn't sleep with the slightest background noise. Even when he had the TV on it was at a volume almost no one else could hear.

I let myself into his office without knocking.

Noel looked up from his laptop, affronted, but then he smiled. Unlike most men, he became more handsome when he smiled. It showed his age; the late-thirties lines around his blue eyes stood out and his face became more weathered. But he wore middle age well, like an expensive luxury accessory, like the suit jackets he wore over his jeans.

'Hey you,' he said, beginning to stand. 'What are you doing here?'

I shut the door, pulled out the second wheeled chair with some commotion and sat down. The office was psychotically tidy, with papers and folders stacked in size order and everything arranged at right angles.

He stared at me, and slowly lowered himself back into his chair.

I raised my eyebrows, damned if I was going to speak first.

'Am I about to be told off?' he ventured.

'Well, I'll give you some credit for realizing you've done something wrong.'

A couple more seconds.

'Ah,' he said, chewing his lip a little. 'Ah. I . . . didn't think he'd speak to you.'

'What kind of excuse is that?' I snapped, reciting a mantra in my head to stay calm, stay calm, stay calm. . . 'So it's OK for you to share my private business about my family with a stranger as long as it doesn't get back to me? Is that your logic here? If Noel Braben shoots his mouth off to a random guy in the forest and Seven doesn't hear, does it make a sound?'

'Well, *you* once shared your private business with a stranger the first time you met them. You had no issue with telling me.'

He never raised his voice to anyone, not that I'd heard. It was unnerving.

I hesitated. Maybe it should have done, but that fact hadn't crossed my mind once while thinking about this the night before. I still wasn't sure why I'd told Noel anything about my personal life in the first place. If I'd been able to share the story of what happened to my family with him so freely, before anything had happened between us, it didn't seem outlandish that he'd thought it might be OK to regale someone else with it.

I am sitting on a mountaintop.

I can hear the wind in the trees.

I am calm.

I am calm.

Noel pushed a silver thermos across the desk at me. 'Do you want some coffee?'

I picked it up without a word and took a gulp of the coffee inside. I never drank coffee. He knew I didn't drink coffee. It was black and disgusting and made me want to gag but I drank it anyway, to avoid speaking for a few seconds longer.

'What did he say to you? It's kinda unlike Mark to do something like that. He's a stand-up guy. I didn't think he'd just start talking to you about it.'

'It wasn't just talking to me about it, to be fair to him. He wasn't simply looking for a fun conversation. He. . . He made me an offer actually.' I fished the business card out of the pocket of my leather jacket and held it out for Noel to see. 'He said he's a guy who solves problems.'

'He. . . Wo. Wow. He said that to you?'

I nodded.

Noel let out a snort of disbelief. 'No, really. I mean, Mark, he's. . . expensive and he's. . . he's *Mark*. Wow, he must be really interested in you. He doesn't talk business with just anybody; he works for the Russians and spends half his time out there doing. . . God knows what.'

There had been a festering sensation of dread and excitement in my stomach that had crept into my consciousness the night before and worsened now.

I am sitting on a mountaintop. . .

He started laughing and clapped his hands together, making me start. 'Fucking hell, this is. . . OK, I know you're pissed off with me and everything but this is pretty fucking amazing, you know. If Mark Chester wants to take an interest in you then maybe you should think about it? Maybe just talk to him? I don't know. You don't have to if you don't want to, but he's serious, he'd probably find out stuff you never would. . .'

I stared hard at the plain business card, with the number and no name. 'So he's kinda a big deal then?'

'Yeah. He's a big deal.'

'You really think he'd find something?' I asked, sceptical. 'After three years? I mean. . . it's almost three years now and there was no evidence then. You really think he'd find something?'

'Well, I'm not one to exaggerate. . . much.' He thought for a moment. 'But I don't think Mark's ever left a job unfinished. I don't think he's ever lost a person he's tried to track down and I don't think he's ever left a person alive who he was paid to take care of. He basically never fails, I think.'

I didn't know if this was what I wanted to hear.

'Are you still pissed at me?' Noel asked, leaning forwards

across the desk and pushing his laptop to one side. 'Look, I wasn't just gossiping like some old bloody woman, I was just. . . Lighten up, OK? This could be a really good thing for you.'

I wasn't sure if he was right or not so I nodded. It wasn't as if I was going to draw an apology out of him.

He tried to prompt a smile from me. 'Yeah? We OK?'

'Yeah.' I forced my lips to twitch, to appease him.

'Yeah? Good, I hate it when you look at me like that, baby.' He reached across the desk and gestured for me to take his hand. 'And you know, I could have done something super smart here.'

As I put my hand in his, I noticed that his wedding ring was back on.

Chapter Two

The first time I entered the Underground I wasn't impressed. I spent the majority of my first impression waiting downstairs in the club for my interview, picking at my fingernails and hunched over.

I'd been sitting there for twenty minutes too long and the barmaid kept reassuring me, 'He'll be down in a minute,' but I was starting to feel insolent.

It's not as if I needed a job right now anyway.

I almost left before my interview, never to come back.

Sometimes I tried to imagine how everything might have turned out if I had.

Even if I was underwhelmed, the club was nicer than I'd expected: not as gaudy and overblown. It was about as tasteful as an erotic club could be. Now, at three in the afternoon, you could almost mistake it for a jazz place in the right light, without all the naked women.

A few men in suits were drinking and talking amongst themselves at tables, while the barmaid appeared to run the place. Some low indie rock was playing from her iTunes behind the bar and the lighting was bright but tinted purple.

There was exposed copper piping hanging from the ceiling.

The man I was waiting for, Noel Braben, was upstairs in his office.

I was to find out that the Underground did in fact have an owner, a woman called Ms Edie Franco, but I was only to see her twice in the time I worked there. Noel and Ronnie O'Connell, his long-time business partner, spoke of her working 'up north' with her other clubs. The two of them had more invested in the day-to-day management of the Underground than she seemed to.

When the door to the stairwell on my left opened it wasn't Noel Braben who walked out of it. It was a woman with dark red hair, metallic and glossy. She had high cheekbones and wide eyes that looked me up and down and full lips that tightened at the sight of me as she looked over her shoulder on her way out.

I watched her go, thinking that she was gorgeous but an obvious bitch and that she probably worked here. . .

A man wearing jeans and a suit jacket appeared in the doorway after the woman had left, looking pissed off and eager to abdicate from this day. Tired blue eyes searched for me from under a mop of hair that made him look like a member of the Beatles, and he frowned.

'You're. . . Seven?'

'Yeah.'

'Seven,' he repeated.

'Yes.' I raised my eyebrows this time and he smiled.

'OK then, come on.'

It wasn't exactly lust at first sight. But it became apparent very quickly that something about me amused him, and something about him fascinated me.

I wasn't used to finding men interesting. Women had more

intricacies; they were harder to please in every sense, harder to read, and the women I had loved I could live my entire life learning how to please and how to read.

But I liked Noel Braben.

I swivelled left and right on the spinning chair as he observed me and asked things like, 'You always lived in London? You don't look English, exactly.'

'I'm half Japanese but my parents moved back and forth a lot so my accent is pretty much English.'

'It's a bit American.'

'Well, that's how we speak English. We watch a lot of American TV.'

'Do you still live with your parents?'

'No, they're dead.'

'Ooh.' A grimace. 'I'm sorry. Was it recent?'

'They were murdered a few years ago, with my sister.'

I think I'd wanted to shock him, or myself. It was the only explanation for why I'd stated it with such bravado.

But he wasn't shocked.

'I'm sorry,' he said, with the blank tone of a guy who considered murder no different from any other form of death. 'Did they ever find the. . . guy?'

'No.'

'And you survived?'

'I was out.'

Another frown. He looked down at his desk, his only hint at a reaction, then back up at me with a smile. 'Can you dance?'

I was surprised he had changed the subject. He didn't bring it up again until we were in bed, three weeks later.

'Um, a bit,' I replied. 'I can dance but not like. . . dance. I've done Ninpo and some martial arts though so I can pick stuff up quickly.'

He leant in. 'Look, this isn't the Royal Opera House. If you can put one leg in front of the other and smile at the same time most people here will be happy. Have you got any special talents?'

'I can sing OK and I can paint. I'm not sure if I'm particularly special at either.'

'Well, I can be the judge of that.' He smiled at me again.

I decided right then that I was going to have sex with him. At some point, whether it was next week or in a few months or whatever, it was definitely going to happen. It had never not happened when I'd decided on it.

'You know how this place works?' he asked.

'It's a strip club, right?'

'Yes. . . and no. Officially, we're an erotic club. I manage it, with my partner Ron. Ronnie O'Connell.' He spread his hands. 'But I'm going to be upfront, cos you don't seem naive. We do a lot here. We're Members Only. People. . . certain people. . . come here to meet. We entertain them, give them free drinks, give them a song and dance, and depending on who they are we send the best girls to their homes for private performances. Are you OK with that? Potentially?'

'With going to some guy's house?'

'They're never just some random guy here. We vet all our members very thoroughly; you'd be safer working here than you would be on the tube. We can promise that.' He became very serious suddenly. 'We've never had a single incident, not with a member.'

I mulled it over, but I wasn't surprised. You'd have to be an amateur at life to go for a job interview at a club like this and not expect to be asked to partake in some mild prostitution.

'Well. . . yeah, I'd be fine with that,' I said, shrugging.

'Great!' He couldn't quite repress the smile. 'Um, before you do that you will need to provide a clear and very recent STD test. Only valid within the last month.'

'OK. I think I'm starting to understand what this place is all about.' I tapped the arms of my chair and looked around the office again. 'I don't think I've made a very good first impression on my co-workers though. I'm pretty sure old bitch-face who just left isn't that big a fan.'

He laughed and sat back in his chair, spinning around a bit. 'Co-worker? You're confident.'

'Well, I've got this job, right?'

'You've got it, yeah. Er. . . Seven.' He rubbed at his stubble. 'Old bitch-face doesn't work here though.'

'Oh, great.'

'She's my wife actually. She works at PWC.'

Fuck. There wasn't anything I could say to rescue myself from that, so I reddened and said, 'Oh.'

'It's OK; she's an accountant. She knows she's a bitch.' He grinned at me, but I wasn't sure if he was joking. 'But you're probably right to say that she doesn't like you. She doesn't like anyone who works here. Sometimes I think she doesn't even like me.'

I looked for the wedding ring and there it was, where I should have seen it in the first place. I'd noticed that his office was eerily tidy, everything in line with something else, or perpendicular to something else, but I hadn't noticed the wedding ring.

'Can you stand up so I can check you over? I can call Daisy up if you want a girl in the room but it's just a look. Nothing weird, don't worry.'

The barmaid had seemed nice, but I didn't feel threatened. On the contrary, I wanted to us to be alone.

I stood up, put my bag down beside me and pushed the chair away.

'Everything?' I asked.

The air in the office was hot and the one window was shut.

'Everything you feel comfortable with, but the top layer has to go. It's so we can check for marks, tattoos and stuff. We don't allow anyone to use drugs here so we look for any evidence of that as well, needle marks. . . weird bruises.'

'OK.'

I took off my leather jacket and put it down on the chair behind me, then my boots. As I unbuttoned my shirt I looked down at my fingers, and then met his eyes as I slipped it off my shoulders, folded it slowly and placed it with the jacket.

His face was expressionless, but he was tapping the arm of his chair.

I slid my skirt and tights down to my ankles and stepped out of them, suddenly more conscious than I liked of what he might think of my skinny and childlike body. I tried to remember in more detail what his wife had looked like. She'd also looked slight of frame, but more athletic than me, with broader shoulders.

With a breath, I unhooked the straps of the black bra and let it slide down my arms.

My body felt hot, inhabited by an exhilarated visceral sen-

23

sation that squeezed my diaphragm and shortened my breath.

I saw him wet his lips, eyes down, away from my face.

'Can you, er. . . turn around?'

I turned around in a circle. As my back was to him I was overcome by the fantasy of him approaching behind me, taking me by the arms, kissing his way down my back, pushing me down on to his desk with his hands all over me. . .

'Yeah, that's fine. Fine, I mean. . . nice. Good.'

'Only good?'

I picked up my clothes and started to dress myself, coy all of a sudden.

He gave me an exasperated look. 'Yeah. Great. Look, stop being a smart-arse and tell me when you can start. Tomorrow?'

Pulling my jacket on, I beamed. 'Really?'

'Bring in some ID and bank account details tomorrow morning and I'll give you a hundred or so to go out and get together some decent outfits, then you'll be good to go. You can shadow one of the other girls for the night.' He was writing something down. 'If you run off with the hundred and think I won't find you, I will, OK? So don't.'

It was the first time I'd felt vulnerable in front of him, but he said it so matter-of-factly that I was pressured to ignore the momentary fear and move on.

I sat down to pull my tights back up. 'Seriously?'

'Yeah. Um, one question though.'

'Yeah?'

Awkwardly, he cupped one hand beside his mouth, as if someone might be listening.

I leant in.

'You won't think it's racist if we play up the Japanese thing, will you?'

I whispered back sardonically, 'No, you're fine. I won't sue.'

'Awesome.' He spun around in his chair again, appraising me. 'Because the whole Japanese schoolgirl thing, the little white socks, the skirts and stuff. It's a total no-brainer.'

Chapter Three

Nausea hit me on the tube the following morning, and I held my forehead in my hands for most of the journey.

In my mind there were images of bumping into my parents or sister. I couldn't imagine what an alien environment my old estate would seem without them, but at the same time I was scared of walking towards my old flat and feeling too much as if I was going home.

Would I have the guts to go inside? Was I going to start crying? Maybe I'd just go crazy and start screaming and hitting things. What if I ran into someone I'd known?

It's OK, I thought. No one had really known me there anyway.

I stared at the shoes of the person sitting opposite me until my stop.

My old block of flats wasn't far from the tube station. In fact you could see it straight away, looming into the sky. They should have knocked it down, or burnt the fucking thing.

The houses, the roads and the pavements surrounding it were drenched in familiarity, but felt too quiet for my memory of the place. It was like walking on to a battlefield in the years after the fight, when there were no traces of blood any more and the grass had grown back, where the calm would always feel at odds with the knowledge of the violence that had taken place.

I stopped walking, midway between my block of the flats and Jensen McNamara's. There had been a broken skateboard in the bushes next to the pavement the last time I'd walked the same route, but it was now gone.

It had been humid then. At least it had the grace to be cold now.

I walked up to the nearest building and buzzed Jensen's old flat, wondering what the hell I was doing here. I knew I was kidding myself that this was a pointless exercise. I knew what I was really doing. I was looking for an excuse, any excuse, to call Mark Chester. I was looking for something to help me overcome my paralysis.

'Hello?'

It sounded like him.

I swallowed. 'Jensen?'

'Yeah?'

'Um, this is Kiyomi. Kiyomi Ishida. I don't know if you remember—'

'Kiyomi? Fuck, er. . . Fuck. Hi?'

'Can I come in for a moment?'

He paused for a little too long to sound polite.

'Oh yeah, yeah, OK, sure.'

I was buzzed up and he met me in his doorway looking exactly the same as I remembered him. Not that Jensen's was a face that had particularly lodged itself in my memory, but there was nothing new or exciting about his features.

'Man, you look different,' he said with a nervous smile.

For a second, he hesitated, as if wondering whether to hug me or shake my hand, but then he just backed away from the doorway and let me come inside.

'You look nice with shorter hair though. It's cool. Do you want a drink or something?'

'You know I don't drink.'

'Well, tea. It's like midday, babes.'

He was just as unkempt as I remembered. His flat smelt the same, so much so that I found it hard to speak.

'Tea, yeah. Anything herbal.'

I followed him to the other end of his flat, where a tiny stove and washing machine were wedged behind a sofa.

'I'm sorry I never got to see you after. . .' He shook his head as he moved about his space, keeping his back to me. 'I'm sorry anyway. It was fucking horrible. I never expected to see you again, to be honest. Didn't think you'd ever come back. Thought you'd just. . . go back to Japan or something.'

'Too expensive for me.' I sat on the back of the sofa. 'I couldn't even afford the flight.'

'Did they ever find out. . . anything?'

'No, nothing. It's not like anyone saw anything so. . .'

Jensen put the kettle on, pushed up the sleeves of his over-sized shirt and turned to face me. 'Ah, that's a fucking shame, I'm sorry. I mean, you'd think they'd have found something. They spoke to everyone round here: me, the Williams kids—'

'They spoke to you? Who spoke to you?'

'Well, most people had uniforms come round to ask them questions. A couple of us had the guy in charge, a guy in plain clothes.'

'What did you say?'

An apologetic expression. 'Uh. . . nothing. He did ask if I'd seen you that day and stuff so he must have known I was lying, but I just didn't want to have to write up a statement or anything and. . . Sorry, I don't think it would have affected their case. I just didn't fancy telling this guy I'd seen you, that's all. Sorry, I know you shouldn't lie to the police and stuff, especially when it's about important—'

'What did he look like?'

I knew straight away whom Jensen was referring to, and my stomach turned with unease.

He frowned. 'Black hair, really greasy, like. Old. I didn't like him, but then who likes police, I suppose? All miserable bastards. All corrupt too, you know.'

'A comb-over? Did he have a comb-over?'

'Yeah, a really shit one.'

Now I was on edge, as though someone might be listening to us.

'I'm sorry I lied. It wasn't cool,' he said, raising his voice over the roar of boiling water.

'No, I don't mind.' I indicated my head across the flat in the direction of my old home. 'What about the Williams kids?'

'Oh, they all wrote statements. Even the younger ones were asked questions. They're still living there if you wanna go speak to them, except. . . Oh, shit, this is sad. You know Nate? The oldest? He died not long after.'

'What?' I wanted to drag Jensen away from pouring fucking tea. 'How?'

'Drive-by. Reckon he was mistaken for someone else. They

got the kid that did it though; he's in juvie. Fuck, it's like your place is cursed!'

Without saying a word, without saying goodbye, I turned away and walked out of the flat.

'Um. . .'

I heard him, dumb with confusion, as I slammed the door.

'Um. . . nice to see. . . you.'

There was one relative in the Relatives' Room. One relative sitting in silence, picking my nails and chewing my lips. The other two people were police officers. Both had given up trying to speak to me a long time ago.

The Relatives' Room appeared more like a haphazard staff-room, with a cupboard and sink full of mugs, a small plastic kettle and boxes of tea left out on the side. A used teaspoon was hanging over the sink, dripping.

I looked down at my hands again, now clean of blood, and observed the yellow foam showing though the frayed royal-blue fabric of my chair.

Drip.

I'd stopped panicking by then. My breathing had slowed and I held my hands still. My face was stiff and my emotions had stopped, rigid. I tore off a piece of nail from the side of my thumb and gnawed at it, obsessing over the tag of loose bleeding skin.

My sister had called something to me as I'd left the flat.

'Kiki, look!'

I hadn't stopped or looked, just said I'd be back soon and left to go to Jensen's because I'd been so bored. All the time. So fucking bored. Crawling with boredom. Boredom that made me want to claw off my own face just for the entertainment.

Kiki, look!

One of the officers kept glancing sideways down my top.

I hadn't been allowed to see my family. Not again. I was already finding it hard to remember walking into my flat and seeing them.

Drip.

A nurse came in, smiled at us, and efficiently made some tea with the plastic kettle and used teaspoon by the sink. She stirred a West Bromwich Albion mug and returned the spoon to where it had come from.

I kept forgetting in the midst of these micro-episodes, things existing and people going about their jobs and their lives, why I was here. Even my memories, erratic and infused with static like shit TV reception, didn't seem like my own.

Thinking back, I could see myself only as an observer. In my memories, I was watching myself enter the flat from behind.

I saw myself stare, throw up, fall, and I followed myself out. . .

I could see the broken bottle of Asahi, not far from my dad's hand.

The hand was split down the centre, fingers parting from each other in their attempted defence against the *blades like this*. His hands were in pieces around what was left of his wrists. . .

I rocked forwards and I saw the officers recoil a little.

'There's a sink,' one of them said.

I remembered throwing up on one of them on the way here and the other one had started laughing and apologizing.

Drip.

The nurse left.

The officers left.

A man walked in.

At first, I didn't see anything strange in both the officers leaving.

The man introduced himself by his intention rather than by his name, badge or rank. He introduced himself by his vile black comb-over and deep-set eyes that looked as though at any moment they could be swallowed up by his face.

He pulled one of the bright blue chairs away from the wall and rotated it until he was sitting adjacent to me.

'Miss Ishida? Kiyomi.'

I hadn't fucking said that he could call me Kiyomi.

'I'm here to ask you a few questions, if that's all right with you?'

It was just the two of us. I wished that the other officers hadn't left.

At the time, I nodded.

'You didn't directly witness anything, I understand? You were out?'

Yes.

I said it first in my head, before I managed to take the breath needed to speak.

'Yes.'

'Where were you?'

There was still boiling water in the kettle. The teaspoon was still dripping.

I saw the top of Jensen McNamara's head, felt the flutter of words against my cunt. . .

'The shops.'

'Really?'

He wasn't asking. His tone was oiled with cynicism. He knew I was lying. I knew that he knew I was lying. What's more, I could tell he'd expected me to lie.

'You didn't have anything with you when you returned,' he said.

'I know. I forgot my money.'

I picked at the yellow foam instead of my lips, eyes down, tapping the leg of my chair seven times, seven times. . .

'You were apparently shouting at some children in the stairwell of your building. A few eyewitnesses have mentioned them. Can you give me their names so I can take their statements?'

'I don't remember.'

'You don't remember.'

'No.'

'Do they live nearby?'

'I don't know.'

'Kiyomi.' He leant forwards, linking his fingers on his lap. 'Anything you can remember, anything at all, could be crucial in finding out who did this. If anyone saw anything, we need to be able to speak to them. Do you understand?'

I wanted to ask him if I could see his ID, but it seemed too aggressive. I felt as though, if I asked him that, he'd have licence to confront me with the lies I was telling.

'I don't remember who they were,' I said, ripping out some of the yellow foam and dropping it on the floor. 'I didn't know them. They were just hanging around.'

They could put it down to shock, maybe. If I faked a lack of memory. . .

'They could give us a lead, Kiyomi.'

'I. . . didn't know them.'

'Could you identify them in a line-up?'

In my mind I could only see their hands, showing the lengths of the blades.

33

I wouldn't identify them, not to this guy, but I nodded anyway.

'And you didn't see anyone?'

I looked at him. If something happened, if he moved too suddenly, I had an idea that I could maybe reach the kettle and throw the boiled water in his face.

'No.'

He put his hand over mine and I nearly vomited again.

'I'm truly sorry for your loss, Kiyomi,' he said.

Then he left.

That was it. My loss. That was what had just happened to me, condensed conveniently down into a fucking four-letter and one syllable word. My loss.

I sat there, aware only of my own breathing.

The officers didn't return.

For a second, I considered cutting my wrists with one of the blunt unpolished knives in the cutlery drawer. Then this, my loss, could all be over. Just like that. . .

But no.

I hadn't seen anyone, I thought.

I hadn't seen anyone.

I left the chair and ran out of the Relatives' Room into the hospital corridor.

But there was no sign of him.

There was no sign of him but I never forgot his face.

Chapter Four

I called the number from the business card with no name and arranged to meet Mark Chester the following evening, as I'd always been intending to. He didn't sound surprised to hear from me; the fluency of his speech was unnerving.

I found him sitting in the window of the café he'd suggested in Covent Garden, on an artfully tacky leopard-print stool just out of the sun. On the counter next to him was a brown leather satchel, like the ones public schoolboys carried.

Something by Roy Orbison was playing. It was the sort of tearoom designed to attract hipsters with iPads.

'I was pretty rude the last time I saw you,' I said, sitting down next to him. 'Sorry.'

'No, you were hilarious. I wasn't offended; I expected that sort of reaction.'

The stool was so high that my feet didn't touch the floor, so I sat there swinging them back and forth in the air like a toddler.

When Mark spoke to me next he had his business face on.

'So, did you think seriously about what we talked about?'

I snorted. 'That's a bit of an understatement, but yeah, I thought about it.'

'Would you like a smoothie?'

'Er, no, I'm good.'

'So what do you think?'

It took concentration to become used to his rapid-fire questioning, especially when I was still unsure of my intentions. 'Look, I'm going to be straight with you. This isn't the sort of offer where you say you'll do something for free and then suddenly a few months down the line some hidden charge appears, is it?'

'Why would I do that?'

'Well. . .' I couldn't find a reply that didn't sound like childish cynicism.

Out through the window I could see a guy in a flat cap was setting up for some sort of show. He was staring at the bare legs of every woman that walked by.

'I totally understand why you wouldn't trust me,' Mark said. 'My flatmate says that I make people uncomfortable.'

'No, it's not that. You seem pretty trustworthy. According to Noel you're up there with the most trustworthy people I've met in months. I think he fancies you, to be honest; he got way too excited when we were talking about you. I could *smell* the man-love.'

'Well, naturally.' A wistful smile.

'I just haven't really thought about all this since it happened,' I continued. 'I haven't thought about any of them. It's weird even entertaining the idea that you could do something about it now.'

'Well, if you don't mind me writing stuff down like a hack. . .' he said, going through his bag for a notebook and pen. 'Can you just tell me what happened? No, wait, tell me about your parents first. Their names, what they did, where you lived, any personal stuff you think is relevant.'

I noticed he was wearing eyeliner.

'OK, that's easy. My mother was called Helena and my dad was Sohei.'

It was easy to talk about my parents like this, as if I was reciting their resumés.

He nodded.

'He worked for a company called Importas. He was manager or something, but he kept moving us between London and Tokyo every few years. We lived in Hampstead in London and Toshima-ku in Tokyo, and then when he lost his job we lived in Tooting. Shit-hole.'

'And Tooting. . .'

'That's where it happened, yeah.'

I paused. For a moment the single high-definition image came back to me. Always my sister. The five-year-old skull cleaved in two. I didn't remember much of Mum or Dad. If I concentrated really hard I could sometimes see the broken bottle, stained red, that my dad must have raised to try and defend them. The glass was embedded in his hands. I'd seen it as I'd fallen to the floor in shock.

Mark was watching the street performer outside. He didn't persist in his questioning, so I answered the silence and the vast expanse of blank space on his notepad.

'I was at this guy's house, Jensen McNamara. He lived just across the road from us. But I got bored. I went home and bumped into these kids in the stairwell. I can't remember any of their first names, apart from the oldest one, Nate. They were just kids in the building. Little scabby boys. All Williamses.'

Blades like this. . .

'They stopped me and said there had been a fight or something upstairs. The oldest one had seen these guys go up. I don't think he said how many. . . Two. *A couple*, he said. With *blades like this*.'

I lifted my hands in the air in front of me, demonstrating.

The bottom of Mark's glass made a gurgling sound as he sucked the last of his drink up his straw, cutting me off.

I raised my eyebrows.

'Sorry,' he said, pushing the glass away. 'But you didn't see these guys though? You didn't see the men the kid saw?'

'No. If I did. . .' I swallowed. 'If I'd been there they would have killed me too. I know that. But by now it's been so long they probably don't care enough to. . . to want to track me down or anything. Sometimes I think about it, you know, if I'm scaring myself at night. I wake up and I wonder if they're still out there looking for me, or whether their job was just done and finished then, regardless of whether I was there or not. I just. . . I don't get why they wouldn't come back for me. Why would they let me go just because I was lucky and wasn't there?'

'They won't still be looking,' Mark stated with some confidence.

I worried he was about to make some sort of inane gesture of comfort or support, like touching my arm or something. But he didn't. Of course he didn't. He wasn't an idiot.

'How do you know they're not still looking?'

'Well, they would have to be pretty shit to have taken nearly three years to track you down.' He pulled the glass back to him again and frowned down his straw at the remaining bubbles

38

of his drink. 'If I ever took three fucking years to carry out a hit I'd retire.'

'And do what? Knit?'

'I've never thought about it. I'm doing what I want to do and. . . we don't tend to retire, we tend to die. But I'm all right with that.' He nodded, and grinned. 'I'm unsure sometimes, whether I'd avoid retiring just in case my job slipped into a hobby. . . and then who knows? No more rules then.'

'Hasn't it already become a hobby with you doing this for free?'

'Maybe.'

Silence.

He added, 'This isn't a frivolous act, my wanting to work for you. I'm not doing this for fun. It's just not very often life confronts you with a real mystery, a chance to solve a real mystery.'

I could hear someone playing *Angry Birds* behind us with the volume turned up to an antisocial level. I straightened my skirt, pulled it down a little and tried to ignore the noise.

'So, you go upstairs. . .' He waved a hand at me, drawing a circle on the page with the word 'Details' written within it. 'You don't have to describe it all to me. Just any extra personal information that forensics might not have picked up on, if it occurs to you. I can find the case file and photos and stuff, no problem.'

All I could hear was the fucking *Angry Birds*.

'Someone called the police?'

I nodded.

'And what happened then?'

'I. . . What?'

39

'What happened then?'

'Wait.' I turned, knuckles white around the back of my stool, and snapped, 'Hey, can you *shut the fuck up*?'

The girl with braided hair stared at me, gormless. People around us fought to restart their conversations before anyone noticed them eavesdropping. The sound of the game ceased and the girl stood up and flounced out.

I am sitting on a mountaintop, I thought, taking a deep breath.

'Your father was never. . .' Mark seemed pensive for a moment. 'Apologies if this comes off as an insult, but your father was never involved with Yakuza, was he? He didn't associate with anyone like that when you lived in Japan?'

I knew he didn't mean it to be offensive, but the very suggestion sent a reactionary shot of anger and defensiveness up my spine. I almost said something scathing about Mark's tattoos, implying sarcastically that he looked more like Yakuza than my dad ever had. But I stifled the comment.

'No,' I said, pursing my lips. 'He might not have died with all his fingers but he had them all before that.'

'It's OK, I didn't think so, but sometimes you have to ask the obvious questions.' He shut his notepad. 'What are you doing now, just working for Noel and Ron?'

'Excuse me?'

'What were you doing before?'

I felt embarrassed all of a sudden. 'Nothing, really. Mum wanted to me to go to uni but Dad was happy for me to stay at home and try to. . . make it as an artist. So I was just doing that, just painting every day. I was thinking about art school a bit but. . . it's all really expensive, higher education, you know.'

It sounded ridiculous, even to me. I couldn't believe now that I'd ever been stupid enough to think anything would have come of my staying at home painting. But Mark didn't seem to share my contempt; he at least humoured me by asking another question.

'And you don't do that any more?'

'Well, I'm only good at two things and one of them was art. You'd have to be pretty damn stupid not to head down the other path if one of the only two things you're good at is art.'

'What's the other thing?'

'Sex.' I smirked. 'Sex and art.'

'Then you're right. Best to stick to the former in this climate.'

I thought of the Relatives' Room, the comb-over and small black eyes, the way he kept saying my name. . .

I'm truly sorry for your loss, Kiyomi.

'Can you let me know the names of everyone you came across that day? Even if they were kids, it would still help to know. They might have seen something.'

'Well, there was Jensen McNamara; he lived across from me. I could find his address for you but I'm sure he's on Facebook. The kids I spoke to were the Williams kids. I can't remember all their names but they lived a few floors below me, I think. And. . . there's something else,' I said, trusting my hunch. 'It was kinda what made me call you actually. There was a man who came and talked to me just after. . . I don't know who he was. We were alone, which was weird, and he asked me a lot of questions but I lied to all of them. But he knew I was lying.'

'And he didn't identify himself as a police officer?'

'No. I would have asked but I was really out of it. I don't know, he could have been anybody.'

41

'Not if you were alone. A police officer wouldn't sit alone with a female borderline minor and ask questions. Don't take this the wrong way but you look about sixteen.'

'I'm twenty-one. I was eighteen then.' I began talking fast. 'It wasn't just me. I spoke to a. . . well, he wasn't a friend, but I spoke to Jensen McNamara yesterday and he said the same man had come to question him too. He described him and said he had a black comb-over. It was the same man. *And* one of the Williams kids, the oldest one, was killed not long after in a drive-by shooting. He might have seen who did it and now all of a sudden he's dead. Doesn't that seem like too much of a coincidence?'

Mark scanned the café behind us, but no one appeared to be listening.

I made a mental note to lower my voice, having forgotten we were in a public place.

'A drive-by could be coincidental,' he said.

'Well, you could check, right? They apparently caught the kid who did it and he's in a young offenders' place.'

It was starting to become dim and crisp outside. We didn't have much longer here.

My heart was racing. I tried to slow it down, slow down my breathing.

'I can check it out,' Mark said, with a firm nod. 'You've definitely given me, as the professionals say, a "solid line of inquiry".'

The last rays of the sun falling on the red overhangs of the shops outside reminded me of Tokyo.

'Noel said you've never failed at a job. Is that true?'

There was no trace of modesty in his expression. 'Yes.'

'Seriously, why are you doing this for free?'

'Because I don't do my job for the money. I never have.' He observed the tattoos on the backs of his hands and his black-painted fingernails. 'That's why I've never failed.'

Chapter Five

To my irritation, the person I always wanted to call first in these situations was Noel. I resented that I felt that kind of attachment to anybody, but through sheer force of persistence he had managed to wind his way into the only parts of my life that demanded one-on-one discussion. He hardly ever talked to me about trivial things; neither of us was good at it.

I called him outside the tube station near his flat, so I could kid myself my intention was still to go home if I wanted.

'Hey,' Noel answered, sounding weird.

'Hey, are you at home?'

'No, no, I'm. . . not.'

I doubted that. At this time of evening the only other place he would be was downstairs at the club, and I'd be able to hear the activity around him.

'You know if it's not a good time, that's OK,' I said.

'No, it's not that! It's. . .'

There was movement, as if he were changing locations.

Just like that, there was a glimmer of sadness.

'You're not at the club, are you?' I sidestepped away from a wave of commuters.

Silence.

'It's OK, I was on my way home and then back to work and. . . I just wanted to check if I could come by for a chat, that's all. I spoke to Mark today, just now.'

'Oh. Cool, cool.'

It was so obvious. It should have occurred to me first; I'd even seen the wedding ring.

'She's there, isn't she?'

'Yeah. It's not really a good time.'

'No, I understand.'

'I'll call you back.'

I wasn't sure whether to hang up, but then he did. I didn't think he was going to call back.

I stood outside the tube entrance for a while, feeling awkward and ridiculed, as if the people passing around me could sense my humiliation.

This had happened once before, and I'd gone three weeks without a callback. But then the wedding ring had come off again and I'd been regaled with another tale of her being unreasonable or hysterical or stubborn or all of the above. The first time I'd believed him, but I was starting to wonder at what point, if all your relationships hesitated and ended the same way, you should start to ask if it was you.

He'd asked me over and over again about my past, about any great loves or failings I might have had, but I never saw why I should tell him about those. I was too young to have had many.

What that person had done and what they were now doing with their lives was none of my business any more.

*

45

I couldn't stop thinking about what Mark had said, even at work. I took five minutes to lean against the bar and chat to Daisy as she steamrollered her way through making the worst Long Island Iced Teas I'd ever seen. But I wasn't listening to her. I stared out into the club, through everybody, and it took a while for me to realize she was addressing me with a direct question.

'What?' I turned, resting back on my elbows.

'I said sorry if I'm staring at your tits in that outfit!'

I looked down at them and my false eyelashes itched. 'Oh. Don't worry, I didn't notice.'

'I'm not like *staring* at them, but they're just. . . *there*, you know.' She mimed a pair of tits in mid-air. 'That bra is fucking insane.'

I sighed and looked around for anyone whose drinks were empty. My gaze alighted on two guys sitting apart from everyone else, not watching the stage much, just talking to each other in what seemed like secretive tones.

Great. I wasn't in the mood to deal with anyone too fucked-up or energetic.

'Bitch, are you even listening to me?'

'Who are they?' I asked, gesturing at the two men. 'Haven't seen them before. You know them?'

'No. Take them these and find out, I guess.' She put a couple of beers on a tray and slid it across the bar-top. 'They look like. . . Actually, they don't look like anyone. They don't even look like accountants.'

I adjusted the stupid bra so the diamanté wasn't digging into my ribcage so much, picked up the tray and walked over to them with a smile.

'Can I get you anything?' I asked, putting on a ludicrous sultry tone.

They both eyed me with the same quiet calculation. White skin and strong cheeks, pretty much identical – so, brothers? – but for the man on the left having thicker hair and a dimpled cheek when he almost smiled. Almost.

'Alcohol, please,' said the brother to the left, with an Eastern European accent.

I put down the tray.

He chuckled. 'Beer is not alcohol, it is lemonade.'

I stopped smiling. It was becoming painful. 'You want vodka then?'

'Please. Just vodka.'

The two of them exchanged glances and I turned around to get them their drinks, curling my lip at Daisy.

She gave me a hesitant thumbs-up after she'd poured the vodkas.

'I haven't seen you here before,' I said when I returned to the table.

'We are aware of Mr Braben and Mr O'Connell's club. We could not resist to visit.' The one on the left, with the more impressive mane of black hair, leant forwards and indicated that I sit down next to them. 'I am Alexei. This is my brother, Isaak.'

'You Polish or something?' I said, sitting down and crossing my legs so that my knee just brushed against Alexei's.

'You have cheek, little girl. We are Russian.' He looked me up and down. 'What are you? Korean?'

I snorted. 'OK, I asked for that. I'm half Japanese.'

'And your name?'

'Seven.'

'Your real name?'

'That *is* my real name. Noel and Ronnie like us to use our real first names, he says it makes this place feel more. . . familiar, I guess. I think some guys like to think they're talking to a girl they're not paying for. Not someone called. . . Crystal or fucking Fifi or something.'

He laughed. Isaak didn't, but then Isaak hadn't said anything yet. He seemed content to sit back and watch the two of us talk. I wondered if it was a weird sexual thing and almost grimaced. What if I got these guys on a house call and they wanted to do some weird incestuous double-act or something?

Alexei was attractive though, in a rabid way, like Marlon Brando, as if he would fuck you while holding you down by the neck. I decided that I could probably have sex with him without much prompting.

'You are funny,' Alexei said, resting his drink on my knee. 'You must know all of your boss's business secrets.'

'Well, I could probably guess Noel's password.' I grinned, swallowing back the anger I could feel rising to the surface at the very mention of his name. 'I don't know his PIN number though.'

How fucking dare he treat me like that on the phone. Again.

I snapped out of my stale bitter thoughts and found Alexei was still staring at me.

He raised his eyebrows. 'What's his password?'

'Oh, I don't know, his wife's name and his birthday? Caroline255? His first dog? Chewbacca?'

'What are you, his mistress?'

'Well. . .' I uncrossed and recrossed my legs, biting my lip. 'Not any fucking more.'

Alexei gulped back the rest of his vodka and I went wordlessly to take his glass back to the bar. He made to grip my arm and without thinking I parried him. There was a silence. I reddened a little, feeling that I might have overreacted.

'Don't leave us yet,' said Alexei. 'I would like to know his mother's maiden name.'

'Oh well. . . I don't know that, I've never met her.' I took a step back and noticed that Isaak was almost smiling again. 'Anyway, I think I'd be a little more than fired if Noel knew I was divulging his inside leg measurement. Though I could probably find that out, for real.'

I laughed, attempting to lighten the atmosphere.

'What if we made it worth your while?'

I hesitated, unsure of what to do with the empty glass, so I sat down again. Before I could think of something to say Coralie prowled up to Isaak from behind and laid her hand on his shoulder. She was so flawless that sometimes I wished she'd chip a tooth.

'Can I help you with anything here?' she asked, practically purring.

'No, please leave.'

Alexei hadn't even looked at her.

Coralie's perfect beam slipped as she made a questioning face at me. I rolled my eyes as if to say, 'Don't even ask,' and she left us. I was glad something had provided a brief distraction. The two of them were still waiting for me to speak and I wasn't sure how to play it.

'Worth my while. . . how?'

'Name your price.'

'Er. . . a flight to Japan and a deposit on a flat.'

The two of them looked at each other, nodded, looked back to me.

I was nervous now and laughed again to hide it. 'OK, you guys. You're funny, but you know this isn't a serious conversation, right? I'm going to get you some more vodka. Try not to bribe anyone else while I'm away.'

As soon as I had my back to them I exhaled for a long time and was grateful for the chance to lean against the bar. What a mind-fuck. I wondered who these guys were and what they were doing here, if they were business rivals. . .

But maybe they were joking? That must have been it. They were joking. They were Russian, after all. Their humour was bound to be dry.

'Can you give me two more of these?' I handed the empty glasses to Daisy, shaking the weird feeling off me.

'He's hot,' she remarked, glancing over my shoulder with approval. 'If you're into that sort of thing.'

'Yeah, he's, er. . . something. Not your type?'

'Na, too hot for me. They get boring when they look like that.' She poured me some more Absolut and mocked deep thought. 'You know, I really love guys with a complex. Bullied as a child, Daddy issues, obvious but undiagnosed symptoms of severe bipolar. . . Fuck, I'm crazy for it. What can I say?'

'That's a flattering description of Nic.'

'He loves it.'

I picked up the vodkas, took a breath and then went back to the Russians, who were conferring in their own language as I approached them. My voice dripped with sarcasm as I sat down again.

'Have you upped the price to include a holiday to Peru?'

'I am offended you do not take us seriously, Miss Seven.' Alexei held a hand over his heart. 'I assure you, we can be very serious.'

A pause. 'OK, no, really, this is inappropriate. I don't think I can serve you any more. I'll send someone else over.'

'You will receive everything you ask for, and also a part of the profits.'

I stopped.

Isaak's voice was lighter than his brother's, less tuneful. It was the first time he had spoken.

'What. . . profits?' I asked.

'The profits from our operations,' Isaak continued quietly. 'We are very organized and, to us, someone like you is invaluable. You could be of so much help, if you were willing to work with us. Of course you could still continue to work here for. . . whatever it is you make that is enough to afford your basic rent and your dresses and fancy underwear. But it will never be enough to afford what you want, will it? What do you really want?'

His English was in a different league to Alexei's.

I didn't think anyone had asked me what I wanted before, in any meaningful way. The answer sprang to mind immediately and it came as no shock. I wanted to go home. More than anything, I wanted to be back in Tokyo, with the one who mattered. Noel, of all people, could have done with being brought down a few rungs a while ago. If he began to realize there were consequences to his actions once in while, maybe he'd stop treating everyone around him as if they were flies.

My reply came out before I'd properly thought it through. 'Give me your number.'

Alexei took a pen from his jacket and wrote a mobile number on the back of a London Underground coaster. I noticed that the two of them were dressed in grey. Just grey. It was as if they had both read the same cheap book on espionage: *Blending In For Dummies*.

I took the coaster and stood up. 'I'm going to go now.'

'I hope you get in touch.'

My heart racing, I walked with as much nonchalance as I could to the dressing room. Just having the number in sight was making me feel ill so I put it in my locker where I didn't have to look at it.

When I mustered up the courage to go back into the club again, the two of them had gone.

Daisy skipped up to me and tucked a wad of notes into the waistband of my knickers. 'I don't know what the fuck you said to those guys, but you must have a flippin' bottleful of charm hidden away under that massive permanent sulk-on of yours.'

'What's this?'

'Their tip. They left it for you personally. They were really insistent on it being for you.' A glance over her shoulder. 'I know they like us to pool it and stuff but I won't tell if you won't. That one was all you, that was. You should have it.'

I flicked through the notes.

It was 150 pounds.

Chapter Six

As prostitution goes – hookerdom, whoring, escorting, whatever you want to call it – my first experience of it was probably one of the better ones. It had been about two weeks. I'd brought in the STD test within my first few days and thought I'd have been asked to do something by now.

I hadn't seen much of Noel since my interview, only for snatches of chat here and there, and never about work. Everything I'd learnt about the club so far I'd picked up from Daisy or one of the other girls. But he appeared that night, intercepting me in the middle of the floor and beckoning without a word.

I was just about getting used to traversing the slick club floors in heels that I could barely shuffle in, though I still glared at Daisy if she gave me more than two drinks to carry at a time.

'Um. . . OK.' I put a tray of drinks down on the nearest table, not caring if that was their intended destination or not, and followed Noel upstairs to his office.

Halfway up I had to take my shoes off and carry them, as I couldn't yet control my balance going up and down stairs. They were about five inches high and almost made me adult-sized. Aside from those I was wearing some kind of kimono-style lingerie. The tassels flapped around the backs of my thighs, distracting me.

Once inside, Noel shut the door for me and looked serious. 'I have something for you, if you're interested. If you're up for it, I mean?'

'What sort of thing?'

He indicated for me to sit, but I remained standing.

'A house call.' He leant against his desk, folding his arms. 'A favour for a pretty good mate of mine. Well, work mate.'

'You want me to go have sex with someone?'

Uncharacteristically coy, he hesitated. 'Yes. If you like.'

'Well, who is he?'

'His name's Darsi Howiantz, he's a psychologist or. . . psychiatrist, I can never remember the difference. Anyway, he works with the police and helps me out a lot with stuff and. . .' He struggled to find the words. 'He's into cool things, like books and art and stuff. Like you. You read, don't you? So I thought it might be good to send you.'

It was almost sweet, how awkward he was being. He looked tired, though his eyes were still alert and unclouded. I noticed that his shoes were under his desk where he must have kicked them off. Stifling the urge to laugh, I realized that he must have absently walked down into the club to find me without putting them back on.

I shrugged and put my own shoes on the floor. 'Well, yeah, sure. I guess I get paid more for this?'

'Yeah, of course, it's always where the real money is. But if you don't want to do it or if you want to leave it a while and just find your feet then that's cool, I can get another girl.'

'No, really, I'm fine. I don't mind.'

It didn't seem as though he'd expected that response. It didn't seem as if he entirely wanted it.

I inclined my head. 'You don't think I'm ready?'

'No no, it's fine. You're fine.' He frowned and cleared his throat. 'Right, OK. We pay for the taxis obviously. You haven't done this before, have you?'

'No, I haven't.' I smiled a little. 'But it's just sex, isn't it?'

A pause.

'Yeah.' He looked at the floor for a moment and then back to me, taking a breath. 'Yeah.'

The intensity in the air was thick for a moment as he stared at me, but then he cleared his throat again and took his mobile out of his pocket. He didn't use it, just held it.

'Um, do you have any questions? The obvious stuff is that everyone always uses protection; it's standard. Nothing that's going to leave a mark is allowed without prior warning, ever. But you won't have to worry about that with Darsi, he's pretty straight-edge. He. . . reads a lot. I don't think he'll be into anything weird.'

I kept nodding as he rambled until he ran out of breath.

'OK,' I said, standing very still. 'Just let me know when I have to leave.'

'You don't have any questions?'

'I don't know. Is he hot?'

Noel snorted and glanced at the ceiling, mocking thought. 'Oh well, er. . . speaking as a heterosexual male who's totally comfortable with his sexuality. . . Yeah, he's all right. He's a nice guy too, he's a good guy. Just. . . be yourself and you'll be fine.'

'Myself? Great.'

He swallowed, nodding. 'Thanks. I'll call him then.'

With another glance at his shoes, I picked up my heels and turned to leave.

'Seven, wait a sec.'

I opened the door and waited by it.

He came forwards, pushed the door shut and kissed me for a long time. I could feel the release of repressed tension in his body, his hands running up me, and then he let me go and I wasn't sure what to say to him. He was close. I could see the tiny strands of grey in his hair.

At the time, I wasn't sure if it was something he did with the other girls, but I went with it anyway. I'd wanted him to do it. Even if I could have said no, I wasn't going to.

'That's all,' he said, and went to sit back behind his desk.

I watched him for a couple of seconds and he was breathing heavily through his nose, but he didn't look up from his laptop again so I left.

Darsi's living room, or study, was full to the point of hoarding. It was the strangest collections of items I'd ever seen, but then I could tell within less than a minute of meeting Darsi that he was a very strange man. He had the awkwardly formal social skills of a reclusive academic, but he was appealing. He also didn't ask any questions about my name, which was a first.

As I repressed my amusement at him shaking my hand, I took in his sharp and thin but attractive features.

'So what's that?' I asked, pointing at a multi-coloured plastic bird with what looked like a lump of misshapen brown playdough for a beak, balanced atop a pile of books.

He followed my gaze and indicated for me to sit in a wide reading chair. My skirt was almost too short to sit down but I managed to avoid prematurely flashing anything by crossing my legs.

'It's a bird with a turd for a nose,' Darsi said matter-of-factly.

'And you just buy that sort of thing. . . around?'

He sat also, in a swivel chair by one of his two desks. There was no sofa or TV.

'No, I made them.'

I looked around the study, at the files and photos and the dolls with dog heads attached to their plastic shoulders and I laughed. 'OK, either you're a Mike Kelley fan or you're a mental serial killer.'

'I spent my PhD interviewing serial killers. It could be both. Would you like a drink?'

I stared at him. At first I'd had no idea why Noel had sent me. I could be perfectly affable in a large group, but everyone could predict I'd be terrible at house calls. I found it too hard to hide my boredom or distaste in a one-on-one situation, when there wasn't a wall of background music and other women and alcohol to distract people with. But now it was becoming more apparent.

'So what do you do?' I asked, too intrigued to acknowledge his offer of a drink. 'Noel said—'

'I'm a forensic criminal psychologist.'

'And what exactly have you done recently for Noel that's so great?'

He sat there, owl-like in his shirt and delicate glasses with his foppish hair, and swivelled. 'Nothing great enough to warrant this but. . . he insisted.'

'Well, I've never done this before.'

'No?' He smiled. 'Neither have I. I don't go into Noel's club, really.'

I couldn't imagine anywhere he would be more out of place. It made me wonder what he was like in bed; whether his bookish

57

demeanour was masking something perverted. The dolls and figurines made me think so.

'So. . .' I hoped my phrasing of the question wouldn't make me sound too suspicious. 'If you've interviewed all these serial killers, could you spot a proper psychopath in the street now? I mean, if you spent a bit of time with them, could you tell who was likely to be a raging psycho murderer?'

'Quite a lot of people have psychopathic traits: it doesn't mean they're going to go out and murder someone. Most of the time they end up owning businesses or running a government department.' He picked up a mug from the desk next to him and checked it for liquid, but didn't find any. 'But the longer I've talked to psychopaths and. . . sociopaths, it does become easier to spot them. A surprising amount of them.'

'Am I a psychopath? Can you tell me that right now?'

'The very act of asking that question, or asking yourself that question, probably means that you're not.'

'Why?'

'A psychopath would almost never self-identify as such, unless it was the result of some cataclysmic event, like a murder for example. They would simply think that. . .' He trailed off, his face tightening in thought. 'They think that the world works in a certain way, and that they're working it to their advantage. They think they're right, in short. They think of others as pawns and opportunities and they also think that's how all people should be, if they want to succeed.'

I snorted. 'Did you just try really hard to dumb that answer down for me?'

'Only a little. I hoped you wouldn't be able to tell.'

'Look, I'm here to do whatever you want,' I said, deciding to propel the situation forwards. 'I'd be happy to sit here and talk to you about your job and ask you questions, but I was also sent here to do other things and. . . I really want you to do whatever you want, even if it's weird or. . . especially if it's weird. I'd like that. I don't want you to think you have to be polite to me or make small talk with me. It's fine for you to ask for anything.'

I wasn't sure if I'd said the right thing, or if girls were even meant to talk this much on house calls, but I suspected Darsi would need some prompting.

'Just be yourself,' Noel had said. Now I understood why.

'Sorry,' I said, covering myself. 'Sorry if that was too forward.'

'No.' Darsi took a long breath, as if he were stifling a large smile.

I waited, trying to contain how eager I was to know the sort of thing that turned him on.

He gestured at his books. Stacks of them. There was a step-ladder wedged between piles, to reach the tops of his shelves.

'Pick a book from here,' he said, taking off his glasses for a moment. 'Fiction.'

Chapter Seven

It took the rest of the night and half a day for me to come to a decision; less time that I'd thought.

I returned home at just after four in the morning, to the shitty flat that had somehow become my base. It used to belong to a friend, whose doorstep I had appeared on nearly three years ago, still smelling of soap and copper and mute with shock. He'd let me stay without hesitation, giving me a bed and space for a permanent easel in the tiny living room. Then he'd gone. I didn't know where. But he left me this place: the one flat in London where the rent never seemed to go up.

I could barely remember the guy's name now. I'd always been more into having acquaintances than friends.

The flat had resembled a Far Eastern opium den when I'd arrived and smelt of incense and marijuana. Not much had changed. I'd come to like it too much.

When I got home I stood in the kitchen doorway holding the coaster in my hands.

Another phone number.

I knew what I wanted to do, much more so than I had done with Mark's business card, but the fear was stopping me. It was just the fear.

It wasn't as if anyone was going to get hurt. If anyone could afford to lose some money, it was Noel. It might even do him good to feel something less than invincible for once. What bothered me were the possible repercussions.

There were no two ways about it: I'd be dead within hours if either Noel or Ronnie found out what I'd done. Noel might have shown me affection, brief flashes of humanity, but I knew that deep down they were both beyond reason in a way that most people would never understand. Violence wasn't a last resort to them; it was how they interacted with the world. I would die and they'd laugh. Fuck, they'd enjoy it.

But it wouldn't get that far. . .

. . . and I could go home.

I slept on it, for about six hours, but when I woke up nothing had changed. It felt like most of the daylight hours had passed me by outside.

I could go home. That was the thought that overrode everything. *I could go home.*

Repeating it over and over to myself, I went into the living room, picked up the phone and called Alexei.

'Thanks for the tip,' I said, sitting on the floor with my toes curled into the rug. 'It was pretty generous. Look, I've had a think about your offer and I'm. . . interested. I think I'm interested. Just tell me in a bit more detail what you guys are actually thinking of doing.'

'You think you are interested?' He was smiling, I could tell. 'Think is not good enough. For what you are asking for, we will need you to prove it.'

'Um. . . prove it? How?'

'Earn your first payment we gave you.'

'My payment?' My newfound resolve wavered a little. 'What, my *tip*? How do you want me to do that?'

'Be clever. Show some imagination. Then we will talk. I would like very much to talk to you again, Seven.'

Racking my brains for a strategy, I came up with nothing.

'Right. OK, I'll. . . get back to you then.'

'We hope so. We do not like it when women lead us on.'

He hung up.

I rested the phone against my chin, trying to work out just how much of a threat his last statement had been. It made me feel uneasy, sitting on the floor obscured by the sofa. It made me look around, as if something were in here with me. I stood up and fixed myself something to eat, making as much noise as I could, so that I could almost forget how alone I was.

Before I went into the Underground that night I found a store full of gadgets, and asked to see some of their voice-activated recorders. They were expensive but, suspiciously, they all came to just under 150 pounds. I bought the most expensive one I could afford within my budget, and a USB stick.

Feeling too on edge to read the instructions back in my flat before work, I took a long bus ride around the West End instead. It seemed easy enough to use, but the more I thought about it the more insane my plans seemed. What was I doing this for? To prove myself to a couple of over-confident Russians who claimed they could pay me enough to return to my old life? Or was I doing it to give the middle finger to Noel?

A bit of both, I figured.

On my way into the club I was painfully aware of the USB and the recorder knocking around the insides of my pockets.

When safely in the dressing room and hidden behind my locker door I transferred the recorder from my coat to the underwiring of my bra, and wondered just how I was going to get Noel or Ronnie to come out of their office.

It would be easier if Ronnie were here. He was the more social of the two.

Daisy let herself into the room behind me and started counting to ten under her breath as she adjusted her hair in the mirror.

I hated it when other people counted out loud. It made me nervous.

'What's up?' I asked, slamming my locker a little too hard and applying some lipstick.

'There are some proper wank-stains out there tonight. It'll be a flippin' miracle if I don't end up *killing* one of them. I stopped serving them a bloody age ago and somehow they still got fucking trolleyed!'

'Is Noel or Ron here?'

'Ron's upstairs; not a clue about Monobrow. I don't think I can get him to chuck them out until they actually *do* something though.'

She backcombed her hair and observed her hip bones, making a sharp edge above the line of her hot pants. Apart from Noel, Daisy was the only person here who could make me laugh. I'd hated her when we'd first met and I was sure the feeling had been mutual. But there was something so compelling about her brilliantly pretty features and reluctance to ever give a shit about anything.

'Think I can *lure* them into doing something vile and start screaming?' she asked.

I glanced down at myself and smirked. 'I don't know. Could I?'

She grinned. 'Or we could just poison them all, eh?'

With an exasperated sigh, she walked out of the room. I followed her and instantly spotted the group of men she was referring to. It was impossible to miss them, even with the club this crowded. They were making more noise than everyone else put together and I didn't recognize any of them.

Onstage, the Chinese girl was doing some contortion act, on her knees bending over backwards until the top of her head touched the floor. I could do that easily, I thought, but no one likes a show-off.

I watched Daisy flirting with the irritating drunkards and kept an eye on them, willing them to cause more of a scene. I held back, trying not to catch any eyes and become occupied by work until I'd had the chance to go upstairs.

Now I was here, actually doing it, my worry about getting caught far outweighed any guilt I felt towards Noel or Ronnie. Ronnie hadn't done anything wrong, but I realized I had zero problem with screwing over Noel a little. All I needed to do was think back to his voice on the phone, speaking as if he suddenly didn't know me, and didn't want to. . .

Bastard.

What did I care if a couple of Russian upstarts took some cash from someone who was rich enough to have offered to keep me in a flat of my own more than once?

I'd always turned him down though. I hated the idea of being owned by somebody like that.

'Eh, sweetheart, can we get some ales over here?'

64

'We don't have. . . Wait.' I waved a hand vaguely in the direction of the voice.

'Hey, are you deaf, sweetheart?'

'Why don't you call me *sweetheart* again?' I snapped, meeting the eyes of the dick sitting at the table to my right. 'I'd really like that.'

He shut up and I moved back and leant against the bar.

Daisy was pretending to laugh along with one of the men: the youngest-looking guy with one of those stupid moustaches that had come into fashion in the more tragic and *happening* parts of the East End. She leant across him to get some empty glasses and he grabbed her ass. You almost couldn't blame him.

'Hey!'

She slapped him with surprising strength. He pushed her. Glasses dropped.

I ran towards them and caught the words 'Crazy bitch!' screamed into Daisy's face before I grabbed his arm, twisted it up behind him and almost put my boot-heel through the back of his knee.

Daisy kicked him again, for little reason. 'Fucking *touch* me. . .'

Even the girl onstage hesitated to stare at us.

'Go get Ronnie,' I said, and pushed the guy away from me on to the floor. 'Now get the fuck out and take your friends with you.'

Daisy winked at me and made an upstairs gesture to another of the girls nearer the stairwell.

'Who the fuck are you, bitch?' one of the others sneered at me, trying to help his friend regain his footing. Their eyes

65

were bleary and aggressive with gin or Bacardi or whatever it was I could smell on them.

'I'm the one who could break your face before my boss even gets down here to throw your sorry ass out,' I said, leaning in. 'So run along.'

I left Daisy watching them with a smug smile and her hands on her hips, running over to the door to the stairwell as the Underground's second manager, Ronnie O'Connell, came storming through it.

He was well over six feet tall, so I barely even fell into his eyeline. He could tuck me under his armpit and carry me around like a clutch bag if he felt like it. He scared me, Ronnie. He scared me much more than Noel ever could.

I slipped through the door before it had even shut and sprinted up to the deserted corridor and the open door of their office. I wasn't prepared for the wave of nerves that hit me when I got there. In a million different mental scenarios Ronnie came back up and found me, his olive-skinned face and cruel brown eyes full of anger and suspicion, and asked me, 'What the fuck are you doing in here?'

Argh, fuck, come on.

I ran my hands along the underside of the desk but it seemed too obvious. Noel kept the place so ordered that there wasn't enough clutter to take advantage of. He emptied the bin twice a day. There was no dust on any of the surfaces. I tried to search for an object that I'd never seen move, that neither of them touched.

There was a printer under the desk. It looked prehistoric compared to everything else in the room. I knelt, stuck the recording device behind it and switched it on. It had something like four days of battery life. Even if they did have to print something they wouldn't find it unless they were looking.

OK, OK, come on.

There was no sound from the stairwell.

I stood up and tapped a key on his laptop. It restarted but asked for a password. There was no time for me to wait around and try to remember the name of Ronnie's wife and kids, so I left it and crept out of the office.

The door at the bottom of the stairwell opened.

Shit.

I turned and ran towards the end of the corridor. Everything else would be locked. There was nowhere else to go but out of the fire escape as quietly as I could, not even shutting the doors properly behind me for fear of making too much noise.

I crouched outside the doors, steadying them with my palms to stop any slamming.

Shit. Shit!

My stiletto heels were falling through the metal grating.

There was no sound from inside.

I stood up and shut the doors fully with a small click.

It was cold at the top of the building. I was suddenly conscious of wearing little more than underwear. Baring my teeth against the bitter breeze, I walked with difficulty down the spiral stairs and into the road running along the side of the club. I looked left and right but there was nothing to see but the backs of restaurants and bars, skips and rats. No people, thank God.

With as much dignity as I could muster, shivering, I let

myself back through the staff entrance and into the dressing room.

The Chinese girl, taking off her make-up, frowned at me. 'Why did you go outside like that?'

'I just. . . really needed a cigarette. Forgot my coat.'

I sifted through the coat rack and through the pocket of my leather jacket for my mobile.

Why the fuck had I mouthed off to those guys? Was it fucking bravado or something? Had I thought it was clever at the time? Probably. Stupid bitch. Now that I had hidden the recorder the idea of potentially having Ronnie O'Connell out for me was terrifying, and very real.

When I found my phone I shut myself in the grotty staff toilet, sat with my feet up on the seat and called Alexei.

Someone had written 'Question everything' on the wall. Someone else had drawn an arrow pointing to it with the counter-question, 'Why?'

'*Da?*'

'Um. . . Hello, it's Seven.'

Silence.

I filled it with sarcasm. 'You know, I'm fine. Thanks for asking. Um, I did it. I put a recorder in their office and it's on. I think it lasts for a few days.'

A pause. 'Good. That is a good idea. More immediately, Noel Braben's password is much more interesting to us.'

'Well, obviously I don't know the password to his computer or anything. I mean, I could guess but after a few tries I think you get locked out.'

'You change your story?'

'No!' I swallowed. 'No, I'm just saying that it's not likely

I'd get it right, that's all. Look, I know I said I could but, to be honest, I don't think there's any way I could get Noel's password. We're not on the greatest terms right now and—'

'Stop talking. I am not interested by what you have to say.'

I faltered, thinking that he might have sounded happier with me after I'd given him the prospect of eavesdropping on Noel and Ronnie's office conversations. 'Well, you obviously are to some degree, because otherwise I wouldn't have this number, would I?'

'I am not interested by your *excuses*. If you do not find this password, things will be very bad for you.'

'But it's just not possible.'

'That is not my problem.'

'But—'

'A name! An address! You cannot get any of these simple things?'

I listened for the sound of anyone waiting outside to use the toilet, and whispered. 'These aren't simple things, OK? I can plant a recorder but things like names and addresses and stuff. . . I'm probably not going to be able to do that. Sorry.'

'Then things will be very bad for you.'

His vocabulary wasn't extensive enough to articulate in any more detail exactly how he wanted to threaten me, but I was glad of it. I got the message.

I searched for the right words, but in the end all I could say was, 'Yeah. Yeah, I understand.'

'You will find something more useful to us. If you call us again with any other questions and no further information, I will tell you exactly how bad things will get for you, so that we have no more cause for time-wasting. Do you understand?'

'. . . I understand.'

He hung up.

I realized I'd been holding my breath and exhaled.

'Fuck.'

I took several deep breaths.

'*Fuck.*'

There was more anger coursing through my system than fear; anger at myself. I thought they would have been seriously impressed by what I'd done, and all I'd offered was sarcasm.

Idiot.

After staying in there for as long as I could get away with, I went and put my phone back in my jacket pocket. I hadn't even had time to put my forehead in my hand and try to calm down when Daisy reappeared, swinging on the open door.

'Hey, where did you go? Ron wants you to go upstairs and confirm what happened with those dickheads.'

'Oh. . . Needed a cigarette.'

'Right. Well, go on then. He's got a proper mood on now.'

For a moment, I wished that I was able to stomach alcohol. But then I composed myself and went upstairs, trying not to let any more emotion cross my face.

Chapter Eight

It was almost half three in the morning and I was sitting cross-legged on one of the club tables watching Daisy wipe the bar down. She had put more clothes on now the place was empty; a lumpy grey jumper with a Velociraptor and 'Clever Girl' splashed across the front.

The floor was sticky.

Daisy was talking about pornography.

'You watch it too, right?' she said, hopping up on to the bar for a rest. 'This isn't just me being a pervert?'

I shrugged and lit a cigarette. 'Yeah, I watch it. Sometimes I can't be bothered though. Too much effort.'

'But you know what I mean, right? You can never find a single decent fucking video if you're a girl. It's an outrage.'

I threw the cigarette packet across the club at her and she caught it and lit one for herself.

'Well. . .' I said, inhaling. 'Depends what you're looking for.'

'Don't tell me you watch *mainstream* porn, it's *disgusting*.'

'Since when were you a porn hipster?'

She flicked stray ash off her jumper and pointed at me. 'Look, *you*, I'm not a hipster, I've just got taste, that's all. You can't seriously say mainstream porn turns you on? All the shit actors and choking and gagging and. . . you know, there's not one genuine fucking orgasm in sight? The way they go on, you'd think we cum at the fucking *sight* of a cock.'

'Yeah, but it's for men, isn't it?'

'I don't know what's more insulting: that they don't even consider me a proper customer or that men are turned on by those fucking amateur dramatics.'

'What do you look for?'

She played with her hair for a bit, giving some serious thought to her answer. 'I just wanna see people fucking who actually *want* to fuck each other. It's what porn is meant to be, watching people really enjoying a good shag! That's where it's all at: the amateur videos. The amateur *lesbian* videos, especially. That's the only way you get anything quality.'

'Didn't know you were into ladies?'

'I'm into all sorts. Cocks, cunts, tits, all of it.'

'So everything's fair game to you, then?'

She took a drag and laughed. 'Well, not ugly people. And I'm stuck with the fella, aren't I, bless his heart.'

I tried to imagine her watching pornography. I tried to imagine her with a woman. I stubbed out my cigarette in the ashtray behind me and motioned for the packet.

She threw it back to me.

'So. . . how's it going with Monobrow?'

I fiddled with my lighter. She was the only other person who knew, or who claimed to know. I had never actually confirmed anything or spoken to her about it properly. That way I could never be accused of lying.

The silence was uncharacteristically tense for us.

'I don't think it's *going* any more.'

She nodded. 'I'm sorry.'

'He's married; it was never going to *go* for long anyway.'

'I think he really likes you, Kik.'

I forced a smile, even though the mention of it all out loud was bringing the anger back. 'He's a prick. . . Actually, no, he's not. He's just. . . weak. Doesn't know what he wants one day to the next.'

'He won't stay with her.'

'He won't leave her either.'

'Go talk to him.'

'Since when did you become a couples therapist?'

'Just go to his house and talk to him! They're dim, girl, they're all really dim. They can't take hints. Go talk to him.'

The cigarette was starting to taste stale. 'Maybe.'

She was right. It was obvious; I did have to go to his house and talk to him, but not for the reasons she thought. At the time, I was sure everything was going to turn out all right, somehow. It was never my intention for anyone to get hurt.

That night I dreamt about Seiko.

One of my earliest memories of Japan, and of my mother, was being taught to deflect a compliment. It was the done thing there, deflection; not being too good, too distinguished. Mum embraced that idea more than Dad ever did. Maybe it was because he was Japanese and she was the other? The westerner? Maybe she just wanted to belong?

The playground was dark and sullen with humidity.

I went to a pre-school in Toshima-ku where they were shocked

I could speak their language, looking as anglicized as I did. I had the straight dark hair, the skinny frame and the demure voice, but I was still clearly the other. My dark green eyes gave me away, the sallow tone of my skin and exaggerated size of my lips and nose.

Mum walked me inside the gates with an umbrella hanging off her forearm, and started talking to some of the other mothers in broken Japanese. They humoured her, told her it was excellent, when it wasn't.

I spotted the only girl I liked, Seiko, and she waved at me.

'Kiyomi is looking beautiful, Helena,' said Seiko's mother to mine.

She was a sweet-faced woman whose teeth were a little too big for her mouth but I thought that only made her look more friendly.

'No, she isn't,' Mum said, smiling.

'She is beautiful.'

'No, she isn't. Thank you.'

It was an ongoing argument between her and everyone around us who disagreed. To this day, I was never sure who I believed was right. But it was the first thing I remember being taught so overtly, how to deflect. No, not deflect. Reject.

Seiko told me I was pretty when we were both a little older, when I had moved back to Tokyo for the second time and when we were both able to understand what it meant. It was a relief, coming back to Japan from London at the age of fourteen. I preferred the way I wasn't leered at. I preferred not having to plan my walks home around the whims of men and their constant over-entitled harassment.

I used to think that it was here, and only here, in this one city, that I felt a profound sense of calm. Now I realized it wasn't the place; it was she.

It was she who started calling me Seven, because of the OCD that dictated I do everything in sevens. I turned lights on and off seven times. I blinked in groups of seven if I got agitated. If I scuffed my heel on the road I had to stop and scuff it another six times. . .

But it was all knocked out of me over time, when we moved to London.

Seiko had inherited her mother's features: the wide eyes and wide smile. I felt less on edge around people with open faces, where motives and thoughts and emotions could play out. It was ironic, given that I had always struggled to move beyond two or three of the most basic expressions. My smile was crooked. The rest of the time, regardless of what was happening, I looked like undiluted apathy.

We were standing on a bridge in the gardens surrounding the Meiji Shrine, watching the fish, a few years before we both discovered what it was to really get drunk. I wished that humans could stand a chance of looking like those fish, with their silver and orange scales. Sunshine was wasted on skin like ours.

Tourists passed back and forth behind us, sometimes pausing to take photos. But it was so quiet here. Even in the tourist spots, it was quiet.

'You're so beautiful, Seven,' Seiko said.

'No, I'm not,' I replied.

Even though her smile was trying to appear sad, she never quite managed to attain it. There was too much light and hope in her face.

'Sometimes I think trying to get to know you is like trying to see through the top of a forest canopy,' she said. 'You don't stand a chance of seeing what lives up there or how it works, but occasionally you can hope that something comes falling down.'

Chapter Nine

The next day I went back to Tooting. I surprised myself. So long with no inclination to return and now I'd visited twice within a few days, without any major breakdowns. They didn't have the power I'd expected them to, my old roads and buildings. I was sure I'd feel differently the closer I got to the flat though.

It was warmer; more like a proper summer and not the sad excuse for a July I'd become used to in England. During the winters the cold didn't bother me; it was the tragedy of the summers that made me miss Japan.

This time I bypassed Jensen McNamara's building and went up to my old block. It looked like it had been refurbished, or at least repainted.

I tried to guess where the Williams kids might have lived, and buzzed a couple of flats. After some silences, a man answered.

'Yes?'

'Hi, is it OK if you let me in? I forgot my—'

'Which flat, love?'

'Well. . .' Of all the people who could have answered I had to get a fucking inquisitive one. 'Flat eighteen. Actually, I *used* to live in flat eighteen.'

He didn't say anything for what seemed like a long time.

'I'm looking for Mrs Williams,' I said, hoping the elaboration would loosen him up. 'I just want to talk to her, or Mr Williams. . .'

'Oh, child. . . You'd better come up here,' he replied. 'Flat six.'

I was buzzed in.

I almost turned and walked away, spooked by his tone of voice, but my bloody-minded need for information made me go inside. The interior was different. It may have been repainted but a stain had been left in the air that was still fresh and raw despite the years that had gone by. It was as if the scene had been replaying itself in my absence, and I was just here for another rerun.

There were no broken syringes under my feet, and no graffiti on the walls, or blood on the stairs.

I only had to go to the second floor.

What had they done with my flat now? Burnt it? Boarded it up? Or, worse, rehoused another family in there? If there was a new family, would they even know what had happened?

The door of flat six was ajar and he was waiting for me, peering through the gap. I recognized him and the name Angus came to mind. I didn't remember him ever speaking to anyone, but I'd seen the face before. In fact, I think I'd rarely seen it in its entirety, only in fragments in half-open doors and curtained windows.

'Oh, it really is you. . .' He didn't move as I approached.

'Hey.' I waved, unsure of what else to do. 'Yeah, it's me.'

'Come in, come in.'

He shuffled backwards behind the door to let me inside, totally hiding himself from sight. It crossed my mind that walking into a random strange man's flat wasn't the best idea, especially as no one knew where I was, but he looked old and physically wasted. I reckoned I might win in a straight fight, if it came to that.

I didn't attempt to look at him as I came in. He would show himself when he felt like it. The inside of his flat was smoky: tobacco, weed and incense. In the corner of the living room was an old-fashioned sprawling red sofa, with a regal pattern like medieval wallpaper.

There was a suspicious-looking ginger kitten darting around the room next to the wall.

'I'm so very sorry.'

I turned.

He was skinny enough to be obscured by small objects, with gaunt features, no hair and at least two rings on every one of his fingers.

'My name's Angus.' He extended a shaky hand.

I shook it and noticed that his fingernails were longer than most women's, and filed to rough points.

'I'm Seven. I lived. . . upstairs.'

'I'm so very sorry,' he said again, keeping hold of my hand.

'Thanks.'

'Please. . . sit.'

I didn't want to, but for fear of seeming rude I backed on to the edge of the red sofa.

'Is the Williams family still here?' I asked. 'Or maybe just the parents? I'd really like to speak to them.'

'Oh, they're gone. They're gone.'

He crouched, rather than sat, across the room from me, directing all of his words at the carpet through the protective barrier of his hands. It must have taken an extraordinary amount of courage for him to let me inside.

'What? Where did they go?'

'I don't know, they just. . . went.'

'When?'

'After.'

The movie posters all over the walls made the living room seem even smaller, trapping heat. There was *Pulp Fiction*, *The Lost Boys*, *Labyrinth*, *The Goonies*. . .

'After I left, you mean?' I said.

'No, after. . . after. . .'

'After one of their kids died?'

'One of them,' he whispered through a hole between his fingers. 'This building is bad luck. It keeps its evil all stored up, in the walls. That's why they tried to repaint it, see. . .'

He giggled and halted, as if the sudden action had shocked him into silence.

My head ached.

'The oldest died, right?' I pressed on.

'The oldest boy, Nate. Not long after you left this cursed place, child.'

I looked around me and felt oppressed by the eyes of the posters. 'I've never been into superstition. How did Nate die?'

'He was shot.'

'A drive-by.'

'The boy was only fourteen, same age as Nate. We're turning the young into soldiers; what chance do they have?'

I thought of my sister and the glass embedded in my father's hand. What chance did any of us have if someone wanted us dead more than we wanted to stay alive? Through sheer force of will you could end anyone's life, at any time. It wasn't until that day almost three years ago that I'd understood the truth of how transient and abrupt all our lives are. If you wanted to stay alive more than someone wanted you dead, then that was all that mattered.

'Did anyone find out why? Was he mixed up in a gang or something?'

Angus shook his head, twitched and shook his head again. 'No.'

'No, no one knows why? Or no, he wasn't in a gang?'

He continued to shake his head. 'No one knows. They weren't in gangs, the children round here.'

I wasn't so sure, but it could easily have been a case of mistaken identity. What I wanted was a connection; anything to hang on to that proved all the deaths in this building were connected.

The kitten leapt up on to the back of Angus's chair and stared at me.

'Did the police speak to you at any time?' I asked, glaring at it.

'I didn't see anything.'

'Yeah, but did the police—'

'That's what I told them, both times.'

I sighed. 'So officers came to speak to you both times?'

'Yes. . . Yes.'

'Just the officers? Did a man come to see you as well? Not a police officer, just a random guy?'

He hesitated and stopped shaking his head. 'A man.'

I almost hadn't wanted to hear it. 'Just the one, on his own? What was his name?'

'. . . I don't know. I thought he was a detective. A plain-clothes detective. He spoke to everyone. When he left, my tabby. . . Kellogg died. Just had a seizure and died right there, by you.'

'Maybe the man was cursed too?' I said, attempting to sound lighthearted and failing.

'No, it's the building. It's the walls.'

Angus chanced a look at me, twitched, giggled, and fell silent.

I didn't want to kill her: the cat. I don't imagine a child could understand the concept of wanting to kill something at that age, when death was still something abstract that was talked about in euphemisms.

The cat was called Audrey Hepburn. She was seven years old and she had a bad leg from where she'd fought with a fox one night. She had a soft brown coat and rubbed her cheek against your knuckles when you stroked her.

Looking after pets is more exciting when you're young. When we visited Grandmother in London in the holidays, I was allowed to treat her like my own pet. Caring for an animal, feeding it and playing with it and brushing its fur, all felt like tiny rehearsals for being an adult.

The logic in my mind was clear. So clear. I took the painkillers that I saw my grandmother take from the bathroom and put them in Audrey Hepburn's food, breaking up the little soluble pills into tiny powder pieces to hide them amongst the jellied meat and biscuits. If I did that, Audrey Hepburn's leg would hurt less.

I don't remember the details so much, just a vague sense of satisfaction at my good deed, and playing in the garden, and later the cat throwing up all over the kitchen and a trip to the vet and then Audrey Hepburn didn't come back.

Mum was cleaning up the vomit, shaken and white. She didn't look at me so my father took me back into the garden and distracted me.

My grandmother slapped me and thrust the empty pill box in my face and I cried and I cried and I cried. Not just because of the shock of being struck – my parents had never even tapped me on the wrist – but because I didn't understand what was happening. Grandmother said Audrey Hepburn was dead. Dead. It sounded a large and ominous word even then. My parents said that she'd had to go away to a holiday resort for poorly cats, or some shit like that. Cat heaven.

Grandmother didn't speak to me again, unless it was in a strained and artificial voice put on to appease my parents. We used to spend most summers and Christmas Days with her, but never again after that. Mum visited her alone usually.

It wasn't deliberate. I knew it wasn't. But Grandmother said, 'The bad will out,' so maybe if deep down you were evil, it didn't really matter if it was deliberate or not?

Chapter Ten

I almost didn't feel like me, walking to Noel's flat the next day, hoping that his wife, Caroline, wouldn't be there for some freak reason. I would never have thought I was stupid enough to try and do it. And it was stupid. It wasn't brave. It helped, as I walked, if I thought of it as a video game; something that had no direct life-or-death effect on my life.

It was getting too hot for jackets but my leather one was like a comforter. I'd feel too exposed talking to Noel in some skimpy outfit trying to find an excuse to get into his private computer.

I didn't like myself if I thought too much about it.

I buzzed my way into Noel's building by pressing all the other buttons at random, and took the lift to the eighth floor.

'Fuuuuuuuck,' I muttered to myself as I knocked on his door.

There was no sound, for a while. I hoped that I'd judged the day wrong and went to walk away when he answered.

He looked about as happy to see me as a police officer or Jehovah's Witness. I hated to admit it but he also looked better than I had seen him for a while. The lines around his eyes were less pronounced and his skin was more youthful. I could tell he hadn't been drinking much or taking as many drugs.

'Seven, what. . .? Hi.'

I felt like the scum of the earth, but he was managing to be almost as big a jerk as me.

'Can I talk to you?' I asked.

'Um. . .'

'Sorry, I wasn't asking. Did I sound like I was?'

With a patronizing smile, I opened his door and walked past him into the flat. It looked different; more cluttered. Not everything had been put away or painstakingly cleaned. I could tell that Caroline had been living here again and it pissed me off even more that it hurt a bit. I'd never been under the illusion that he would leave her, but I'd never had her paraded around in front of me like this.

His laptop was on the dining table, open.

I pulled out one of the chairs around it and sat down.

'Can I get you anything?' Noel asked, sounding exasperated.

'An explanation as to why you blew me off the other day would be nice.' I looked pointedly at his wedding ring.

His hand hovered in the air as if he were about to hide it from view, but then he rested it on the back of a chair. 'I was going to tell you about it, but it just didn't come up. I hadn't seen you for a while and. . . Caroline doesn't come running at my beck and call. How was I meant to know she'd come back?'

'Because she's come back *twice* now and you keep saying it's the last time.' I threw up a hand. 'Look, Noel, I never asked you to leave her. I never asked you that or thought you would, even when you were crying all over me that she'd walked out again and all that shit, so. . . can I get a little respect here, please?'

To my surprise, he didn't become defensive. Instead he pulled out another chair and sat down also.

'OK,' he said. 'Let's talk, if you want.'

I'd hoped it wouldn't be this easy. I needed an excuse to pretend to dissolve into hysterics and make him leave the room to make me tea or something. If anger wasn't going to be on the cards, I was going to have to play for emotional devastation. I forced myself to think about my sister, and tightened my face to mimic a dramatic repression of tears.

He tensed. 'You think I haven't been. . . fair.'

I hated sounding this pathetic, but it was necessary.

'Did you even care about me at all?' I said, doing my best to sound strained.

'Jesus, of course! I mean. . .' He lowered his voice. 'Of course, it's just. . . It would kill Caroline if she knew. I mean, that would be it.'

There were no photos of them together in his flat. I had another look around for some while he'd been forcing out the last couple of sentences, but there was still nothing. Whether they were together or not there was never any photographic evidence of it, not even a self-satisfied out-of-date wedding photo. I wondered if they both had Facebook accounts with albums of posed couple photos. Maybe that was where all their public affection was?

I glanced at the laptop. 'So, you think she'll stay this time?'

'I don't know. Maybe. If I can stop. . . drinking and. . . well, drinking.'

I'd never seen him ashamed before, but that changed when he talked about alcohol.

'If I hadn't come and seen you today, were you just going to ignore me until I got the message?'

He looked at his hands and shrugged. 'Honestly. . . I'm not proud of it. I might have done. I'd have. . . Christ, I'd have ignored you right now and run away if I could. Is that sad? That's fucking sad. What a prick.'

'At least you're upfront about that.'

'Being a prick?'

'Yeah.' I went to take a packet of cigarettes out of my bag and hesitated. 'Am I even allowed to smoke in here now?'

'No, she, er. . . doesn't like it.'

'What do you do?'

'Smoke out of the window.'

'Jesus. . . Pussy-whipped.' I put the packet away again, keeping the laptop in the corner or my eye, and sniffed. 'Fuck, I'm not going to lie. . . This sucks.'

'We're friends, aren't we?'

'Are we?' I saw the chance for an escalation and took it, my eyes welling up. 'Are we really gonna be friends, Noel? Caroline's just gonna let us hang out and, what, go. . . fucking bowling or something? Carry on going to art galleries and shit like nothing happened and you're not married and. . . not even allowed to smoke in your own fucking flat?'

I dropped my bag and cigarettes contemptuously by my feet, put my head in my hands and started crying.

'Seven. . . Shit.' He got up and stood over me, flapping, not sure whether to touch me. 'Please, come on, stop crying. You shouldn't cry over me anyway—'

'You're not going to fire me, are you?' I looked up at him with tear-streaked eyes, smudged mascara, and his expression was one of sheer terror. 'Am I going to be able to carry on working?'

'Yes! God, yes, Seven, I'm not going to fire you. Come on.' He put his hands on my shoulders and I continued to sob for a while.

'I'm sorry,' I said, thinking that I should be awarded a fucking Oscar. 'I'm sorry, I don't know what's got into me. . . I just. . . I really care about you, you know.'

For a moment the crying almost became laughter, but I pulled it together. I could only imagine I had dragged Noel into his worst living nightmare.

'Can I. . .?' he ventured, giving my shoulders a squeeze. 'Shall I make you some tea or. . . coffee?'

Fucking yes.

I nodded, shielding my eyes.

'Yeah, I'd really like that.' I clutched his hand for good measure. 'I'd *really* like that.'

He never fucking remembered that I didn't drink coffee.

With a barely audible sigh of relief, Noel left me and crossed the living room into his kitchen, shutting the door behind him. I could see him leaning against the side and taking some deep breaths, psyching himself up for the return, making the coffee as slowly as possible.

Doing my best to block out the horrific reality of the danger I was in, I slid the laptop towards me, found my way on to his day-by-day planner that was open next to his emails, and scrolled through it for any names.

The name 'Issa' came up a couple of times over the last fortnight. I clicked on one of his emails and saw nothing but a date and time. No place.

I paused, trying to hear anything over the sound of the kettle boiling that might warn me if Noel was coming back in.

Nothing.

I started scrolling again but everything else in his email history seemed innocuous. I wiped my eyes and searched his inbox again for the name Issa. This time I opened a couple of emails between Noel and Ronnie, discussing a drop-off. Issa was copied in. Full name Issa Taggart.

I noticed his most recent email was from Caroline and paused, a lump in my throat.

A cupboard opened and shut in the kitchen and I jumped, snapping back from the laptop.

The top of Noel's head appeared, tentatively, around the half-open door.

'Sorry, I don't remember how you take it?'

I almost couldn't speak, my heart pounding and jaw locked. 'Um. . . white. Sugar.'

He nodded and disappeared again, not even glancing at the laptop. The kettle had boiled, so I had a few minutes. I knew it was an idiotic thing to do, only more likely to get me caught, but I clicked on the email from Caroline anyway.

'*Heeeey, going to be late home. Hitting gym with the girls. I'm so proud of you for everything you said this morning! You can do it. :) I love you I love you I love you! xxxx*'.

Fuck, it was horrible.

I read it again, when I shouldn't even have let myself read it the first time.

As in if in a trance I went to his Sent Messages to find a reply.

'*I mean it. I love you I love you I love you. N xx*'.

He'd never written like that to me. It was as if I was reading correspondence from another human being entirely.

I read it again, but just the 'I love you's' this time, and closed everything down with a loud sigh of relief. It took me a while to stop shaking and breathe normally. I'd stopped fake crying when my head had started to ache from the effort.

When Noel came back through with the coffee I wasn't that interested in seeing the charade through. I was too angry with him to pretend to be hurt.

He put a cup of coffee down next to my hand and I ignored it.

'Are you even happy?' I asked. 'Really? I mean, I can't help but think that in a few months you'll ring me up and everything will just start all over again, except every time you'll sound a little bit less happy and a little bit more unhappy.'

That part wasn't insincere. I decided that part I actually meant.

'You're probably right,' he said, sitting down, unrepentant.

I snorted. 'I'm probably right, huh?'

'Yeah, I . . . Seven, I respect you too much to lie and say nothing is going to happen again. We have history, you know. That means something, right? But I promise, I truly fucking promise it'll never affect your job.'

My job. Christ.

I almost couldn't believe that he had the gall to say that to me, and then he had the audacity to reach across the tabletop and take my hand. The gesture didn't help the level of fury that was building in my stomach every second I was looking at his stupid faux-earnest face.

What did he want, a fucking gold star for being honest?

When I first met him I'd thought that his overly frank and unapologetic manner was admirable, but I was starting to believe that maybe he was just a raging dickhead who couldn't be bothered to spare a thought for how to conduct himself around people who weren't sycophants.

I picked up the coffee, looked at the white carpet beneath our feet and poured the entire boiling cup over his lap and on to the spotless floor.

'*What the fuck?*' He flew up, knocking his chair backwards. 'Fuck, Seven, what the *fuck* was that for? That fucking. . . Jesus, *ow*, fucking hell!'

I put the cup back down on the table and sneered at him swiping at his crotch as I skirted around him in the direction of the door.

'Wow, I hope that doesn't. . . Looks like it's going to stain. Asshole.'

I lit a cigarette on my way out of the flat and I heard him call after me once. But it was just the once and he didn't follow me.

Chapter Eleven

An old man stared at me for my entire tube journey. Every time I caught his eyes he licked his lips and at one point I was certain he was masturbating across the near-empty carriage. Feeling unwashed and revolted I got off two stops early, even though it happened so often I should have been used to it.

All I wanted to do was curl up on the sofa and go to sleep, or maybe fantasize about punching Noel in the face for a bit. But it was as if I could sense an atmosphere before I reached my street and the front doors of my building.

At first I wasn't sure if it was he, but a few more steps and Alexei's face and build came into focus. I walked more slowly for a moment, eyeing him and his brother standing either side of the entrance like a pair of scrawny black crows.

I sighed. 'Well, hi.'

'Thank you for planting the recorder for us,' Alexei said, with a nod. 'You did well.'

After his attitude the night before I wasn't prepared to take anything else he said at face value.

I shrugged. 'Thank you.'

'Come with us.'

Alexei indicated behind me at the road, where a car with blacked-out windows was waiting half on and half off the kerb. Every nerve in my body screamed against it. I would almost certainly die in that car if I allowed them to coerce me inside. But aside from running, I didn't see that I had another choice.

'How the hell do you know where I live?' I asked, folding my arms and taking a step back.

'We followed you.' Isaak stared at me, still and matter-of-fact, as if he hadn't spoken.

'And why would you do that?'

'What's to stop you from backing out of our agreement if we don't keep track of you?'

'Keep *track* of me? I didn't sign a contract here, I said I could maybe help you and—'

'*Maybe, maybe, maybe.* You twist your words.' He inclined his head. 'Who exactly did you think you were talking to? A couple of amateur thieves?'

When Isaak did speak he was calm and to the point. Too calm. Horrifying.

I looked back and forth between the vehicle and Alexei's ill-practised smile, and decided to do as they had asked. I walked to the car and got into the back. After a minute or so Isaak joined me. In the front, next to Alexei, there was a driver whose face I couldn't see owing to a pair of large reflective sunglasses.

We started to drive.

I started to talk.

'Anyway, I just had a look at Noel's computer and there's not much on there. I mean, nothing you guys would find interesting. But him and Ronnie were swapping emails about a guy called Issa Taggart. He might be one of their dealers. I don't know, I don't think they'd talk openly about drugs by email. Anyway, I think that's the name you should go on. There wasn't any mention of an address. . . No reason, I suppose.'

I clutched my bag against my lap, struggling to sound confident, trying to remember if there was anything in there I could use as a weapon.

'Issa Taggart,' Alexei parroted, exchanging a look in the overhead mirror with Isaak. 'Issa Taggart?'

'You recognize the name?'

'Yes, we do. He is one of a list of names we have from. . . surveillance, but obviously we cannot search all of their houses. An address, we can find.'

'How long have you been watching him?'

'. . . A long time.'

I cleared my throat. 'Why are we driving?'

'To talk,' Alexei said, turned away from me.

'Well, we're finished, right?' I spread my hands with an animated smile, daring to think for a second that it might be over now that I'd done what they wanted. I was finished now. I was ready to jump ship and never try and be smart about anything ever again. 'Good luck with the whole. . . robbing thing. Don't mention it was me. Um. . . can you stop the car?'

Isaak made a strange little twitch next to me.

'No, we'll need more,' Alexei said. 'We'll need you to continue finding us these locations when the drugs and money start moving. This is an ongoing project, not a fucking. . . what do you call it?'

'Shoplift,' Isaak offered.

'Yes, shoplift. Did you not understand what I told you?'

'I understood,' I hissed back. 'But that's not what you asked. You just asked me to come up with something and I have and. . . you know, I don't even care about the flight or the profits any more. I'm done, I'm out.'

'No, you are not.'

'Well, *sorry*,' I said, raising my eyebrows. 'I'm not your little dog with a bell on it waiting for commands like this guy over here.'

I gestured at Isaak, who smiled at his brother.

It was way too cramped in the back of this car. If I were killed no one would know. He could strangle me and even if someone looked straight at the windows they wouldn't be able to see.

We drove in silence, turned a few corners.

Alexei's voice came from the front.

'Well, if the girl will not honour her agreement. . . Kill her then.'

I punched Isaak in the ear and he elbowed me in the chest, pinning me against the window. Air left my lungs. There was a knife in his hand with a long serrated edge.

Fuck, it hurt; it hurt so bad I thought my collarbone had cracked.

'No!' I screamed, scratching at the arm that was holding me down. 'No wait! Wait! I can help you! I CAN HELP YOU!'

Alexei raised a hand without looking back.

No words, and Isaak let me go, taking his arm from across my chest. He sat back in his seat in the middle of the car, aloof and ready. The knife was lying across his knee. I couldn't take my eyes off it.

'What have you got to say now?' Alexei asked slowly.

'I can give you something. . . better.'

'Like what?'

I didn't have a fucking clue. I'd only said it to stop Isaak from disembowelling me.

The car halted.

I was shaking.

The driver cut the engine and Alexei turned to look at me. 'What? What have you got to say? You talk far too much. You are one of those sluts who do nothing but talk. But you have one last chance to open your mouth, which should be wrapped around my dick, and say something that might save your fucking life. Do you understand me now? You fucking Asian *cunt*.'

Breathing was difficult.

'I'll. . . I can get you everything.' I was almost paralysed with fear, my throat clamming up. 'Everything, the drugs, the money. . . Every stash, I can find out where it is. I. . . I know Noel, OK, he'd tell me anything, *anything*!'

It was becoming unbearably claustrophobic, as if I was already pleading for my life within my own coffin.

'Anything,' I repeated, meeting Isaak's eyes too. I didn't think he would be more reasonable, but he might be able to see the long-term benefits in what I was offering. 'Think about it. Noel Braben. . . Ronnie O'Connell. . . You'll get a free shot through me. You'll get loads of free shots. No one would suspect me, least of all them! You'd barely have to be involved; they'd never be able to find you.'

Some thought for Noel's welfare should have crossed my mind, but it didn't. Either I died, or I did this. It was an obvious choice. I would have offered them anything in exchange for my life. Everything was expendable in comparison.

Alexei stared at me. I didn't know how to interpret the smile on his face. I just prayed that he cared more about the money than he did about his dislike of me.

'You think this is. . . how do you say it. . .? Leverage?' the driver said suddenly, impassive behind his sunglasses. He had the same accent. He raised his face to the overhead mirror to address me from behind the lenses. 'Take away your face and your body, your smart mouth and that hole between your legs and what power do you have over anybody, really?'

I was desperate for Alexei and Isaak to miss the fact that he had a point.

Forcing myself to remain calm, I glared at him past a sweep of my hair and said shakily, 'I have more power to get the things you want than you do.'

My breathing was audible.

The driver's eyes were front again, completely indifferent to my false bravado.

A siren passed us in the distance.

I realized I was sprawled against the corner of the car and I made a more conscious effort to sit up straight, even with Isaak encroaching into my space.

The decision was with Alexei, but I felt that if I said anything else I would most likely talk him into killing me just to shut me up. These guys weren't exactly feminists. A woman talking back at them was probably more offensive an idea than gutting me in the back of a parked car.

I noticed Alexei had been chewing gum when he took the

small white ball out of his mouth and stuck it in the drinks holder.

'OK,' he said. 'OK, Miss Ishida. You have our attention. You may explain. You have one minute.'

I began talking for my life. 'I can get into the houses for you, where they keep their money. I'm a girl. Some of the dealers even know me. There's no way a gang of you will be able to get in and out without leaving traces of a struggle. All I would have to do is ask. . . or make up some story, and most people would let me in.'

I deliberately avoided looking at the knife. If I did I'd start to fall over my words.

'Think about it,' I said, trying to appeal to their logic rather than non-existent reason or emotions. 'I could get in, find whatever I need to find and get out without any sign of forced entry. If I was disguised I wouldn't draw any attention to myself. What were you lot going to do? Wear balaclavas to the front door? Imagine, I could get in and out and you wouldn't even have to leave a fingerprint. No one could ever connect you to it.'

'Think that is your minute gone,' Isaak said, eyes on his brother.

I clenched my fists. 'You know it makes sense. Let me live and I can do the legwork for you. What have you got to gain by killing me anyway? You wouldn't even have tried. You wouldn't even know what you could be gaining. All you'd be doing is leaving evidence around for people to find later.'

Isaak snorted. 'This is ridiculous.'

'No, it's not,' the driver said.

'You're going to listen to a stupid *girl*?'

'Shut up!' Alexei snapped. '*You're* being a stupid girl! Do you not hear what she is saying?'

'And you trust her?'

'What's the worst that can go wrong?' I cut in. 'I fail, I get killed? Just a longer way around to the same ending. . . except if I don't fail you reap the benefits.'

Alexei turned to the driver and they conversed in Russian.

Isaak shouted something but was reprimanded.

I shut both eyes, desperate to speak again but not wanting to push my luck any more.

Alexei mixed his Russian and English for a moment, and then addressed me.

'You know, if you are lying, we will kill you, and it will not be as quick as the death we were going to afford you now.'

I nodded. 'What does it matter if it's between you or someone else? What reason would I have to lie? To give myself, what, an extra week? An extra month?'

It was lucky, I realized, that they all thought I was dim-witted because of my gender. They probably didn't think I had the mental capacity to lie at this point, and I would just be begging for my life like a typical weak female in movies.

'Alex, you don't believe this bullshit?' Isaak spat.

'Isaak,' Alexei gestured at me, 'what can she do? Are you really that scared of her?'

Isaak fell silent, but glared at me.

I tried not to look too smug, but I hoped my expression was pissing him off.

'We will be watching you,' Alexei said. 'In the meantime, you will wait for our instructions.'

Isaak rolled his eyes but said nothing further.

'Now, get out.'

I had to regain control of the situation somehow. If I let them leave it like this they'd never listen to anything I had to say again, so I didn't get out right away. Instead I looked at Alexei and said, 'I want a passport'.

'You *what*?' Isaak looked at me as if I'd said I'd wanted to publicly defecate.

'Well, I assume if I'm still holding up my end of the agreement you're both going to uphold yours?' I raised my eyebrows. 'I can't get to Japan without a fake passport, can I? Noel will just have me followed. You think I'm stupid?'

'You f—'

'All right.' If I wasn't mistaken, I thought I saw Alexei wink as he said this. 'That is fair.'

'I'm going to want to see proof of it.'

Isaak drew back a fist. 'Get the fuck out *now*, before we change our minds!'

I put my hands in the air and retreated back into the corner. 'Fine! Fine, I'm going.'

The driver unlocked the doors and Isaak pushed me out so hard that I fell to my knees in the road outside, scraping my hands. I got up, shaking, as the car pulled away.

Across the street a woman was walking her dog but all she had done was quicken her pace.

I looked over my shoulder for the vehicle but it was too far away to read the number plate.

Chapter Twelve

I lay awake for most of the night in the living room with the light on, trying not to count, trying to meditate instead, meditate myself to sleep.

Everything I'd said in the car had been from panic and now I couldn't see a way out. It was only going to afford me an extension at best. I was certain they'd kill me when I was no longer useful to them, but I'd have to deal with that when it came to it. Until then, all I could do was plan ahead as much as I could and be prepared.

I began to think of other times in my life when I'd had to convince people to do things for me. It had never been difficult. Getting into a drug dealer's house wasn't going to be the hard part, but what the fuck was I going to do once I was in there?

I'd need a gun: it was the only weapon you could defend yourself against other guns with.

It was still and clammy and silent outside. I kept sweating.

Every so often I'd think back to reading Noel's emails and feel like shit, even though our perverted sex triangle was the least of my problems. The last time I was feeling this down Noel took the day off work and took me to an art gallery.

It had been a novelty to be taken anywhere in public. Not

that I'd minded. . .

I sat up, sick of my thoughts and wondering if I had any sleeping pills.

My phone rang.

It was five past three and the Caller ID said 'Mark'.

'Aren't you concerned about waking me?' I answered.

'Well, if you were asleep you wouldn't answer. You don't sound very tired.'

I shrugged. 'No, no I'm not tired. What are you calling about?'

'Are you free for a prison visit at some point?'

'What?'

'Can you come with me to a prison sometime?'

'Um. . . Well, yeah, I work evenings. Wha—?'

'Nothing's set in stone yet but I'm waiting on the name of the kid that shot the Williams boy. Even if his death is unconnected I thought it wouldn't hurt to double-check, and I thought you might want to come if you want to stay informed about everything?'

I couldn't help smiling. 'And the perfect time to call and ask about this is three in the morning?'

'I just got home, I don't keep regular hours like you *working girls*.'

'OK.'

He paused. 'You sound sad.'

'Well, my. . . family were killed in this machete incident. You might have heard about it?'

A dark laugh. 'Fine, but if you have any reservations about what I'm doing, I'd really like you to tell me. It's your job, not mine.'

'No, I'm fine.'

I thought about asking him about the Russians. He did work for some, after all. But I was still too shaken by the day's events to talk about them. If I told him about the Russians Mark might find himself with a conflict of interest and decide to pull out.

I cleared my throat. 'Call me tomorrow if you end up going to the prison.'

'Have you ever been to a prison before?'

'No.'

'Fascinating places, from a strictly anthropological point of view. Brings out the base instincts in people. I've heard prison guards take bets on arranged fights and then "accidentally" fail to lock up certain cells. Something about uniforms, or cramped hierarchical environments.' A pause. 'I've never been asked to go after someone inside a prison before, but sometimes I plan how it might go. . . for the challenge.'

'Mark. . . It's three in the morning.'

'Sorry. Point taken.'

I rubbed my eyes. 'Thanks.'

'Sleep well,' he said, before hanging up.

I was alone in the room again.

There was no point staying awake all night chewing my lips to shreds so after a while I turned the light out and went to sleep.

I couldn't help wondering if the Russians had planted something in the flat to watch me. It seemed plausible: plausible enough an idea for me to torture myself with. But at that moment I couldn't be fucked to look.

*

I wasn't sure that I loved Noel, not properly. Not in the way that people were meant to love and care about each other, but the one time I thought I might have done was when he took me to the art gallery.

It was the National Portrait Gallery. Lucian Freud. He walked me around, not because he particularly liked art, but because he knew I did. It was the only time he ever really deviated from his routine for me.

'Had an eye for the larger lady,' he remarked.

'He liked the way they moved.' I tried to put it in a way that he would understand. 'Look at the skin; there's so much texture in the different shapes, so much shade. It's much more interesting than a skinny human body. It's like a landscape.'

He pulled a face. 'I know you're into this kind of thing, love, but you know. . . this guy was almost certainly a massive raging sex offender.'

I snorted. 'Well, yeah. Maybe.'

'I mean, that one of his kid on the floor.' Noel shook his head. 'Not right. Not right in the head. If I had a daughter I wouldn't. . . Fuck, I'd take the face off any guy who looked at her like that. It's all. . . urgh, look at it, it's all sexual and wrong.'

It was the first time I'd heard him talk about kids. He was godfather to both of Ronnie's but he'd never shown much interest in having children himself. I was dying to know if he'd ever talked about it before. Had he wanted them? Did Caroline want them? I wanted to know everything about Caroline. Sometimes I thought that I was more fascinated by her than I was by Noel. I wanted to know what it was that made him love.

I nudged him. 'Are you trying to say I'm not right in the head for liking this?'

'You. . . You're not right in the head, no, but that's fine because I fucking love your head, it's beautiful.' He kissed my hair. 'I'm your head's biggest fan. I'd go see your head headline Wembley.'

'Nice one.'

'You see what I did there? *Headline*?'

'Get off.'

But I loved it when he spoke to me like that. I just wasn't able to do it back.

We walked around and around for something like four hours. Noel stopped in front of one painting, perturbed.

'What's up?' I asked, stopping beside him and slinging an arm over his shoulder.

'That's freaky.'

I read the title: Man with a Feather. It was a self-portrait, but the colours were flat and the arms were too long. Behind the man stretched a body of dark water, with stepping stones, and a house. The house should have been reassuring, but it wasn't, because the windows were full of the same dark water. In one was the silhouette of a crude bird. In the man's hand was a feather.

'I don't know, it's probably the least rapey thing in here.'

He couldn't help smirking. We loved the word 'rapey'. Daisy used it a lot. Everything to Daisy was 'a bit rapey'.

'Yeah but. . . he's just stuck out there, isn't he, and those things are in his house. Those things are all in his house.'

He stayed in the same spot for a long time, looking at that painting, but that wasn't what scared me. What scared me were the painted women: textured and trapped inside the frames, beneath the ominous shadow of the painter. The longer I looked at these women, the more I thought about my own situation. It was then that I decided I'd never be owned by somebody, because to be owned just put you in a painting. It trapped you for the rest of your life, looking out at the world with dull eyes.

That night Noel offered to pay for a flat for me, a flat of my own. I turned him down, and I turned him down every night he offered after that. I barely so much as let him buy me a drink.

He pretended to be exasperated by it but I knew that he wasn't. He liked it.

It was only now that I realized it was because it reminded him of Caroline.

Chapter Thirteen

I met up with Mark late in the morning and he was shaking his head by way of greeting. He'd requested that we meet at a nearby library, which I found odd. But then Mark was so thoroughly odd sometimes that I felt able to dismiss it. The outside was grand and stone, with something Latin written across the entrance. There were a couple of alcoholics sitting on the steps outside.

'No prison visit then?' I asked.

'No name yet,' he replied, stopping to finish off a cigarette. 'But I wanted to ask you a few more questions and. . . this might seem unorthodox, but I wanted to try something. An experiment of sorts, if you've got a good enough memory for it.'

'I've got a pretty good memory. What did you have in mind? Anything to do with why we're here?' I gestured up at the library.

'Yes, actually. I need quiet. Come on, let's go inside and wait in the café. I could kill someone for a soy latte. Not literally but. . . Well, maybe literally.' He smiled.

'What are we waiting for?'

'Someone who may be able to help. He won't know anything about you or this job. It's all completely confidential.'

'How can he help then?'

'You'll see.' He threw away the cigarette and indicated for me to precede him inside the building. 'How's Noel?'

'He's. . . I haven't seen him in a while.'

Mark walked us both into the bright library café and bought me a green tea with a knowing smile on his face. He sipped his latte and let out an orgasmic sigh of satisfaction. Behind him, a bespectacled student obscured by an Apple Mac watched us disapprovingly.

As we sat down he took a breath and said, 'You and Noel are more than friends, aren't you?'

'Noel's not friends with any of us, he's our boss.'

'Your mouth moves differently when you talk about him. This side kinda goes up. . . It's like a twitch, you probably don't even realize you do it.' He spread his hands. 'Look, I don't care and I'm not trying to be smart or sound like your therapist. I just noticed. It's my job to notice things like that.'

I wasn't sure what to say. It was hard not to fidget and keep adding to his visual cues but the chairs were so damn hard. . .

'Do you want cake?' he asked, unable to hide the curious glance he shot down at my scratched palms.

'No,' I said a little too quickly, before I laughed at myself. 'Sorry, it's just a weird subject for me to be talking about like this. Why do you care what Noel does with his spare time anyway?'

'I don't, I just love gossip. I like *knowing* things, even if it's just trivial stuff. Knowledge is power and all that.'

His tone was reassuring.

He took another sip of his coffee. 'But is he good in bed? Because I've always been quite curious about that.'

I grinned and gave him the finger.

'I'll take that as a yes, but I won't hold out for any details. I've always had him down as a strong but tender kinda guy.'

I looked over his shoulder at the entrance, stifling the urge to laugh.

No one was making their way in our direction yet.

'Who is your friend that's coming and what does he do?' I asked, anxious to discuss something other than Noel.

'He's my roommate actually; we share a flat. He's one of my best friends and he has a real talent for drawing. Much like you, he's an artist, but he's best at portraiture. He can really capture a person.'

I frowned. 'And you want him to. . . what?'

'I want you to describe the man who spoke to you. The man you couldn't name who was dressed normally. My friend can draw him so I have someone to look out for. While we don't have a name, it may be the best we can do. Do you think you can do that?'

There wasn't a single detail I couldn't recall about that man's face. I'd never thought about drawing him myself. My talent had never been for replicating people. People weren't abstract enough for me.

'Yeah, I can do it. When is he coming?'

'In a moment. He's coming from north of the river. Can I ask, did you ever meet another officer in charge of the investigation into the deaths?'

I racked my brains. 'No, never.'

'No one ever introduced themselves as such?'

'No. Why?'

'I'm having some trouble getting hold of the case files

and I've. . . It's peculiar. I've never had this problem before. Everywhere my informants look they can't seem to find it. No reports, photos, no evidence logged. Quite a lot of it seems to have been moved. Can you think why this might be? Maybe the Japanese authorities wanted to look into it because a Japanese citizen had been murdered?'

'Maybe. I never spoke to anyone from Japan either.'

'I don't doubt that, it's just. . . It's not what I expected. It's usually the simplest stage of looking into any case. They're all usually just there. Accessible, you know.'

I stiffened even more in the chair. 'What does that mean?'

'Maybe nothing. It might just be a miscommunication.' He gazed outwards, to the shelves and shelves of books. 'Reminds me of this other job. . . No, it's nothing. Reminds me of nothing. Don't worry about it.'

I saw a man enter the café, search the place until he saw Mark and walk towards us. He wasn't as tall as Mark, with tanned skin and a face that I couldn't define as attractive or not. I recognized him, but I wasn't sure where from.

Mark turned and stood up to hug him. 'Hey, Nic, thanks for coming.'

Nic. . .

Nic hugged Mark without taking his eyes off me. They were shockingly blue and hidden partially by his fringe and wayward hair. I went to shake his hand and as I did it dawned on me where I'd seen him before.

'Oh, you're Daisy's. . .? Sorry, you know Daisy, right? I work with her. I think I've seen you pick her up a few times.'

Nic stared at me uncomfortably as I stammered out my greeting, but then smiled and let go of my hand. He had a

Roman nose and sharp canines not dissimilar to Mark's.

'Yeah, I'm Daisy's. . . I know Daisy. And you're called. . .'

'Seven.'

'Seven?'

'Yeah, you heard it right. Like the number.'

'Right.'

We shook hands and Mark looked between us as Nic sat down.

'I didn't know you two knew each other?' he said, looking amused.

'We don't,' I replied. 'I work with his. . . girlfriend. Daisy. You probably know her if you guys live together. Obviously you must know her, I guess.'

Fuck, I thought. If only I could find a way to be present at a dinner chat between these two. I'd have to ask Daisy about it the first chance I got.

'You wanted me to draw something?' Nic said quietly, sounding keen to move the conversation on to something else. He reached down into the bag he had dropped beside his chair and started to take out a notepad and some sharpened pencils.

Mark sat forwards. 'Yes. If Seven describes someone to you, do you think you can draw something close to what she can remember?'

'Um, yeah.' Nic looked at me. 'Only you will be able to tell if it's accurate or not, but yeah, I can certainly give it a go. You'd have to remember the face in some detail – will that be OK?'

'Yeah. How long do you think it will take?' I asked.

'As long as it takes. I guess. I've got most of the afternoon if it takes ages.' He smoothed his hand over the paper a few times, as if soothed by it.

Nic seemed nice, I thought. Nic Caruana. But I couldn't imagine him and Daisy together. Unless he had a zany and talkative hidden alter ego that came out when he was drunk, he seemed too humourless and awkward for her to be able to cope with.

'I can write down build and stuff,' Mark said. 'Just try and remember the face, that's what I need in detail. Sorry, Nic, do you want anything?'

'I'm good to go.' Nic smiled at me, pencil in hand. 'This is the nicest thing you've called me to help with in years.'

I realized that everyone was waiting for me to say something, so I thought back to the Relatives' Room and conjured the scene again. The yellow foam, the dripping from the teaspoon, the way the officers left. . .

'He has a wide face. . . with slight jowls. Not really any chin. He's about fortyish, maybe. I'm not good with ages. He's older, anyway. He had a round face with er. . . not much hair. But the hair he does have is swept into this thin comb-over. It looks really greasy. It was horrible actually. But he might not have any hair now, I suppose.'

'Like this?'

I watched the blank page as Nic's pencil swept across it, creating shape with self-assured speed. Every so often his jaw jutted out a little with concentration.

'Maybe. With the jowls it's more like a collapsed rectangle. Sunken in at the bottom.'

Nic nodded and paused. 'Eyes? It's easier to work from eyes first for me.'

'Small, dark, almost black, heavily lidded, with more lines underneath. There weren't that many at the edges.'

'Like this?'

I took a breath as the eyes formed within minutes, and stared out at me from the table.

Nic was looking at the piece of paper like a lover, in an almost trance-like state. His eyes were half closed. I was surprised he could work like that but I was impressed; I could kinda see what Daisy saw in him, in this silent humble self-expression.

'Is this OK? Please tell me if it's shit,' he said.

'It's not! No, it's really not shit.'

'No, it's not,' Mark agreed.

I noticed that Mark was watching Nic too, with an affectionate yet wistful expression on his face that almost made me feel like I was intruding. No, not wistful. Pained. He probably didn't realize that he was doing it either. . .

'I'll photocopy this when I'm done and leave one for both of you,' Nic mumbled, shading and shading. 'You might find it useful; it might. . . jog your memory more. I don't know. I hope this is OK.'

I wasn't sure how much I enjoyed the idea of having the image floating around the house for me to look at every day, but I could see his point.

'Don't you want to know what this is about?' I asked, surprised that he was going to this amount of trouble.

I expected him to take the bait but Nic smiled.

'No. Really, no.'

Chapter Fourteen

When my grandmother, my mother's mother, died, my mother refused to let me see her on her deathbed.

It was during our second phase of living in London. I was eleven years old and sitting outside in the hospital corridor with the rest of our family. Everyone was crying but me. Of course I was old enough to understand death by then; I just didn't care in the same way they did. She'd never given me anything that would cause me to miss her. I was sad because my mother was sad, but I was also aware that it was nothing more than an emotional formality.

She died of some terminal lung disease, inflated with pain-killers and drowning in a combination of her own bodily fluids. The only things I remembered about her later were her poorly-knitted jumpers, the thread veins in her cheeks that had fascinated me, and what she had said to my mother about me before she died.

I wasn't meant to hear it, but oftentimes the only way my parents could communicate anything of worth to me was indirectly. Eavesdropping, they called it. Loitering, hidden by doorways, was the only way I learnt anything worthwhile as a child.

My parents were sitting opposite each other at the kitchen table, my father with his back to me. He was pretty useless in situations like these, but occasionally he'd reach over and hold her wrist, like an anchor, just keeping her here.

I sat on the floor outside the door with a drink, in my pyjamas.

'Why didn't she want to see Kiyomi?' my father asked, at some point.

'Oh, you know how she is.'

'What did she say?'

'Exactly the same as every other time we tried to make her see her.'

'I always thought that was all just heat of the moment? If she misbehaves, I understand that—'

'She's a very superstitious woman. . . Was a very superstitious woman.' She sniffed and wiped her eyes. 'She was raised very differently to you and me.'

My father took his hand from her wrist. 'But no one really believes in that sort of thing nowadays. Not even the lunatic Christians in America really believe in. . . you know, the Devil and hell, all that stuff. It's not of this time.'

'She's not of this time. I mean, she wasn't of this time. Her father was a vile man, a vicar. A sadist, if I ever met one. I was always amazed she remained as sane as she did. Her own mother didn't.'

There was a pause.

I sipped my tea.

'But to say those things about Kiyomi—'

'She killed her cat, Sohei. In her state, you can hardly blame her for being shaken by it.'

Another silence.

I'd been so young at the time that I'd almost forgotten about the cat.

'But to call her a Devil-child. You can't put that thought in a girl's head,' my father was saying.

Outside it had started raining. A winged insect was crawling up the opposite wall towards a picture of me and my mother at a beach. She had my hand and was walking me into the sea. There were white cliffs in the background. I was still wearing nappies then and my face was open with glee and shock at the white foam around my ankles.

My mother wiped her eyes again.

The silence was oppressive when no one was speaking. The rain was like white noise in the room.

'One of the last proper conversations we had was about Kiyomi. She wanted me to put a lock on her bedroom door.'

'Oh, please—'

'But we almost did once, remember! When she kept creeping out at night, we did talk about it. But we didn't because she agreed to stop doing it if we bought her that. . . God, that dinosaur toy that she broke. Can you remember trying to explain to her the difference between right and wrong? She laughed in our faces, Sohei. She found it funny. She looked at us with such contempt—'

'She was five! You can't be contemptuous at five; she wouldn't have even known the word!'

'Well, it was horrible, OK, thinking we'd never be able to make her understand that. That's the only. . . that's the most important thing you can get a child to understand; it's the first thing you make them understand. My mother didn't like it, OK? It scared her.'

'Did it scare you? Is that what you're saying? You're actually trying to justify your mother not wanting to see her own grand-daughter?'

It didn't even properly sink in at the time that they were talking about me. It wasn't until I was older that I attached any significance to the conversation. I just wanted to know why Grandmother hadn't wanted to see me.

I chewed the skin around my fingernails.

'She only stopped creeping out when we gave her something,' my mother said. 'Not because she knew it was wrong.'

'Kids do that all the time.'

'She laughed at me and I didn't like it! It didn't seem normal, OK!'

'You're just upset. You don't really believe everything you're saying—'

'Do you remember just before that, when her friend came round to play and she broke her dinosaur toy, and. . . she didn't even ask for another one, but she said that to make it fair we had to break her friend's toy as well?'

'What has that got to do with anything?'

I turned, just to look around the doorframe again, and my mother was staring at him. She always looked really beautiful just after she cried. It was like the tears washed something off her face. Stripped-down and shiny-eyed, she was enchanting.

'Isn't that wrong? That's. . . not the way a girl thinks.' She clenched her fists in front of her on the table and spoke down to them. 'That's not the way any kid thinks! You break a toy, you ask for a new one, sure, but to. . . demand, like it makes sense, you break someone else's. Isn't that scary to you? That her first thought was to make some other kid cry too?'

'I don't know what you're trying to say. Are you going to sit there and say she is evil too? Just like your mother? No, wait, your batshit-crazy mother, because remember that's what you used to call her. . .'

'No!' She hesitated. 'I don't know what I'm trying to say.'

When I was older she did a lot to feed my paranoia, but at this point my eleven-year-old self felt I had nothing more to learn from the conversation and went upstairs. I swatted the insect with the sleeve of my pyjamas and flicked its broken wings on to the floor.

Chapter Fifteen

I trained for the first time in weeks, went over sequences of moves and blocks and rolls and kicks and sit-ups and push-ups until I was dehydrated and couldn't do any more. I hadn't moved from the floor, meditating in silence, for at least three hours, when the intercom buzzed.

The room had fallen into total darkness.

'Fuck.'

I assumed it must be the Russians and got up, stretching my stiff and aching limbs before making my way to the front door and buzzing them in. I switched some lights on, squinting. My stomach was empty. I poured myself a glass of water and looked at the food in the fridge, weak with hunger, but couldn't face it. I doubted I could keep anything down after exerting myself that much.

Nic's photocopied drawing of the man with the comb-over watched me from the kitchen work surface.

There was a knock at the door.

I felt sick as I went to answer it.

But it wasn't the Russians; it was Noel.

I almost started crying then and it took all my willpower to stop myself, but I wasn't sure I disguised it very well.

He smiled nervously. 'Can we talk?'

'How do you know where I live?' I asked, my voice shaking a little.

'I had you followed ages ago. Just so I knew.'

'Jesus. Overstepping the mark much?'

He just stared at me.

I didn't have the energy to be indignant without becoming upset, so I waved him in. Against my better sense I was glad to see him.

'Are you OK?' he asked.

I sat down on the sofa and sniffed, hiding my face. 'Ah. . . no. No.'

'What's happened?'

'Nothing, it's nothing.'

'Is it me? It's me, isn't it? I know it's me.' He sat down next to me and tentatively put his arm around my shoulders, as if he was about to say something monumental. 'Look, I was coming round here to say I've been a massive dickhead, if that's any help? If you were still pissed off I was really going to ask you. . . to forgive me and stuff. But if it's not me. . . Well, I can have them killed. Really. I'll have them killed.'

I laughed but it wasn't proper laughing. It was crying with a smile.

'No, I don't think it's anything to do with you.'

'Really?'

'Really. Though I still accept your apology. They're practically an endangered species, I'll take them where I can get them.'

'Want to talk about it?'

'No.' I met his eyes and looked away just as quickly. 'No.

I. . . I'm just going to have to find somewhere else to live within the next month, that's all.'

'Fuck, is it landlord problems?' He frowned. 'Because, seriously, I can sort those out for you.'

'I don't think you can.'

His arm suddenly felt heavy across me.

'I can find you somewhere.'

I sighed. 'We've talked about this before. I don't want your. . . charity. I'm not your fucking adult child. I don't want a trust fund.'

'Oh come on, that's unfair.'

The arm fell away and we sat shoulder to shoulder instead.

'I've already told you I don't want to be kept.'

'You don't need to be!' He stopped himself from rolling his eyes. 'You don't need to be if you pay your own rent, albeit a bit lower. . . if you like. Your name can be on the tenancy agreement. I'll just. . .'

'What? Be my landlord? No thanks. Like I'm going to call you about things like the boiler packing up or something? Come fix a broken washing machine? God, no.'

'You're so difficult.'

But he didn't look pissed off. It was said with affection. He liked difficult women, he'd told me so enough times. He couldn't be with anyone for too long who didn't cause friction and tension and challenge him. He actively rebelled against anything like happiness and contentment and I understood it; I was much the same.

'You can look for a place for me,' I said, attempting a compromise. 'You can help me look. But it can't be some place you own.'

'Done.'

He held out a hand to shake mine, and his grip lingered. I looked away.

'How is it going with Mark?' he asked, ignoring the tension. 'Did you speak to him?'

I nodded.

'And?'

'He's looking; he's got some leads. He's a cool guy actually.'

'Is he confident?'

A shrug. 'He strikes me as the sort who's always confident.'

'And how do you feel about it?'

I was thrown by the question. Noel never asked about feelings. Even the most perfunctory 'How are you?' was done begrudgingly, with a little panic in his tone, dreading a real reply. Once he had made the mistake of asking one of the girls how she was three hours after she had broken up with her boyfriend. She had cried all over his suit while he made SOS signals to me over her shoulder. All Daisy and I had done was laugh. Noel didn't come back into the club for a fortnight.

'I almost don't want to know,' I said, giving him enough credit to think of a serious answer. 'I've got so used to not knowing that I was almost OK with it. It's the prospect of finding out why that actually makes me feel. . . sick.'

'Well, that's normal, I reckon.'

'What if I find out something about them that I didn't want to know? What if my dad really was mixed up in something bad in Japan? I gave Mark shit for asking if he was involved in Yakuza and stuff like that but the truth is. . . I don't know. I don't have a fucking clue. And they were my parents. Isn't that sad?'

'They did have lives outside of you, you know. Even though it's never that nice to think about, is it?' He snorted. 'It's like imagining your parents having sex. Even though it's obvious it happens. . .'

I grimaced. 'Well. . . that was unnecessary, Noel. Thanks.'

'Pleasure to help.' This time he patted me on the back softly.

'So why are you here?' I asked, not wanting to let him feel it was this easy to win back my favour. 'Caroline left again, has she?'

He had the grace to look ashamed. 'No, she's still here. I just forgot how much easier it was to talk to you. You know, me and her, we don't have that much in common. The only thing we do have in common is that I love her. . . and she loves her, and she loves that I love her. That's pretty fucked up, right?'

'This thing with Mark and my. . . family. You know I never really cried about it, I never did that "stages of grief" thing. Aren't you meant to feel something?'

There was a long silence.

He put his arms around me and squeezed. 'You know. . . you can talk to me.'

I nodded, feeling closer to crying again now that I was in his arms. I detested the effect he had on me, but it reassured me in that it made me feel more like a normal person. I'd rather die than cry for real in front of him.

'I think half your problem is that you don't talk.' He took my scraped hands in his. 'You're like me, you don't talk, you. . .'

'Argue.'

'I was gonna say "drown".'

Sometimes his eyes became so fucking wise I couldn't handle them.

I looked at the blank easel in the corner of the room.

'You seem to be feeling something now,' Noel said, jogging my shoulder. 'You just like to bottle things up. Don't worry, you're probably just emotionally retarded and repressed, like us blokes.'

I laughed.

He gave me an animated smile. 'You'll probably turn to alcoholism or build up some great anger-management issues.'

'Great, well, that's made me feel better.' I wiped my eyes, but I wasn't lying.

'Take the next few nights off, if you want. Take as many nights off as you want.'

'Urgh, no, can't think of anything worse. I'd rather keep busy. Plus, I need the money.'

He was about to offer to lend me money. I could sense it in his body language and hear the words forming in his mind, but to my surprise he stayed silent on the matter and I was grateful for that. It had only taken several hundred refusals for the message to sink in that I didn't want anything from him. Tragically, I realized that I didn't want anything from him except his company and attention.

How weak, I thought.

'I'm sorry for being a bitch,' I said, suddenly feeling like shit for everything I had done, for everything I had promised to do.

It wouldn't hurt him, I kept telling myself. It was just money. I would never hurt him.

'Don't worry about it.'

I linked my fingers, turning them around and around each other.

'Did you come here to fuck me?' I asked, turning to face him.

He gave his response some thought, which obviously meant yes.

'If we don't, I won't mind.'

I took the side of his face in my hand and kissed him. I didn't even care if the flat was bugged any more. Let them listen. Let them watch. The calm washed over me like fucking Valium and I'd missed it.

It was always so much easier to do this than it was to say anything else, and at least it was more real than thinking about Seiko.

Noel was sleeping against my back, with one hand on my thigh and an arm wedged under my neck like a flight pillow. He smelt of sweat and sex but it was impossible to get away from him when he was sleeping; he seemed to gravitate towards human contact in his sleep, which meant that I spent most of our nights together awake and overheated.

At about four in the morning I carefully eased my way out of his embrace and out of the bedroom. It was the first time I'd slept there in weeks. I tended to sleep in the living room on the pull-out sofa bed; a habit I'd never been able to break. The bedroom didn't feel like mine.

I switched on one of the dimmer lamps, red-tinted, and paced naked around the living room, trying to work out where I would be hidden if I was one of those little microchip-sized recording devices.

Maybe they were in multiple rooms? They'd had so many opportunities to plant them if they knew where I lived. They could have been in and out of the flat like ghosts.

I found my mobile on the floor next to the sofa and took it into the kitchen with a packet of cigarettes, shutting the door.

While psyching myself up I ate cereal dry out of a bowl, and then called Alexei.

I listened for a moment to check that Noel was still asleep, but there was no sound. He barely made any noise in the night. Sometimes I couldn't hear him breathing and thought he was dead.

It rang out the first time but I called again, and again, until Alexei answered. I'd taken the time to devise a semi-script in my head. I couldn't rely on any of my own courage to carry me through; it would have to be like slipping into a character.

'Fucking bitch, what?' His voice was thick with sleep.

'Morning. Have you got my passport yet? Because, you know, I'm going to want to be seeing that soon.'

I could hear the sound of him sitting up, wiping sleep out of his eyes, standing up and walking out of the room. He muttered something to someone in Russian. Maybe he had a wife? He continued walking, down some stairs, clearing his throat. Maybe he had kids?

'You put on quite the show earlier,' he said after he had stopped once again. 'Were you trying to turn me on?'

I heard him fill a glass of water from a tap.

'You like what you saw?' I said, my skin crawling as the words came out.

'It was like music to my ears. All clever talking girls like you need fucking hard.'

I smiled, revolted by him. At least I now knew there was no video recording in the flat. If it was only audio, I could work with that.

'Interesting', he continued, 'that you think you're in a position where you can demand things.'

'I hardly think you're in a position to accuse me of making unreasonable demands.'

'You called for anything else? Or did you just want to piss me off?'

I took a deep breath away from the line. 'I want to go over a couple of things. The terms of my payment. I need to be clear on what's in it for me before I do anything more for you.'

He laughed, but it was a better response than anger. 'And what makes you think we won't just kill you if you don't cooperate with us?'

'Then kill me. As you well know, I'm close enough to Noel to find out anything you want, things you wouldn't even get a sniff of on your own. Also, your plans will end in fucking disaster without my help and you know it. Either the police will catch you within weeks, with all the evidence you'll leave all over the place and with all the witnesses who'll see you, or Noel and Ronnie will. Personally I'd hope for the former. Ronnie would cut your dick off and feed it to you. . . but I imagine yours would go down easy, wouldn't it? You could knock the whole thing back like a tiny little oyster, right?'

He didn't rise to the bait. 'What do you want?'

I hesitated and hoped it wouldn't cost me. 'I still want enough of a cut to buy my one-way flight back to Tokyo to start over, and I need you to get me a passport. I want to see the passport soon. I want to actually have it in my hands.'

'Is that all?'

'You want to run it past your boss?'

'There will be no need. He trusts my judgement.'

'Then fine.' I swallowed. 'That's what I want.'

I wanted to say so much more, about the graphic ways I was fantasizing about killing him, but that would have to wait for tonight.

Alexei mulled it over.

I covered the mouthpiece of the phone to take a few breaths, my heartbeat bashing against the inside of my ribcage.

'Done,' he said.

'What? I mean. . .' I said, before I could stop myself. 'I mean. . . good.'

Fuck. I berated myself. You had to fuck it up right at the end.

My hands were shaking.

'Was there anything else you wanted?'

He was so infuriatingly and eerily fucking calm.

I tried not to start stammering. 'Just. . . can you keep me informed about what you want me to do? I'll let you know about anything else I. . . need.'

'I like you,' he said.

It was too easy. He was going to kill me when they were done. He wasn't even bothering to be discreet about it; his tone was dripping with glee at the prospect.

'I like you too,' I replied in my sweetest voice. 'Oh no, wait, I hope you die in a fire.'

'Not before I pay you, you don't.' He chuckled to himself. 'Goodnight, Miss Seven Ishida. I'll be thinking about you tonight.'

The line went dead.

I refilled my glass of water and downed it, trembling all over. My body was slick with perspiration and not because of the humidity.

Sliding my feet across the tiles, I opened the kitchen door again to listen for Noel, but he was still passed out from what I could hear. I shut the door and lit a cigarette to compose myself, going through the small amount of information I'd gleaned from the discussion in my head.

I thought it had gone well. It had gone according to plan. I'd just thought I'd feel better about it afterwards if that had really been the case.

After finishing the cigarette I went back through to the bedroom and lay back down. Noel found me without even waking up, pulling me back against his chest where I'd been before. I was still shaking a little, but not too long after I was wrapped in his arms the shaking stopped.

It was fine, I kept telling myself. It was fine, as long as I never thought too long and hard about my betrayal or its many worst-case scenarios. It was fine. Plus, the more I did what Alexei wanted the more likely it was that I would come across an opportunity to stick a knife in him. At least, that was what I hoped.

Chapter Sixteen

Mark called me not long after I'd fallen asleep, at eight in the morning, talking fast and high-pitched like he was wired on caffeine.

'Do you ever sleep?' I asked, yawning and still seeing my room in double vision.

'Yes, just not the normal hours. They're so restrictive. Did you know that the natural human sleep pattern is four hours asleep, two hours awake and then four hours asleep again? Makes so much more sense. . . Anyway, I'm calling because I found the Williams kid's file. Nate Williams. I know the name of the boy who shot him and where he is. Want to come visit with me? It's one of those mental right-wing places that would rather offenders rot than "reconnect with their community" and all that touchy-feely liberal bullshit. . . as they'd call it. We'll have no trouble gaining access if we have some ID. I'll make a few calls. You still there?'

'. . . Yeah! Um. . . tell me where to meet you. I can be out in twenty.'

Noel was waking up, looking mortally offended as he did every time he was forced into consciousness before nine, so I got out of bed and dressed in the living room.

I threw on some shorts with a cropped top that Daisy had lent me and left Noel to sleep a while longer. I wasn't a tender-kiss-goodbye kind of person, but I felt confident that the next time we saw each other things would be back to normal. No matter what happened or how much we pissed each other off, slammed doors, threw coffee, rolled eyes. . . we would always come back to each other. We couldn't find anyone else as interesting.

'Hey, sexy!' some guy yelled at me through the window of a café as I was looking for Mark's car, banging on the window. He had tramlines shaved through his eyebrows.

I stopped and slammed my middle finger against the glass just as hard.

He jumped, as did his group of mates.

'Fucking lesbian!' he shouted after me.

Pushing up my sunglasses I scanned the roadside and spotted Mark waving at me from across the road. He was sitting in the front of a navy Porsche, with the roof down. There was a suit jacket slung across the back seats and he was wearing a smart white shirt and trousers, tattoos in plain view.

I crossed the road and got into the car beside him, matching his smug grin with one of my own. 'Now I can see why people pay you to blend in.'

'You're not paying me.'

I held up my hands as he reversed out of his space. 'Why can't we just take the underground?'

'Feltham. Easier by car. You look lovely, by the way.'

'Huh, thanks. So, what's going on here?'

Mark had Nate Williams's case file in the back of the car and two fake police IDs in his bag. He had also brought a tiny suit for me to change into.

'It was the only way I could arrange a visit at this short notice,' he explained, looking again at my hands and shouting over the sound of the wind in our faces. 'Do you have a really bitchy cat or something?'

'Oh. . .' I automatically hid them under my thighs; I'd been unaware that the grazes from my fall were still visible. 'No, I'm just clumsy. I fall over a lot.'

'But aren't you a martial artist?'

I glared at him. 'How do you know that?'

'You told me the first time I met you, and you're built like one. You're small but I bet you could floor a man my size. Am I correct?'

We stopped at some lights.

'Yeah, yeah I could. Probably not you specifically but someone untrained who wasn't expecting me to fight back, yeah. My dad was obsessed with self-defence when I was growing up. He was making me take lessons in Ninpo when I was four and I took all these classes on how to throw big guys off you and. . .' There was a silence. 'Maybe he had good reason. Crap, I've never thought of it like that before. You think he made me learn all that stuff because he knew something bad was going to happen?'

Mark shrugged. 'I didn't know your father. It might have just been the way he was.'

The idea had unnerved me. 'Did you ever find their case file?'

'No.' He looked troubled behind the sunglasses. 'No, not yet.'

'Exactly how weird is that?'

A gritting of the teeth. 'Weird. I don't really know how to tell you but the last time it was this hard for me to find a simple case file it was. . . an inside job. That's what all this has been reminding me of. The. . . job. . . The, er. . . man I was tracking down turned out to be a police officer, deep undercover. Sorry, it's hard to explain when it's all confidential. I shouldn't really be discussing past jobs with you.'

I rubbed at my forehead, trying to take the idea in. 'Did you ever find the file?'

'Yes, I did. But it was in his house.'

'So my parents' file is probably in comb-over's house? That makes him. . . fuck, a police officer?'

'Maybe. That's a lot of assumptions, but. . . maybe.' Mark jabbed his thumb at the back seat. 'Come on, Inspector Mishima, get changed. We're almost there. I promise I won't look.'

I undid my seatbelt and climbed into the back, snorting. 'What? You just pick the most famous Japanese name you could think of?'

'Be thankful I'm Oxford-educated. You could have been DCI Jackie Chan.'

Oxford-educated. I was surprised. I hadn't expected that either.

Feltham Young Offenders' Institution was surrounded by high red walls, plastered with official seals and caged off from the world with a heavy iron gate that looked as though it belonged in medieval times.

Inside it was mostly tile and brick. The rooms were all small with barred windows and every so often we passed a desk. The atmosphere was clouded, thick with testosterone and sterility. No one smiled.

Mark and I waited for over an hour in a makeshift inter-rogation room for the kid to come out, chatting about music and artists. He liked Mike Kelley and I was impressed enough to carry on talking. Most people who said they were interested in art could name-drop Georgia O'Keeffe and have Hokusai's wave on a poster at home, but as soon as you started on the history of the nude or Frank Auerbach they just stared.

I wished that Mark was straight, and I was certain I wasn't the first girl to wish that. He'd give hope to us all if he were able to fly the flag for heterosexual masculinity. I wondered if he'd ever had sex with a woman, or whether he still did. He didn't seem the type to place any kind of rigid label on sexuality.

The kid's name was Leo Ambreen-King.

I'd never worn a suit before but I was sure I looked fucking fantastic. Even without the fake IDs I was willing to bet the wardens would have let us in just for an excuse to stand there gawping, which they were, albeit at a distance.

We were both playing *Angry Birds* on our phones when one of the wardens walked over to us and asked sheepishly, 'He wants to know what this line of questioning is about?'

'Nathan Williams.'

The warden nodded and disappeared again.

I glanced at Mark, who pulled a face. We both looked around us at blank walls and dirty floor.

Leo Ambreen-King appeared in the doorway at the far end of the room and walked over to us slowly. He was tiny. I'd forgotten how small some teenagers actually were. He looked as though he had one Indian parent, and he had mid-length curly dark hair framing his baby face.

'Hi, Leo,' Mark said, standing. 'I'm Stephen Abbott and

this is Naoko Mishima. We'd like to ask you some questions, if that's OK?'

He remained standing, hands in pockets, even though we sat back down. 'About what?'

'Nathan Williams. Nate.'

A shrug. 'Ain't nothing left to tell. I'm here.'

'We'd like to talk about who paid you to do it.'

The boy's entire demeanour changed. His hands came out of his pockets and the wardens watching us tensed and took a few steps forward.

'I'm not talking to you,' he said, backing away.

Mark stood up. 'Leo—'

My heart started racing.

'No comment!' he screamed back at us, storming away. 'No fucking comment!'

I went to follow him without thinking and Mark grabbed my arm.

The wardens came forwards to seize him but Mark said, 'No, it's OK. Let him go. We'll come back.'

He let go of me and I rounded on him, hissing, 'What? You're just going to let him go?'

'We'll come back. Next time we won't have shocked him. He'll have had time to think about it and come up with a story that we can pick apart.'

I watched the doorway through which Leo had vanished, willing him to reappear. But he didn't, and he probably never would.

Mark took my arm, more gently this time, and said under his breath as he walked me back to reception, 'Don't worry. I've done this before. Trust me, I've got this.'

Chapter Seventeen

When I'd returned home, I spent the earlier part of the afternoon silently ordering weapons on the internet. Nothing completely illegal and traceable. But enough to make me feel better. The ones I chose had handles that were a dark and seductive green, with dragon carvings twisting around them. They looked as if they would be easy to hold, with blades that rippled and curved and were short enough to hide but long enough to kill.

I had started carrying a small kitchen knife taped into a makeshift holder in the small of my back. The tape irritated my skin and it was going to be an annoyance having to wear a jacket in such hot weather, but it would be worth it, I thought. It would be worth it if I needed to defend myself.

I phoned the club to take the night off work at about three, and the Russians took me on a drive-by past Issa Taggart's house. It was in a relatively nice area. There was a people carrier in the driveway with a 'Baby on Board' sticker in the back window.

I leaned forwards from my infantile position in the back seat and peered past Isaak. 'How many kids does he have?'

'Just the one, a few months old,' Alexei said, exhaling cigarette smoke out of the window.

'So a wife?'

He nodded. 'It is of no concern to us if you need to kill her.'

'Well, for that I'd actually need to have a weapon, wouldn't I?' I replied, hoping that I'd been able to hide my disgusted reaction.

'You will be given a weapon when you need it.' Isaak looked me up and down. 'I assume you know how to use a gun?'

Truth be told I had never fired one. The only time I'd ever come across a gun was when Noel sent me on a house call to shag some arms dealer, who had taken a perverse pleasure in seeing me handle a firearm while he jerked himself off. I knew how one worked. I knew how to tell if the safety was on. I knew how to check how many bullets there were. I knew how to aim. I just didn't know what it would feel like to shoot something, someone, for real.

'Obviously,' I said.

I told myself that it couldn't be that difficult if men like this could do it, and kids who weren't even old enough to drink. How different could it be from a movie, really? It had to be easy. Worryingly easy.

'So, if you are so confident that he will let you into his house willingly,' Alexei said, squinting over the top of his sunglasses, 'how do you plan to do it?'

'I don't think you have to know.'

The driver shifted in his seat and I could tell he was watching me, but he said nothing.

I looked at them all. 'Well, you don't. Either I come back with what you're looking for, or I don't come back at all. Surely that's a pretty failsafe way to work out whether my plans have worked or not. Why should you have to know any other details?'

Isaak rolled his eyes.

'She's right,' the driver said. 'If she dies, we have no need to know what she did or did not do. If she comes back, then we have little need to worry about her methods.'

I was beginning to get some sense that the driver had the most authority of the three. They all acted as though they deferred to Alexei, but I wasn't so sure about that now. When Alexei changed his mind I found it hard to believe it was simply because he was responding to a reasoned argument.

'So when do you want me to go in?' I asked.

'Tonight.' Alexei turned to face me, looking eager to see my reaction. 'Any problems with that?'

'No,' I lied. 'Are you going to tell me what I'm looking for?'

'We'll tell you when you leave. The less time you have to think, the better.'

Bullshit. He was going to wrangle as much control away from me as he was able.

The best I could do was act as though this didn't bother me at all, and pack for every eventuality. It struck me that I wasn't even entirely sure what Issa Taggart looked like.

'Meet us outside tonight at half past eight.' He looked at his watch. 'Four hours enough time for you? You can wash your hair, paint your nails, whatever it is girls do.'

I looked back out at the house and didn't think the small knife taped to my back was going to be enough after all.

'Better take me home then,' I said.

In a state of frenzy I emptied out a small travel bag and packed a couple of kitchen knives in addition to the one on my person, some strong tape, some socks that I could use as gags, some hairspray, cigarettes. . .

I realized too late that they hadn't given me time to find a way to disguise myself. As I sat in the back of their car on the way back to Issa's house, I realized that maybe that had been their plan all along. They knew I couldn't take the risk that Issa might identify me later, so this was a test of loyalty. They expected me to kill him.

'How do you feel?' Alexei asked, grinning at me.

I am sitting on a mountaintop.

I didn't reply, doing my best to clear my mind and meditate. I was sure there had to be a way. There had to be a way of getting in and out of the house without any death. But if there was, I couldn't think of one.

My teeth hurt and I realized I was clenching my jaw.

'We are expecting you to find up to sixty thousand in cash and some cocaine. Though we do not know how much of that.' Isaak turned to me. 'Nervous?'

I might have predicted that amount of money, but hearing it said out loud seemed ridiculous. I'd never touched even a fraction of that sort of wealth before. 'Do you have any idea where it's gonna be?'

'That is for you to find out. You are the one who can find out *anything*?'

Every time Alexei spoke I wanted to kill him. It was going to take every shred of self-control I had not to shoot him as soon as I was given a gun.

'Right,' I said. 'Do I get a weapon?'

Isaak smirked, and handed me something that looked as though it should have become obsolete a century ago. It was barely bigger than my palm, despite being oddly heavy.

'What the fucking fuck is *this*?' I snapped, holding it up.

'I'm going to want him to tell me where the money is. If I shove this in his face he'll just laugh and offer me some fucking Lego to play with!'

'It's a Derringer,' the driver said. He was still wearing sunglasses even in the low evening light. 'You only get one shot. You'll only need one. We have been watching the house and his wife is out.'

'Pilates,' Isaak added helpfully.

I scowled at the tiny weapon.

'We couldn't give you enough shots for all three of us, could we?' Alexei smiled. 'But then, you said you could use a gun so you will have no trouble with that, I am sure.'

They wanted me to fail, just to save them the effort of killing me themselves. They didn't think for a second that I would come back with the money.

I looked out of the window for the rest of the journey until the driver pulled over and I got out of the car without a word.

The people carrier in the driveway was gone.

Sitting on a mountaintop. . .

'I won't be more than an hour.'

Alexei might have said something but I'd already swung my bag over my shoulder and slammed the door.

I'd chosen to wear my black jeans, sexy black high-heeled Dr Martens, lace vest, leather gloves and no jacket. I'd moved the knife from my back to the inside of my boot, as a jacket would have been too restrictive. I paused to apply some dark red lipstick in my hand-mirror, took a deep breath and carried on walking.

I could feel them all watching me from the car, wondering what on earth I was going to do.

I am sitting on a mountaintop...

Oh, fuck off.

I waited for a moment, then rang the doorbell, hoping that an adrenalin kick would carry me through.

A tall silhouette appeared behind the glass.

When the door opened I saw that he had no need to put the safety latch on. Issa Taggart was a huge black man in his early thirties, with a friendly face and the biggest hands I'd ever seen; hands that looked as though they could wrap around my skull and crush it.

'Hi,' I said with a professional smile. 'Mr Taggart?'

'Yeah?'

'Noel Braben sent me.' I looked up coyly from beneath a sweep of my hair, playing up the submissive Japanese stereotype as much as my urge to vomit would allow. 'As a thank you for all your hard work for him. A gift, free of charge.'

I figured it could only work to my favour if I spoke a little like English was my second language. It made most men speak to me as though I was mentally retarded.

Issa Taggart scanned his road over the top of my head, decided that no one could see us and stood aside to let me in.

I bowed my head to him and did as he indicated.

His house had the appearance of one that was in the midst of the awkward transition from home to a young rebellious couple to family haven. Ornaments and cheap-looking nude oil prints were all jam-packed into high places while the stairs were shielded by a child-gate.

He led me into his living room, which looked as though it wanted to be messy but had been forced into a state of unnatural cleanliness, namely by shoving all items into the

141

corners of the room or stacking them under chairs and coffee tables to hide them from sight.

There was a derelict fireplace that had obviously never been used, but there was a holder full of pokers and tongs next to a flayed leather sofa.

'My, um. . . wife will be back in two hours.'

I put my bag down without much noise. 'I will only stay for as much time as would please you, sir.'

He seemed to relax a little the more he stared at me.

'Would you like a drink?' he asked.

'Whatever you would like.'

He smiled. 'I like Asian chicks like you. I'll bring you wine. Where are you from, Thailand?'

I gritted my teeth as he left the room to go to his kitchen, and silently moved one of the pokers from its holder to slide it down behind one of the sofa cushions.

There were a couple of photos of his young wife and new-born baby above the fireplace. His wife was extremely pretty; about the same size as me.

'Japan, sir,' I said.

'Ain't no woman called me "sir" for a long time!' he called. 'You can come again! Bet I'm too broke to afford a chick like you every day though. Am I right?' He laughed to himself.

It never ceased to amaze me how stupid men could become when they were offered sex. I couldn't imagine any woman letting a stranger into her house on the promise of being able to come multiple times within an hour.

I waited for him to come back through to the living room.

He handed me a glass of red and I pretended to sip it, even though the smell alone was almost enough to make me gag.

I was starting to seriously doubt my ability to knock him out and restrain him. He was so fucking big. It would be like hitting a shed. If I was a second too slow he would smash me to pieces.

Taggart sat down on his sofa with his wine and appraised me.

'Noel ain't never done nothing like this for me and mine before,' he said, baring a set of distractingly white teeth.

'Mr Braben is very selective.'

'So you're here for as long as I want? You do whatever I want? Really?'

I nodded, malleable as snow.

'Take something off,' he said with a glance at his watch.

I pulled the lace vest over my head.

I wasn't wearing a bra.

'Come here.'

He put his wine to one side and beckoned me forwards.

I approached him, took both vast hands in mine and strad-dled him. What felt like paralysing fear to me would probably just look like sexual arousal.

'Close your eyes, sir,' I said, undoing his belt and pulling at the buttons on his jeans.

With a last wistful look at my tits he did as he was asked, with this big stupid grin on his face.

I took the heavy iron poker out from behind the cushions and stepped back and out of his grasp. Before he opened his eyes I gripped it tight in both hands and brought it crashing downwards and sideways, as if I were swinging a baseball bat, into the side of his head.

There was a sound like someone dropping a melon.

He made a dull protest, flattening against the sofa as a trickle of blood ran down his jaw.

His eyes were half open.

Holding my breath, I swung the poker again. Not quite as hard, but hard enough.

His eyes closed.

After putting my top back on I dragged Taggart's vast bulk to the floor and set about wrapping him in so much masking tape that I was on the verge of mummifying him. Once I was sure that he wouldn't be able to move either his arms or his legs, I stood up, sweating, and called the Russians to let them know that I had Taggart under control and I was going to find the money.

'OK.' Alexei sounded surprised, but sceptical. 'Call when you do.'

I rang off, muttering, 'Well fuck you very much, dickwad.'

Putting a cautionary piece of tape over Taggart's mouth, in case he regained consciousness while I was absent, I started walking from room to room, trying to put myself in the mind-set of someone who had a lethal sum of money to hide.

I stared at the kitchen and opened and closed a few cupboards.

It was fruitless; I could tell already. The money wasn't going to be put in any old place. Chances are he had a concealed cabinet, a loose floorboard, a cupboard with the top and back removed, or a hole in the wall behind a bookcase. Fuck, it could have been in the baby's room.

There were dirty clothes slung over the banisters and some socks had fallen down on to the stairs. I surveyed the landing and put my head around the doors to the bedrooms and

144

bathrooms. There was an attic too, situated ominously over the stairs, with no visible way of reaching it.

I sat down on the master bed for a while, hugging a cushion. I thought I'd feel more shaken by having to bash the man's head in, but I didn't feel much at all. I had become strangely accustomed to that.

There was a book on physics on their bedside table called *Parallel Worlds*, by Michio Kaku.

I took it downstairs with me and put it in my bag.

Sighing, I knelt beside Taggart and gave him a small shake. When he didn't respond I got his glass of wine and poured a little over his face. After a few seconds his eyes flew open.

I stood up and leapt backwards as if he was going to grab me, and remembered that he couldn't.

The eyes widened, refocused on me, narrowed, and then he began shouting from behind the tape.

I walked away, breathless, and retrieved the stubby little gun from my bag.

'Look,' I said, returning to where he could see me clearly. 'Look, this is nothing personal. I don't know you. I'm working for someone else. Just tell me where the money is. I have these. . . I have these knives in my bag and if you start screaming and stuff when I take that tape off your mouth I'm gonna take a finger or something, OK? So just don't do it. . . Because I really don't want to do that. It'll be really fucking gross. OK?'

I leant down and ripped the tape off.

'Who the fuck *are* you?'

'It doesn't matter. Now can you just tell me where the

money is? Because if I don't have it when your wife gets back, and your baby, I'll kill them.'

I wasn't sure if I meant it.

He seemed pretty sure, spluttering, 'Fuck! Fuck, this is fucked-up! *Fuck. . .*' while blood dried on his face.

'Hey!' I snapped, waving the gun at him. 'Money! Now!'

'If I tell you, you gonna kill me anyway.'

'Maybe, but. . . You know what, I probably will because now you've seen my face and stuff, since I didn't have time to bring a goddamn fucking wig, I'm gonna have to so that you don't rat me out to Noel.' I spread my hands. 'But I promise I won't kill your wife and kid. I won't if you just tell me where the money is.'

'*Fuck. . .*'

'You think *you're* fucked? I didn't want to do this! I'm not. . .' My voice was getting shrill. 'I'm not a bad person, OK? I'm not a fucking psychopath!'

'You are psycho bitch!'

'I'm not, I. . .' I stopped and sighed, my face in my hand. 'I'm not. I've just got to do this. So tell me where the money is and I won't kill your family.'

He was breathing unnaturally fast. 'You gonna kill me, fuck. . . Please. . . Please!'

I felt the tears rising in my throat but I forced them down. 'It's you or me. Now where's the money?'

No answer, just breathing.

'Where is it?' I shouted.

Nothing.

I put the gun down, took the kitchen knife out of my boot and rammed it into one of his exposed fingers.

He howled.

I dropped the bloodied knife, stood up again and kicked him. 'Where the fuck is it?'

'Please please please. . .'

'I'll cut your fingers off, I fucking promise I will!'

Nothing. He just screwed his eyes tight shut, thrashing on the floor and shaking his head from side to side. For a moment I was worried that the tape wouldn't hold, then the energy left my legs and I sat down on the carpet.

I tried not to look at his slashed finger. It made me want to cry.

'I'm really sorry,' I said, cross-legged and hunched over. 'But I really need to know where the money is. If you don't tell me I'm gonna have to kill your wife and I don't wanna do that, OK? But I *have* to kill you, you get that, right? You've fucking *seen* me!'

'If you hadn't got me all trussed-up I'd break your fucking neck, right, bitch. . .'

I couldn't help but laugh. 'Thanks. No, really, thanks. More of that and I'll stop feeling so bad about it.'

I stretched both my legs out and got to my feet, making a load of strenuous sounds as if I had a bad back or hip.

Looking at the clock, I saw that I still had just over an hour.

'Where's the money, Issa?' I shrugged. 'Or I will cut your fucking finger off.'

He just glared at me. It was almost scary imagining what he must have been thinking: a million different ways to kill me horribly.

Without a word I picked up the knife again, knelt down by him and jammed it into his already bleeding finger. When he cried out I just twisted it harder, and harder, feeling the blade collide with bone and work its way through the skin on the other side.

I retched a little.

'FUCK! OH FUCK OH FUCK OH FUCK OH FUCK!'

'Where is it, you fucking sack of shit!'

'Microwave! Fucking microwave!'

'What?'

I withdrew the knife and he screamed, 'The microwave isn't a fucking microwave!'

Dropping the knife again I ran back to the kitchen and opened all the small rectangular cupboards until I came across the microwave. It looked normal from the outside, but when I opened the door there was nothing behind it but a hole in the wall.

I reached inside, feeling around until my hands gripped the handles of a heavy bag, and dragged it out.

It fell to the floor with a solid thump.

There was nothing else in the hole so I dragged the bag back through to the living room.

I realized too late that I had dropped the knife right next to Taggart's hands, and he had been sawing through the tape with a violent flailing motion.

He had one arm free when I ran for the gun on the floor.

I felt it wrap around my ankle and drag me down.

There was blood in my mouth and I was being wrenched backwards.

I kicked and kicked until I felt my feet connect with flesh and then I scrambled for the Derringer and turned and fired it into his face, which caved in under the bullet and showered me with blood as the recoil sent the gun spiralling out of my hands and the sound of the shot impacted against the inside of my skull and my ears began ringing.

I'd bitten through my bottom lip when I fell and it hurt like fuck.

Hands over my ears, I struggled into a kneeling position.

Issa Taggart was dead. He was really fucking dead.

I hadn't been this close to a dead person since my parents and sister. I kept watching him, sure he was going to move, because he was human-shaped and humans always moved, but he didn't. The human in him was gone. Now he was just a lump, like the sofa he was lying next to.

Grimacing, I stood up and put my knife and empty gun back in my bag. I went upstairs, dragged the duvet off their bed and took it downstairs to put over the body. Hopefully his wife would know he was dead on sight and wouldn't feel the need to look, wouldn't scar herself with the memory of seeing her husband wrapped in masking tape, sans finger, sans face. . .

I pulled a bag on to each shoulder and switched the lights off on my way out of the room, so I didn't have to look at the body or the photos of his wife and baby.

At least he didn't make me kill them, I thought.

I let myself out of the house and walked shakily down the driveway and a little way down the road, to where the Russians were still waiting in total darkness in their car. They had turned around while I'd been gone.

The last of the daylight had died while I'd been inside.

Isaak opened the back door and shifted over to let me in.

I swung the bags in before me in silence.

149

Everyone looked at me.

I looked at my hands.

The driver started the car and pulled away.

Alexei grabbed the new bag from the middle seat and unzipped it. His eyes widened in the yellow intervals of light from the passing lampposts.

He muttered something in Russian, and Isaak undid his seatbelt to lean forwards and look.

'All there?' I asked.

Alexei zipped the bag back up and pushed it into the footwell. 'Yes, it is.'

I nodded.

'Is he dead?' Isaak turned to me, his face blank with shock.

'What do you think?' I said, taking the leather gloves off and stuffing them in my bag. 'I want my cut tonight so you might as well count it now.'

Alexei picked up the bag and rested it on his knees, apparently lost in thought.

The driver looked at me in the overhead mirror and said, 'Well done.'

I heard him but tried to think about nothing. Not even the mountaintop or the leaves on the wind.

Chapter Eighteen

I'd seen it in loads of gangster and war movies: the scene where some inexperienced youngster takes their first human life, often by accident, as I had just done. They always ended up standing fully clothed under a shower sobbing into the tiles, writhing and gurning with flashbacks, clawing at their hair and face, plagued by sleeplessness and hallucinations of blood on hands. Hell, fictional women had thrown themselves from castle walls over it.

I didn't have any of that.

Feeling weirded-out by the strained car journey, I left my travel bag, now heavy with money, in the living room and let myself drop face down on to my bed.

It was almost midnight.

I refused to think any more about what had just happened. In the car I'd started to dwell on the idea of Taggart's wife returning, picturing the changing expressions on her face, but I dismissed it. It was like a fire door closing in my mind. If I didn't want to think about something, I shut it off and let it burn itself out without my direct attention.

My limbs were limp with exhaustion, but I made myself get back up, put Bob Dylan on my iPod just inside the bathroom door and go for a shower.

I didn't cry in the shower; just washed.

When I came out of the bathroom I fell straight back into the bed still wrapped in my towel. I must have fallen asleep because the next thing I remembered was being woken up by the sound of my phone ringing in the living room.

I launched myself off my bed, thinking that it might be the Russians, or Noel having found out about the body and money. . .

But it was Daisy.

'Can I come over?'

I shook sleep out of my eyes and glanced at the clock, but I wasn't that attached to the idea of sleep anyway and she sounded uncharacteristically glum.

'Yeah, go for it. You OK?'

'I'm outside actually, pissed and. . . I have Smirnoff Ice.'

I smiled while simultaneously kicking my travel bag out of sight down by the side of the sofa. 'Come up. I'll buzz you in.'

'Wheeey! Thanks, bub.'

I buzzed her in and quickly made sure the bag was hidden before letting her in, holding the towel in place under my armpit.

Daisy swayed inside wearing a jumper and tights, and handed me a Smirnoff Ice. 'I don't know why I bought them. Imagine if I'd been hit by a bus or something, I'd have *died* with these things. People would think I was the sort of girl who drinks Smirnoff Ice at one in the morning.'

'I'll keep that in mind for an epitaph.'

'I'm a cheap date, me. I think I'm just pissed on the E numbers.' She hopped around on one foot taking her ankle boots off and collapsed on to the sofa, putting her feet up on the arm.

'Sometimes when I talk to Nic I think he's just pretending to be dense so that he doesn't have to say anything. Seriously, I ask him a question and he just stares at me, like "Huh?" It's like living with Kevin the teenager.'

'Have you guys had an argument?'

I sat down on the rug and opened the Smirnoff Ice with my lighter. It didn't even count as alcohol in my mind. I wasn't even sure you *could* get drunk on it.

'Yeah and no, not really. I just didn't want to stay there; he drags such a fucking atmosphere around when he's sulking.' She smiled to herself. 'I never thought I'd ever have to like him that much, that's the problem. Let alone say it or. . . show it or anything. I thought people who did that should be euthanized.'

I shrugged. 'Suppose so.'

'Did that happen with you and Monobrow?' she asked, sticking her legs up in the air and looking at them.

I sipped the syrupy liquid. 'What do you mean? Fuck, this is disgusting.'

'I know, right!' She cackled. 'It's bottled diabetes and it's so fucking good. . . I mean, that's how you tell, isn't it? You start off looking happy and then after a bit just them walking around *existing* makes you sad. Fuck knows Nic is really pissing me off with all the *existing* he's doing right now. Even the way he eats Frosties makes me wanna punch him in the face, you know? Just. . . *right* in the face.'

'Not so much. I don't think I've ever been into someone enough to want to punch them in the face.' I shrugged. 'I want to punch random people in the face all the time though so I don't think I discriminate on the grounds of whether I want to shag them or not.'

'Bull.' She rolled on to her side. 'So if it's not Monobrow, who is it?'

'Who?'

'Your bottled diabetes.' She giggled, and carried on giggling for a while at her own joke. 'Come on, I moan to you about Nic all the time and you've never told me anything about you. What about this guy you used to live with? Is he on holiday or something?'

'That guy, um. . . No, he's away for good, I think. And we were definitely never a thing.'

'Then who is it? Come on, who's the guy?'

I didn't answer her. I was finding it weird enough having this discussion when not even two hours ago I'd shot a man in the head. I felt guilty even replaying the memory in my mind. I felt like Daisy would almost be able to see it.

'Does Nic ever talk to you much about his job?' I asked, finding it difficult to talk about him as if we hadn't met.

In truth, I'd thought about him a lot since he had drawn the picture for me, the one that was now in my kitchen. He was a hard man to stop thinking about. Unlike Mark, who wore much of his cunning and delight in his profession on his face, Nic had the air of a naive introvert, as if, given the choice, he wouldn't speak to strangers at all. It was compelling. I hadn't been able to envision it before, but he and Daisy must complement each other with their antithetical approaches to life.

'Oooh, nice evasion, Seven, how *very* smooth.' Daisy winked at me. 'Yeah, sometimes.'

'Like, details?'

'Well, not names and stuff but if I ask he tells me things. Think he doesn't get much chance to talk about it and. . . this might be bad, but. . . I find it really interesting. Does that mean I'm sick? Some kinda psycho?'

'You are a psychopath.' I grinned at her.

She covered her mouth. 'No way, I'm a sick puppy, right! I can't believe I'm telling you this but. . . fuck, I enjoy hearing about it. Sometimes. . . I think I even find it attractive. There, I said it! I dig it, I think it's hot!'

I mock-gasped. 'You find danger hot? You *deviant*!'

'Well no, I wouldn't find the idea of *me* being in danger hot, but it's just a fantasy thing. Sometimes. . . fuck, this is *wrong*, you can't tell *anyone*! But sometimes I have this fantasy that he's just gone out, been in this big fight, has blood all over him and then he comes home and fucks me.' She screwed her face up. 'Argh, God, it's *horrible*, isn't it! I'm a *horrible fucked-up* person!'

'Please, like every woman who has a rape fantasy *wants* to be raped? Of course not, it's fantasy, you don't actually want it to happen to you in real life.'

She thought for a moment.

'No,' she said, grimacing. 'Ew. I bet you're into all that too, right?'

I shook my head, taking another gulp of Smirnoff Ice and feeling thirteen years old. 'Uh-uh. Not my thing.'

'What? You're seriously telling me you don't get sick of being your oh-so-empowered self sometimes and just want a guy to. . . throw you down and. . . *do stuff* to you?' She looked positively giddy at the thought.

'You're such a westerner,' I said, knowing how patronizing I sounded. 'Where I come from a lot of girls are. . . Well, it's got better as generations go by, but girls where I come from are so *agreeable*. It's not the done thing to be loud and brash or. . . opinionated in front of men, really. Here you can do and say what you like. You can fetishize being dominated because it's a novelty for you. Westerners wouldn't know self-restraint if it smacked them in the face with a dildo. Though you would probably like that!'

Daisy cackled, but appeared to be thinking. 'I never thought about it like that. Man, I don't know if I could hack it where you come from.'

I sighed. 'I'd go back and live in my old street in a second. I miss how clean everything is.'

'Why don't you?' She snorted to herself. 'Fuck, I don't mean that in a bitchy way! But why don't you, if you want to?'

'Well, I can't afford it, and there's no one there.'

'No great star-crossed love? Some guy? I thought there might be. . .'

I stared at her until she relented, sitting up and spreading her hands.

It seemed to have irritated her. 'OK, OK, I fucking give up. You know *everything* about me and, as ever, I know sweet fuck-all about you.'

'For the love of *fuck*, Daisy, there isn't some guy!'

'All right, *chill*, *Winston*!'

'It's a girl, OK.'

Daisy's expression fell into confusion, then picked up so as not to seem offensively surprised. I wondered if she'd ever suspected or given it any thought. After she recovered from the initial shock, she shrugged.

'So, you're bi?' she said.

'You don't have to sound so alarmed. I thought you said

you were into *all sorts?*'

'Well, yeah, in porn and in. . . my mind but I've never. . .' She reddened a little. 'I've never got down and. . . *down* with a girl. I mean, I've kissed friends when I've been drunk and stuff but, man, I've never actually had a real vagina in my face.'

Not long after that I managed to force her back out of my front door so I could get some sleep, but my ribs still hurt from how much I had laughed.

When I awoke at around twenty past five it felt as though I had a mild fever. I pushed the cover off me and hung my feet from the edge of the bed until they were brushing the carpet, but within a matter of seconds I was shivering and I pulled the duvet back across my body again.

I turned on to my side and checked if I was sweating.

I wasn't.

My limbs felt large and awkward and I was overheating again.

I turned until my back was exposed to the air but my front was under cover, and that almost worked.

A shooting pain crossed the side of my head and I sat up, instantly becoming too cold.

Was I having a brain haemorrhage or something?

I lay back down, tried to get comfortable and turned my pillows over so my cheeks didn't have to keep pressing against the bed's unbearable heat. But the more I tried to keep myself still the more agitated I became.

My throat was dry so I got up to pour a glass of water, but drinking that didn't help, and walking around just caused my hands and feet to go numb with cold.

I tried lying back down but another muscle spasm darted across my stomach.

'Fuck sake!'

The next time I sat up I felt lightheaded, so I lay on top of the duvet, my leg spasming, certain I was dying and thinking should I call somebody?

Worried that I was going to pass out and that would be it, I walked to the kitchen again and drank some more water. Should I call NHS Direct? Should I call an ambulance? It took me a while to notice I was counting to myself, waiting for a heart attack or a stroke or a total blackout. . .

But it didn't come.

I stayed awake, hot and cold, racked with muscle spasms and crying intermittently, until about nine in the morning. My feet kept twitching.

'Onetwothreefourfivesixseven. . . Onetwothreefourfive sixseven. . .'

It was the first time for years I'd felt the urge to do that, whispering it under my breath. I made myself stop it and broke the never-ending chain of thought. I thought of Seiko, teaching me how to meditate the first time, making me visualize the mountain, the leaves, the wind. . .

I forced myself to eat a couple of slices of toast, even though I was barely able to raise them to my lips, and then fell asleep for an hour.

When I awoke the second time I felt totally normal.

When I asked Daisy about it she suggested that I'd had an anxiety attack.

I was to have anxiety attacks every night for a month before they went away. As penances go, I think I got off lightly.

Chapter Nineteen

'Vaughn died yesterday in his last car-crash. During our friendship he had rehearsed his death in many crashes, but this was his only true accident. Driven on a collision course towards the limousine of the film actress, his car jumped the rails of the London Airport flyover and plunged through the roof of a bus filled with airline passengers. The crushed bodies of package tourists, like a haemorrhage of the sun, still lay across the vinyl seats when I pushed my way through the police engineers an hour later.'

I paused, and spread my legs a little wider. 'Is that. . . OK?'
'Perfect.'
Darsi Howiantz was on his knees in front of me. Over his shoulder were the ranges and valleys of books, papers, odd figurines. He was holding one of those large circular back massagers against my clit, which somewhat obviously was making it an ordeal to read out loud, but it was what he wanted me to do so I obliged.

'In his vision of a car-crash with the actress, Vaughn was obsessed by many wounds and impacts – by the dying chromium and collapsing bulkheads of their two cars meeting head-on in complex collisions endlessly repeated in slow-motion films, by the identical wounds inflicted on their bodies, by the image of windshield glass frosting around her face as she broke its tinted surface like a death-born. . .'

'Ah – ". . . Aphrodite. . ."' I gasped and halted again, blood rushing to my face and between my legs.

He had told me to keep reading for as long as I could, but surrender was what he was after. It was only my second time here, but I loved that I was Noel's go-to girl for Darsi's house calls. It was refreshing, being with a guy who was so completely turned on by someone else's pleasure.

The book was *Crash*. I'd read it before, the first time, when we were having sex and I had a finger up his ass and I was practically screaming the words.

I was glad I wouldn't have to spend the entire night in the club waiting to see Noel or Ronnie and the looks on their faces, the distracted scowls etched between brows that at any moment I envisioned being directed towards me, because they knew, somehow. . .

'Ten days ago, as he stole my car from the garage of my apartment house, Vaughn hurtled up the concrete ramp, an ugly machine sprung from a trap. Yesterday his body lay under the police arc-lights at the foot of the flyover, veiled by a delicate lacework of blood.'

My hands started shaking a little. 'Hm. . . "The broken postures of his legs and arms, the bloody geometry of his face, seemed to parody the photographs of crash injuries that covered the walls of his apartment".'

My hair was beginning to stick to my face and I took one hand off the book to brush it away.

He was moving the device against my clit with a rapid pulsing motion.

'"I looked down for the last time at his huge groin, engorged with blood. Twenty yards away, illuminated by revolving lamps. . ."' I shut my eyes, legs tense, momentarily distracted by the low hum below me. 'Um. . . Sorry. ". . . the actress hovered on the arm of her chauffeur. . ." *Fuck*. . .'

I grabbed a handful of his hair. It was all I could see. My whole body was rigid. I was so close, so close, but then the urge to come subsided for a moment.

'Vaughn had dreamed of dying at the moment of her orgasm.

'Before his death Vaughn had taken part in many crashes. As I think of Vaughn I see him in the stolen cars he drove and damaged, the surfaces of deformed metal and plastic that for ever embraced him. . .'

'*Oh. . . oh. . . fuck*. . .' I gasped and the book sprung shut across my finger. My limbs shuddered as I cried out, every violent breath shaking me from the inside. I arched my back, slid down in the chair, moaning until the tremors began to subside.

My first instinct was to laugh with relief but I stifled it.

Darsi had switched the device off and stood up, tentatively stroking the side of my face. 'Can I get you a drink?'

I'd been so wrapped up in my own orgasm that I hadn't even noticed him come as well, but he must have done. As he stood up, he discreetly wiped his right hand off on a tissue that he must have had in his pocket.

I pulled myself up straight in the office chair again, breathless and smiling. 'Um, yeah, sure.'

As he crossed to the other side of his study to pour a glass from the two bottles of champagne I'd been sent with, I pushed my leather skirt back down again. He hadn't even requested that I undress this time, apart from quietly slipping off my knickers. They were lying on the floor and I became anxious over whether to go and get them or not, but in the end I didn't. Why did I even care anyway?

I put *Crash* down beside my feet and tried to forget about it.

An aftershock of the orgasm shot up through my abdomen and I jumped, crossing my legs. I couldn't even remember the last time a man had been able to get me this wet.

Darsi handed me a glass.

I'd forgotten to specify something non-alcoholic but accepted the drink anyway.

'I'm glad I was sent to see you again,' I said, almost bashful.

'The sentiment is shared.'

'I wanted to talk to you more last time. Not that the other stuff wasn't. . . great.'

He eyed the champagne bottles with bemusement, as if he couldn't understand what they were doing in his house, and shrugged. 'You seem to be interested in human nature.'

'Well, only the interesting parts.'

'The criminal parts.' He understood. 'It's why I went into criminal psychology.'

'What's the actual definition of a psychopath? I know you kinda told me before but how would you spot one?'

'I could lend you some of my articles if you want? I've got some journals, if psychopathy particularly interests you.' He sat back in the swivel chair and drifted left and right. 'There are lots of different symptoms that define a psychopath, but put most simply I think it's a person who lacks a basic capacity for feeling empathy of any kind towards another human being. So combine that with a lot of other contributing factors, like childhood trauma, upbringing, education. . . so many things. . . you could end up with an unrepentant killer, yes. Serial killers are rare, in the way that *CSI* portrays them. That's why they all become famous.'

I thought about the gunshot, covering the body, the strange episode in the night, and felt somewhat reassured. But with the mental image came the sudden fear that he knew. Could he see it in my face that I'd killed somebody? It was his job after all.

I almost drank to mask any discomfort but the smell made me grimace so I lowered the glass again.

'Could a psychopath *act* as if they had empathy?' I was keeping myself unnaturally still.

'That's more of a typical sociopathic trait, someone who mimics human emotions to manipulate people, but yes.' There was a line between Darsi's eyes that looked permanent, even though he couldn't be over the age of thirty-five. 'This is all very simplified though. That's why I'm still researching it.'

'And you help the police?'

'When I can. I work with prisoners and patients too.'

I considered telling him about Leo Ambreen-King, if he was so open to working with people. But now wasn't the time. I wanted the chance to talk to him more first, not least because I'd never had any dealings with a bent police officer or their ilk before, and wasn't sure how it was done.

'Will I be coming back here again?' I asked. 'I mean, will you still be doing favours for Noel to repay?'

'As Noel probably well knows, in the real world I couldn't even afford you.'

'The real world?'

'The one where you don't pay people by sending champagne and beautiful women to their houses.' He smiled, and I realized I'd misjudged how much he knew about Noel's work. 'In the real world, violence is a thing that's controlled and legislated against, it's something that happens to states and armies, but not people. In his world, it's. . . just communication.'

I left him my number written on a packet of Rizlas.

Chapter Twenty

Darsi didn't live that far from me so I walked home instead of taking the pre-booked taxi. I needed the fresh air.

I used to love coming into an empty house. Now it felt like walking into a mausoleum.

I crossed the road to avoid a group of teenage boys arguing about splitting money to pay for something in Tesco before it shut. Maybe it was because I had witnessed more death than most people, but I was definitely paranoid. In the last few years I'd developed a habit of looking at different people in the street, in a shop or on the tube, and imagining how they might kill me.

The last time I did it I imagined a guy standing up from his seat on the Northern Line and coming over to stab me. It freaked me out so much that I had to get off early.

By the time I got home I was almost certain someone was following me, but I put it down to my usual paranoia and just turned every light on in the flat to make myself feel better. A parcel had been left outside my postbox: too big to fit inside, so left out in the hallway for everyone to see or steal.

Thank fuck the knives were still there.

I put them down in the living room, changed out of my leather outfit into a white Beatles T-shirt with holes in the back, then sat down on the floor next to my sofa bed to hack them open with a pair of scissors.

The box wasn't decorative and it was wrapped in several layers of bubble wrap, but it had a sheath to protect it. There were two of them. Not true Tantōs; they were too expensive for me. But they looked like the real thing: about thirty centimetres long and the front third of the blades were double-edged.

They were brilliant. Perfect for hiding in boots or under a jacket.

I held one of the daggers in my lap for a while and imagined jamming it straight into Alexei's eye and out the other side. The thought gave me a sharp physical thrill, not dissimilar to what I'd felt earlier when I was reading the later paragraphs of *Crash*.

Making a mental note to track down some kind of strap to carry the daggers behind my shoulders, I slid one under the sofa bed and another under my pillow.

I slept in the living room with all the lights on. It didn't make much difference. In fact it made me feel worse, being able to see what I thought was coming.

The second time my mother forced me to talk to a therapist was the second time we moved to London and she complained I was becoming withdrawn, as if I hadn't been inclined to introversion my entire life.

Mum was the sort of person who viewed introversion as a personality flaw that needed to be eradicated. Her ideal world was one in which everyone spoke to everyone else at parties in increasingly hysterical levels of volume until you could no longer distinguish words. Ironically, what she saw as confidence I'd always seen as cowardice. Extroverts engaged with the world in a never-ending barrage of small talk and superficiality, shunning the opportunity for any real connection or feeling. Introverts, when they did engage, shared things that mattered, and listened in return. Anything else wasn't worth the energy.

Shoot me if I ever have a conversation about the weather, or anything else that could be interpreted by simply bothering to look at it.

More in an effort to shock than anything else, I told the man, the same one as before, about the time an American tourist tried to drag me off a subway train in Roppongi. I didn't tell him the whole story, but he attributed enough importance to it to claim it was why I distrusted other people so much.

I couldn't be bothered to tell him I'd always been uninterested in most people. Not much in my life had ever been changed by some cataclysmic event. At least, not that I could tell. My personality was a constant. It had become less forgiving, harder and less capable of shame and tolerance and, sometimes, fear. But it felt much the same to me. I'd never indulge in anything as childish as an epiphany.

It was one of the only times during my teens that I'd gone to another classmate's house for a party. I was sober but mildly happy, having spent the whole evening sitting on the floor talking to Seiko. Later on I had bumped into her coming out of the bathroom and I'd kissed her in the hallway because I was feeling brave and because she was drunk and didn't mind.

I was still wearing my school uniform. At the age of fifteen I resembled a twelve-year-old, but I'd learnt not to mind. I figured I'd appreciate it when I was old.

Just before we passed through Roppongi, having missed my

167

original change in a daydream, a drunk American guy staggered on to the train and announced he was trying to get to Shinjuku.

I didn't understand why tourists found our metro so hard. Were they all fucking colour-blind?

'Change at Aoyama-Itchōme.'

'Where are you getting off?' he asked, sitting down next to me and slinging an arm around my shoulders.

I took his hand off my shoulder and moved away without a word.

'Hey. . . bitch, I asked you a question.'

Oh fuck off, I thought, ready to get off at the next stop to distance myself from this whining asshole, even if it meant hanging around in Roppongi for a bit with the tourists and foreign businessmen who had no interest in ever learning our language.

There were only three other people at the opposite end of the carriage and one was standing up to leave.

The doors opened.

I was grabbed by the back of the neck and dragged forwards and off the train. It took me a second to realize it was the American guy. Up close he had overgrown eyebrows and smelt of pungent leather.

'Fucking. . . ignore me. . .' he was snarling.

I ducked and tried to twist out of his grasp but he yanked a fistful of my hair and groped for my legs under my skirt.

He shook me like a kitten and screamed into my face, 'The only reason Asian sluts like you exist is so we can fuck you! Fucking bitch!'

I was covered in alcoholic spit. This time he made a grab for my underwear and I parried his hands, kneeing him hard in the stomach. Grunting, he seized me by the collar of my jacket but I leant back and kicked him in the chest. When that didn't make him let go I whipped my penknife out of my blazer and stabbed him in the kneecap with it, hard enough for the blade to stay embedded in his leg when he howled and dropped me.

A little musical jingle was playing across the platform, signifying the train was about to leave.

I sprinted back on to it and the doors slammed shut.

I sat down, shaking, and realized I'd lost my penknife.

The American was still on the ground when the train pulled away, blood on his hands and crying out for help.

There was a ring of bruises around the top of my thigh and the tops of my arms for a week or so.

No one around me had done a thing. They never did. But at least it wasn't as bad as London. The last time Daisy had been sexually assaulted by some prick grabbing her on an underground train she was told to shush for causing a scene. She'd kicked him in the testicles to make him stop and left the train. When she told me about it later she had become angry at herself for crying.

Maybe it was easier to become more hardened to the fucked-up state of the world if you were a girl? We had to become accustomed to our own harassment and public invasion on a day-to-day basis. I suppose it's easier to remain unsurprised and unshaken by the repulsiveness of others if you live a daily war to keep your body your own.

Chapter Twenty-One

There was someone in the house when I opened my eyes. I wasn't sure if it was the noise of them breaking in that woke me, but I grabbed my unsheathed dagger from under my pillow and rolled off the sofa into a crouch without even thinking about it.

Looking back, if it had taken him one kick to open the door rather than two, I'd probably be dead.

If the lights had been off and I hadn't been able to see him at the moment he appeared in the living-room doorway with a balaclava over his face, I'd probably be dead too.

He was holding a machete.

The sofa separated us and we stood there for what felt like a long time, waiting to see which way the other would run.

He made the move, to the right.

I leapt over the back of the sofa and ran for the front door but he backtracked and cut me off, swiping at me.

The machete swung into the wall.

There was nowhere for me to go but back, as the blade was ripped out of the plaster and I rolled sideways back over the sofa on to the floor.

He lunged after me.

I picked up a pillow and it was almost sliced clean in half in front of my face. My dagger jabbed upwards and there was a grunt of frustration as I sliced open his hand.

'Fuck!'

He dropped the machete but wrenched me back towards him with a strength that almost dislocated my shoulder. Grasping my neck he threw me down and pinned me there, crouched over me like a child with an insect. Blood from his wrist trickled on to my shirt.

I couldn't breathe.

Air rushed into my mouth and out of it but nothing was happening.

His eyes were pale and too far apart.

I found the handle of my dagger and rammed it through his trainer and into his foot.

Suddenly my lungs were full again and I was free.

While I had the chance I kneed him in the balls.

He sank to his knees beside me, legs together, shouting and cursing with no accent.

I scrambled to my feet as he clutched at his groin and this time I shifted all my weight on to my back foot and side-kicked him in the chin.

His head snapped back with such force I thought I'd broken his neck and he fell to the floor, rigid like a tree.

I reached under the sofa bed for the other dagger and slammed it with all my strength into his chest. It sank in, through the breastbone. I pulled it out and did it again, wrenched it out again, stabbed him again, and again, and again, until I was sure he was dead. Blood ran from his mouth and he jerked as though he was having a seizure, before lying still.

I let go of the dagger's handle and stood up, breathing too fast and too hard.

Barely able to walk, I stumbled through to the kitchen and found a paper bag from a coffee shop to breathe into, until my body was flooded with enough carbon dioxide to stop fitting. The bag filled and emptied, filled and emptied, and I sat down on the tiles with my back against the cupboard and the cold tiles against my legs.

'Shit, oh shit, oh shit, oh shit. . . oh. . . oh shit. . .'

I put the bag down and looked back through at the living room. The man was still there, part of a red blade and ornate green handle sticking out of his stomach.

But it was meant to be me lying there, just like before.

After years of suspecting it was coming, for whatever reason, this had been my time to go.

I started counting before I could stop myself, glad there was no one there to see me, and remembered the front door was wide open—

'Shit!'

I was up on my feet again, running down the hall and doing my best to wedge the door shut again. But the lock was shattered, more fragile than I'd thought. I sat against it for a while, hands over my face, unable to stop the adrenalin pumping through me.

Why now? Why had it been my turn now? Who would have found me? The Russians? I imagined them doing the same thing I had, picking their way through the remains of the front door and finding my mangled body, skull cleaved in two. . .

My face felt puffy and flushed.

I stood up, after an unknown amount of time had gone

by, and walked slowly to the living room. These felt like the normal emotions one experienced when seeing a dead body: the urge to throw up, the urge to run. . .

Instead I stepped over his huge bulk and, with my eyes shut, pulled the dagger out of his foot and then, retching, out of his stomach. It made a sound like a blade slicing through lettuce.

I took the daggers through to the kitchen, washed the blood off them as if they were dirty plates, dried them and sheathed them again.

That was the easy part done. I didn't have a fucking clue what to do with the body.

I sat on the sofa and stared at him for a bit, and only when I decided I would have to call Mark did I think to take the balaclava off.

He was foreign, in his late thirties maybe, huge. . .

It didn't make a difference.

There were no familiar features.

I had never seen him before.

I had absolutely no idea who he was.

I couldn't have called Noel or Ronnie, not with the money and drugs still in a bag pushed to the back of the wardrobe. Mark probably did this sort of thing all the time and, furthermore, this wasn't coincidence. The longer I thought about it while waiting for him to arrive, in the shower and then finding a change of clothes, the more I understood this was a sign. This was a sign that we had got close to something, somehow, without even realizing it. It wasn't random, not just my turn to die. It meant that whoever was responsible for sending men up to my flat in Tooting almost three years ago was close enough to have seen or heard of what we were doing.

In a bizarre way, it was a good thing. We were on the right track.

It was almost three in the morning when I'd called Mark, but he didn't sound as though he'd been sleeping. He also didn't sound panicked or surprised when he was asking for my address, but I guessed that it was his professionalism kicking in.

'Keep yourself armed and don't move. I'll be there in twenty minutes. Jam the door if you can, I'll knock ten times.'

Anything less than ten, he'd said, and it could be anyone knocking.

My hair still wet, wearing a skirt and faded grey Slayer shirt with the sleeves cut off, I sat cross-legged on the kitchen worktop smoking and smoking until I heard Mark at the door.

'Where is it?' he said, striding in with a rucksack on his back and another in his hand.

It.

He took a look at the man on the floor in the living room and then turned and put a hand on my arm.

'Are you OK?' he asked.

I hadn't thought about it. I hadn't even looked down at my own body in the shower. 'Yeah, yeah, I'm fine. Just, um. . . No, I'm fine.'

'Really? No need to be macho on my account.'

'Really, I'm fine.'

He searched my face. 'If you say so.'

Mark paced around the body with an appreciative expression on his face, as if he was wandering around an art installation. There was no indication of disgust, just a desensitized silence.

'Big, isn't he,' he remarked.

'Is this the most common thing you get paid to do?' I asked, arms folded, watching.

'Yeah, it is actually.' He smiled. 'It's so much more common than you'd care to speculate. But it keeps my pay regular.'

'It must be the same guys,' I said, trying to stop myself from speaking too fast to be comprehensible. 'It's the same everything – the machete – it can't be a coincidence, right? I mean, this isn't just random, this has to be because you've been close to finding something out?'

Mark had crouched and given the body a small shake with gloved hands. He looked up at me, as if he was deciding how much to say. 'Leo Ambreen-King.'

'Really?' I raised my eyebrows. 'Why him?'

'I was thinking about it in the car. Who else would it be? If he was paid to do something for someone then it stands to reason they would still be in touch. If you want someone to sacrifice a chunk of their childhood to commit murder for you then you'd surely come up with some sort of arrangement. Compensation for when they're released? Something like that. Unless it directly jeopardized his future prospects in some way, why would he be so fearful of speaking to us or being seen speaking to us?'

I took a step back. It seemed obvious and that was why I didn't like it. 'And this didn't occur to you before?'

He paused. 'Did it occur to *you* that this might happen?'

'. . . No.'

He stood up and pulled a face. 'Truth be told, it did occur to me. But I got the impression that that was a chance you were willing to take simply by asking me to pursue this for you in the first place. . . What did you stab him with?'

I was about to tell him when I remembered the bug, and gestured at the kitchen. 'A knife. I just grabbed it when I heard someone kicking the door in. Mark. . . How would he even know I was living here?'

'Your name not on anything? Bills? Internet?'

'Yeah, everything. But normal people can't just get that information, right?'

'Well, maybe. Someone working with the police would be able to find out easier though.' He nodded at me. 'I hope this doesn't sound incredibly patronizing but. . . speaking objectively, you're a very small woman and you should be dead. In a close-combat situation as well, I'm amazed you're OK. I mean that as the highest compliment.'

'Thanks. Well, it's thanks to my dad.' It was the second time I should have been dead, really.

'OK, pack any stuff you're going to need and go wait in the car. I'll drop you somewhere you can stay for the night and come back here.'

I gestured at the body. 'But—'

'Trust me, this part of my job isn't a spectator sport.'

Chapter Twenty-Two

I spent the day sleeping and pacing and feeling lost, really fucking lost, in the sparse flat that Mark had taken me to, and didn't go into work the following night. I'd wanted Mark to get back to me but when he had, in the early afternoon, he had nothing to say and nothing to add. He didn't tell me what he had done with the body or what state the flat had been left in.

I'd showered, dressed in clothes that would cover the bruises running up my sides and down my arms, and walked to the Underground in time to watch Daisy leaving, but not locking up.

That was a sign that Noel was still in there.

It was never Ronnie at this time of night. He had too much to return home to.

For the first time in a while I felt fragile. I'd become all too aware of everything that could break, shatter, puncture, die. My eyes were hot and loaded with fatigue.

Consciousness was a bitch.

I crossed the road to the front entrance and let myself in through the black featureless doors.

The Underground was so calm and welcoming when it wasn't polluted with sad and desperate men. Nearing four in the morning it had the sweet smell of the aftermath of a wedding reception, hopeful and innocent.

Noel was sitting on the floor with his back against the bar, mixing himself a Whiskey Mac. He looked up and, thank fuck, his first instinct was to smile.

'Thought you were Daisy,' he said, patting the floor. 'What are you doing here?'

'Fancied someone to talk to.' I sat down on the floor also.

The walls, tables and drapes loomed around us.

'Daisy made up a new word for me today,' he said, snorting. 'It was getting busy about midnight, and she comes up to me and says, "It's totally rammo-jammo in here." You ever heard that phrase? *Rammo-jammo*. It really tickled me, that one.'

'That's not new,' I said, prodding one of his feet with mine. 'You're just old.'

'Watch it, whippersnapper. You're not too old to put over my knee.' He smirked and shot a filthy grin in my direction. 'Darsi speaks very highly of you, by the way.'

I adopted my best impression of coyness. 'Why did you think that with Darsi I'd make an exemplary house call all of a sudden? You know me, I make small children cry.'

'I could tell you'd make grown men cry. Too smart-arse for your own good.' He shook his head. 'I can't tell you, you'd never get your head back out the door.'

'Oh, go on!'

He raised his eyebrows. 'Honestly, he didn't really want me to send anyone, even though I definitely owe him a couple of favours. . . and he said it was because I wouldn't be able to send anyone intelligent enough. If I could send someone who could hold up a proper conversation for more than ten minutes he'd accept. That was the bet, and apparently I won.'

'And you sent me? To win a bet?'

'Seven, come on. Who else was I gonna send? Coralie mixed up "paediatrician" and "paedophile" when she was trying to read the paper the other day. . . though her English isn't that great.'

'What about Abigail? She's the history student.'

'Seven.' He looked serious all of a sudden. '*Obviously* I sent you.'

I accepted the compliment and changed the subject. 'To be fair, if I looked like Coralie I wouldn't even have bothered learning to speak. I'd just wait around for people to keep turning up and offering me stuff. Why would you want anything audio distracting people from a face like that?'

He shrugged. 'Meh, she's all right. She's just. . . French. They all look the same.'

After an intense stare, Noel picked up his drink and held it up next to his face for me to observe.

'Does this look like a problem to you?' he asked, as if the question had been bothering him for a while. 'Does this look like a suicide?'

'Um. . . no. Not yet anyway. I've never seen a suicide up close.'

He looked sideways at the glass and put it down in front of him. 'Do I look out of control?'

'No. I'm not sure. What are you talking about?'

'Just some bad stuff.' He shook his head, and unbuttoned his shirt a little more. 'Something happened with work and we've fucked up a bit. But it's weird how your personal and professional lives start to mirror each other after a while. No, not weird, I mean. . . fucking sad.'

'What do you mean, *does this look like a suicide*?'

He picked up the Whiskey Mac and drank it in one. 'Caroline says I'm trying to kill myself with it. That I'm just too much of a pussy to do it another quicker way and put a gun in my mouth or something.'

I would have taken his hand but he was too far away. Moving towards him would seem too self-conscious a gesture. I just let him talk.

'When I was about your age I tried to top myself.'

I couldn't disguise the sharp intake of breath.

He looked up at me and I was embarrassingly close to crying. 'What?'

'Just. . .' I looked down, locking my jaw and tightening my throat against the tears. 'Sorry, I just. . . You can't just tell me stuff like that, you know.'

'Oh, love.' He reached out an arm for me. 'Don't get upset about it, it was ages ago.'

I pulled myself forwards with my feet and wedged myself under his arm as he mixed another Whiskey Mac several inches from my face. It wasn't where I wanted to be most in the world, but it was damn close. He smelt like his office and smoke; his clothes smelt like four in the morning, when the drink and sweat, drugs and shouted conversation had soaked into them.

However much I didn't want to, I realized he probably wanted to talk about it, and asked, 'Why did you do it the first time?'

'Why did I try?' He shrugged, putting the bottle of whiskey down between my legs. 'It's hard to say really, cos I was young and when you're young everyone just thinks you're being dramatic. I even thought I was, when I woke up and I was on the way to hospital. I thought it was a bit pathetic.'

I looked up at him but he wasn't looking at me.

'I, um. . .' He smiled. About what, I wasn't sure. 'I wish I was a bit more working class growing up. It would have given me an excuse to say it's been a struggle, but it hasn't been. I had everything I wanted. Money always came easily. . . My parents had this holiday home in Devon and I was staying there for a long weekend with them. The first night I was on my own and I went down to the beach and into one of the caves while the tide was out. . . and I necked a load of paracetamol.'

'Right.' I nodded, as if it was nothing.

'I mean, I didn't realize at the time that that's the worst of the ways to do it. Espccially if it was a cry for help or what-ever. Because paracetamol is weird, it fucks you up slowly from the inside, so you wake up in hospital, think you're OK, but get told you're going to die in a couple of days anyway.' He took a smaller sip of his drink. 'But mine wasn't a cry for help, I really tried. But it's hard, much harder than you'd think. I threw most of everything up and a sea swimmer who saw me go into the cave found me and called someone.'

Alongside all my other aches there was a physical jolt of pain in my chest.

I choked out, 'Why?'

He rubbed his forehead and pinched the bridge of his nose, beneath the slight monobrow that Daisy always made fun of. 'I. . . think I just find it all hard. I find living really hard. They never tell you how hard it's going to be, do they?'

I swallowed.

181

He hugged me a bit tighter and met my eyes. 'I think that's why we get on. You know what I mean, don't you?'

I nodded, gritting my teeth.

'I thought it was just a young-person thing, but it's not. It never went away. Sometimes I wake up and I'm just fucking. . . crushed under how fucking difficult it is to be *here*.'

'And you're always asking me why I'm into *all that meditation shit*?' I didn't manage to smile for very long. 'Fuck, Noel, I'm. . . sorry, it's just hard for me to hear you say things like this. What's brought this on?'

'Argh.' He waved a hand in front of my face. 'Work stuff, and a bit of Caroline stuff. But at least the work stuff can be sorted out.'

'Yeah?' I repressed a shudder.

'Yeah, luckily we can hire people to sort stuff out for us.'

I searched for the best way to ask. 'People like Daisy's fella? Whatsisname. . .? Nic?'

He laughed in a way that made my skin crawl and he hugged me. 'Ha! Yes, precisely. *Exactly*, in fact. We've got him staked-out and. . . It doesn't matter, you don't wanna know about all that bollocks.'

Fuck.

I wanted to extricate myself from his embrace but it would look wrong, so I sat there, tense and certain he would be able to feel the lies.

'I need to stop,' he said, handing me the other Whiskey Mac. 'You have it.'

'Come on, you *know* I don't. Jeez.'

'Yeah. Why is that?' He cocked his head. 'Are you like me? Is it your *thing*?'

'No. I just don't like things that make me feel out of control.'

'I hate control. When I drink it makes me feel like I don't have that pressure to remember to keep breathing. Otherwise it's just like. . . in and out, in and out, in and out. . .'

Sometimes I had been afforded a glimpse, a real sign of the struggle, but I'd never known before how unhappy he could be. I thought of him now, walking into a cave with a bottle of pills and a bottle of something else. As suicide methods went, it was very him. He wasn't exhibitionist or callous enough to do it in a way that would traumatize too many innocent people, like jumping in front of a train or hanging himself for a friend or family member to find.

I opened my mouth to tell him everything. I knew it was the right thing to do. But there was too much everything to even start.

My heart sped up.

But there was no opening sentence that would make him understand, no singular phrase that could adequately excuse everything I'd done, and I doubted I'd be given the chance to elaborate much beyond that.

'Maybe you're right,' I said, instead of anything important. 'Maybe you should stop then.'

'My dad was an alcoholic.'

I didn't know what to say to that.

'I'm sorry,' he said, buttoning his jacket up. 'I'm starting to over-share. It's weird, sometimes I feel like if I tell you everything you'd be able to sort it out. Basically I think you're the Oracle.'

He stood and pulled me up with him into a fierce hug, so fierce that my back began to hurt. When he loosened his grip a bit he held my face in both his hands and I started praying so hard that he would take me home.

'Want to come stay at mine?'

It felt as though he was holding me upright, stood there with his forehead against mine, so close that the flaws in his face blurred.

'Yeah, yeah, I'd really like that.'

I'd considered taking the daggers with me in my bag, but they mattered less if I was at Noel's. I went back to his flat and slept and woke up and fucked with my eyes half closed and no one tried to kill me. I thought about going back to Mark's temporary safe house, carrying on living, and it made me feel so empty inside I wanted to die. But Noel reached out for me in his sleep and made everything seem OK, for this one night at least.

Chapter Twenty-Three

In the morning I awoke before Noel and paced around his flat, anxious to move about in space, oddly claustrophobic. I was a rat in a corner spitting and scratching and hissing but it didn't make a difference, because now I knew Nic Caruana was going to kill me anyway, and there was nothing I could do about it.

I dressed and sat down in the middle of Noel's living-room floor and tried to meditate, remind myself of myself. I still had control. No one else was master of this body, so I could still find a way out of this.

Don't die, I thought, deciding it should become my motto, my one rule to live by.

Don't die.

Noel had asked about my bruises and I told him I'd had a scrape with a car.

'You're lovely,' he'd said anyway.

I wanted to speak with Leo Ambreen-King again, but I had to wait for Mark to call.

I wanted to know whether the Russians wanted or needed my help any more.

I wanted to leave, just leave, but that was out of the question.

I was sick of waiting for everyone.

Standing up, I went back through to the bedroom and looked at Noel from the doorway. His expression was serious and scowling in sleep. I took a step forward, as though I was going to kiss him on the forehead or something, but then left, resisting the urge to rifle through his flat looking for. . . something.

I closed the front door quietly and walked down the corridor feeling lost.

At the elevators I stopped, waiting for one to rise, and the doors opened.

A woman hesitated in front of me for a moment, wearing a pencil skirt and blouse, with bare legs and a leather shoulder bag and dark red hair that looked dyed, but I knew it was natural, because I knew her, and I was certain she knew me. She was pale, gamine, blue-eyed with a fierce stare: the sort of woman who wore her intellect on her face.

She only hesitated for a moment, then stepped out of the elevator. She wasn't wearing her wedding ring but she saw me look for it.

We swapped places.

I looked over my shoulder and she looked over hers before disappearing from view.

Forgetting to press a button, I stood there staring at the wall outside, feeling short and awkward and plain and sick. I'd never been interested in comparing myself to other women before. As far as I was concerned, most people looked the same. I didn't attach much importance to exceptional facial features, so this particular brand of shame and inadequacy was unfamiliar.

Caroline was so beautiful I felt like a pre-pubescent idiot looking up at the adult they wanted to be when they grew up.

I came to and smacked the ground-floor button too hard, leaning against the back mirror as the doors closed, wondering what the fuck I was doing here. What the fuck had I ever been doing here really? As if I was seriously competing with her, the woman who looked like *that*.

'Jesus,' I said to myself, blinking back tears. 'Stupid. *Stupid.*'

I left the building, trying get Caroline's expression as she'd looked at me out of my mind, and Mark rang me.

'Are you at home?' he asked, meaning *his* home.

'Um, no, I'm. . . out for a walk.'

'I've got some things for you to look at, and we're seeing Leo again tomorrow. Can you be back within half an hour?'

'I guess.'

'Make sure you're not followed. I don't think Mr Machete is going to be the last one they send looking for you.'

I glanced back up at Noel's flat and realized it was likely being watched. It was muggy: the hottest day of the year so far, but overcast. Everyone in my line of vision was sweating but despondent in the lack of light. No one was searching for me here.

I looked up again, realizing that Caroline would be able to see me from Noel's window, and hurried across the road towards the tube station.

I was still mentally comparing myself to Caroline, even after I'd returned to meet Mark at the new apartment. My overnight bag was still in my new bedroom, packed with the essentials and full of money, ready to leave again at a moment's notice. I hadn't stepped foot in the kitchen, so reluctant was I to accept the imposition of this new space. My old flat, tainted as it was by my attempted murder, still felt like my base.

Mark had arranged a load of photos on the floor, paper-clipped to different pieces of paper. It was a strange, unnerving, unsmiling collage of middle-aged male faces.

'Who are they?' I crouched down and lifted one of the photos.

'DCI Edward Casey. Age: 58.'

'They're a compilation I got together of a section of the DCIs working in London around the time your parents were killed. From what you said I reckoned that if he is police. . . and that's a big *if*. . . we're likely looking for a plain-clothes high-ranking officer, so this is a selection. These are the highest ranking; I'm working on getting names of lower-ranking officers from other boroughs.'

'How the hell did you get these?' I sat cross-legged, mouth open in disbelief. 'You can't just walk into stations and get this stuff.'

Mark shrugged, but he looked pleased with himself.

'Recognize any of them?' he asked.

There were too many to stand up and cast a casual eye over them searching for a face, so I moved on to my hands and knees and worked my way through each one methodically. I didn't entirely trust my memory. Whoever that man had been back then, he could look different now. I might have made up his eye colour or exaggerated the description of his hair. What's more, these men all looked the same.

'No. . . No. Um, no, not him.'

I moved photos to my left, picking my way left and right down the rows. The further I progressed, the more frustrated I became with myself. Maybe he was here, and I'd just overlooked him?

'No, I. . . Shit, what if he wasn't even a police officer? He was alone – he could have just posed as one. The file could just be. . . lost.'

'Well, hold off on the panic at least until you've discounted this lot,' Mark said with a smile.

I looked sideways at his legs and carried on.

Just under halfway through, almost dead in the centre of the living-room floor, I faltered at the eyes of someone I recognized. It was of man with black eyes, a bald head and—

I'm truly sorry for your loss, Kiyomi.

I picked up the photo and held it close to my face, heart pumping hard and repelled by the image.

'DCI Kenneth Gordon. Age: 60.'

Older than I thought or remembered. . .

I put the photo down to my left.

'Him?' Mark asked, leaning down.

'I'm not sure,' I said, lying and unsure as to why.

Had I just reached a point where lying came so easily that I did it now for no good reason? Or was there a good reason? I couldn't tell any more.

For the sake of appearances, I put another couple of photos down on my left. They looked like him, could be easily confused, but not by me. Rage was coursing through me the likes of which I hadn't felt in years, before everything had become so deadened. I couldn't pick up another photo for fear that my hands would shake and give me away. I expected to feel more relief, but there wasn't relief; there was just the anger, the desperate all-encompassing need to know, stronger than ever before.

I wasn't sure whether Mark had noticed. I kept my eyes down. He probably had. He knew I was lying. I wondered if he'd accuse me of it, or just hold the knowledge within himself until he knew what to do with it.

Eventually, I stopped.

'Can I keep these three?' I asked, still on the floor. 'I want to look at them some more, try and get. . . something. I'm not sure. I only met him once and it was just after it happened; everything was a bit. . . fast.'

'Sure.' He took them off me briefly to look at the names. 'In the meantime, do you want me to start researching them? Addresses and work and a more detailed history?'

I nodded. 'If you like.'

Mark held up the first man I'd picked out and said, 'It's him, isn't it?'

I suddenly wished I wasn't still on the floor.

'I'm not sure.'

'You worry me, Seven,' he replied, turning the photo over and reading the details underneath, 'because you're not as good a liar as you think you are.'

I wasn't used to being called out and my first response was to redden and push away the threat of brattish tears.

'I did already know that it was likely to be one of these few, if not him, because. . .' Mark took Nic's drawing out of his pocket, unfolded it and held it up against the photo of 'DCI Kenneth Gordon. Age: 60'.

It was a pretty decent match.

'Why did you lie?' Mark inclined his head at me, but he didn't look grave or even annoyed.

'I was afraid you'd want to be the one to kill him instead of me.'

I hadn't been sure that this was the reason until I said it out loud.

He sighed, but lightheartedly. 'Look, I'm your servant here, Seven. I do what you want. You don't have to lie to me. I'm not here to interfere, I'm here to help you. As long as you let me advise you because we don't want you getting arrested or anything unnecessary like that. . . Also, please keep in mind that we don't even know for certain it's him yet. But it'll be easy to find out, I think.'

I hadn't expected this response. I was glad he hadn't been cross with me. 'Is it normal for people you work for to want to kill someone themselves?'

'I don't usually get that so much, but bear in mind, people who hire me usually want me to remove people precisely so they don't have to. It's a matter of forensics. I'm simply less likely to get caught because I'm, well, professional.'

A falsely modest smile and spread of the hands.

'But I don't think you're strange for wanting to,' he continued, 'if that was the actual question you were asking. We all have to vent, in certain ways. Do you want to keep this photo?'

I shook my head. 'I'll just look at it too much. Can I keep the rest of the info though?'

'Yeah sure, I can get another. I have them all as PDFs, I just printed these off.'

DCI Kenneth Gordon.

I was glad I wouldn't have the photo. I already felt the creeping obsession with looking into and into his face as if I could find some proof there. It was better to let Mark leave with all the temptation to dwell on it and try to provoke some emotion to drown in.

'OK. Well, be careful in the meantime and I'll call you tomorrow before we go and see Leo in the afternoon, OK?'

I nodded.

Mark gathered up the rest of his compilation. The floor was slick wood and it took him a while to grasp the edges of the papers. I wondered if he was the sort who would keep them, as mementoes.

'You work with Russians, right?' I asked suddenly. 'Noel said.'

I tried to make it sound like casual conversation as I stood up with my hands on my hips waiting for him to go, so I could pursue my own line of investigation.

'Yeah, sometimes. Why?'

'A few of them come in the club sometimes, that's all. Just wondered if you knew them. They're called Alexei and Isaak and there's another one, older. Think they're brothers.'

'There are far too many Russians called Alexei.' Mark smirked. 'You might as well ask me if I know a guy called Dave.'

'Figured.'

'I'll call you tomorrow.'

'OK.'

I counted down ten minutes on the clock as I changed into a clean set of clothes from my bag, and left the apartment again, with a renewed sense of purpose. Nic's drawing was in my bag. Fuck Noel hiring Nic Caruana. He wasn't a superhuman. He was a man and men were all movable objects. So much more movable than any of them would care to admit.

Chapter Twenty-Four

He looked surprised to see me. It was a Sunday so I knew he'd be home.

I was only a little offended that he hadn't called me, even to chat, but then he seemed shy. Maybe he was just one of those guys who needed more time to work up to a bold move like that?

'May I come in?' I found it cute how his expression became coy and awkward. 'I need to talk to you about something. It's kinda work. Your work, not mine.'

'Um, Seven,' he said, saying my name as though it was a word he didn't understand. 'Of course.'

Darsi Howiantz's house brought a sense of calm over me. I felt safe here. There were no negative associations or memories for once. It was so eccentric, like another dimension, that I could almost kid myself we were no longer in London.

The room in which he kept his landscape of papers and his models was kept in dim light, with the curtains shut.

'Can I sit down?' I asked.

'Oh, yes.' He picked up a pile of books from the chair I'd sat in last time. 'What was it you wanted to talk about?'

'You work with the police, you said?'

'Yes, I do.' He positioned himself across from me, also in the same place he had sat last time. 'It's one of the only ways I can apply my research. Otherwise I'm just. . . blagging my way through an easy life of academia.'

A nervous smile.

'Have you ever worked with a DCI called Kenneth Gordon?'

There was a flicker of recognition that he didn't seem to realize was visible to me.

'Why do you ask?'

'So you know him?'

'I'm. . . not sure. Why do you ask?'

I cast my eyes about the room. Did I tell him the truth or not? Was lying safer or was it just the preferable easy option? The lazy option.

After a long pause, I took Nic's drawing out of my bag and handed it over to him. It was the original. Mark had the photocopy.

'He could be responsible for a violent crime and I was wondering whether you knew him.'

Choosing his words with care, Darsi held the drawing closer to the light emanating from his desk lamp. 'If he is responsible for a violent crime, isn't this a matter for the police?'

'No.'

There was almost no way for me to tell the truth without coming off like a delusional female. When I was going through a phase of watching grotesque and disturbing horror movies every night, not long after I'd first moved into my old flat and was trying to force my body into feeling a genuine human emotion again, I'd watched something called *Rosemary's Baby*.

It scared me more than most of the others. I wasn't scared

195

of the supernatural but I was scared of the people. I was scared by the way a female was never to be believed; called hysterical, insane, delusional, dangerous; locked-up, medicated. . . It was my worst nightmare. I had dreams about it for weeks. In those dreams something faceless was trying to kill me and when I protested a police officer locked me in a cell, in the dark, for the thing to find me.

I began talking, deciding that I had to, whether I came to regret it or not. 'A couple of years ago some guys killed my whole family while I was out. When I was in a Relatives' Room waiting for. . . whatever, just waiting. . . a man came in and questioned me alone. He asked me if I'd seen anything and if I knew anyone who'd witnessed anything. But it wasn't normal. It might *sound* normal, OK, but it wasn't, it was bad. It was like I was being threatened. So I said I didn't know anything and he left. It was that guy, right there, Kenneth Gordon. DCI. Except he didn't introduce himself as that when he came to question me. He didn't introduce himself at all.'

Darsi stared at the drawing.

'Um. . .' He shook his head. 'Sorry, this is a lot to take in.'

'I know, I'm sorry and I know this sounds like I might be making things up or that I'm hysterical or something but I promise you I'm not. This actually happened and that's why I need to know who he is and—'

'It's a very serious accusation.'

'I know. That's why I can't go to the police.' I paused and added an embellishment to reassure him. 'At least not right away.'

He took his glasses off and rubbed his eyes. 'What do you believe will be the result of you asking me about him? I have heard of. . . I've come across him, yes. But what would you want me to do about it?'

I didn't have a lie for that one.

'You're the only person I know remotely connected to the police and. . . I guess I just wanted to talk to someone about it who knows him, that's all.' I hated that I felt stupid, even though I knew I was in the right. 'Also, not long after my parents and sister. . . another boy was killed. He was the only one who saw the guys who did it, and he was killed by a kid who's in a juvenile detention centre who *I know* was working on someone else's orders, someone who's promised him some sort of compensation if he keeps quiet.'

Darsi observed the drawing again.

I looked away. 'You don't believe me, do you?'

He put his glasses back on, took them off, rubbed his eyes again, put them back on. 'I'm not sure what to believe. Do you have evidence for this?'

'Well, it's happened to me, isn't that enough evidence?'

'No, unfortunately, not in a court of law. That *it's happened* won't be enough.' He seemed to rue the terseness that crept into his voice.

Standing up, he took the drawing with him to his bureau, where he rifled through what looked like old case folders and photos and professional memorabilia.

'Have you seen *Rosemary's Baby*?' I blurted out.

He turned his head. 'Yes?'

'It's like when she goes to the doctor and says, "There are plots against people, aren't there?" But no one believes her even though it's so obvious, and it's just because she's a woman, really. So if a guy came to you and said that this had happened, would you be more likely to believe him?'

He frowned a little.

The guy who made models out of decapitated animals and dolls was starting to think I was sounding crazy.

I trailed off and waved a hand. 'Never mind.'

Bemused, he carried on searching for whatever it was he was searching for, muttering to himself, barely audible to me.

'We were on a team-building exercise a few years ago that I was invited to because. . . I don't know, I hate the things, but I get on with the people there and they wanted me to come,' he said. 'His wife was very sick. She'd been sick for a while, I think. Still is, maybe. This is the man you're talking about?'

The photo that he held out contained a group of men all dressed in camouflage gear, holding paintball guns, striking different macho poses. To the right, smiling next to a non-smiling and squinting Darsi Howiantz, was DCI Kenneth Gordon. Only he had hair then. A comb-over.

A violent urge to throw up punched against my gut from the inside and I had to avert my eyes.

'Fuck, um. . . Fuck, sorry. Yes. Yeah, that's him. Sorry, I'm not sure what I wanted you to do or even if there was anything you could do.'

'Have you considered getting the police to question the boy in the juvenile detention centre?' he asked, sitting back down.

'Well, yes, but he won't talk. Obviously. Someone's going to see him tomorrow but I don't see how that's going to change anything. I think he's been promised money or something and it's probably a lot.'

There was a silence.

Watched by the eyes of the figurines, I sighed, realizing that, even with a name, DCI Kenneth Gordon was so far away, so unconnected, so well protected, that ascertaining his guilt, let alone exacting any sort of revenge, seemed about as likely as bringing my parents or sister back from the ether into which they had disappeared.

My sister would be almost eight now. She'd have grown into her own distinct personality. Already, at such a young age, she'd been talkative. *Bolshy*, someone had said.

It wasn't something I often thought about.

'I believe you,' Darsi said. 'I don't think you're lying. I think you need to be 100 per cent sure of your theory before you take it anywhere else though.'

For the first time since Mark had begun pursuing this job for me, I encountered the thought: What if it wasn't him?

It had to be, now. It had been him for so long in my mind that now it simply had to be.

'I think I might need a drink,' Darsi said, glancing in the direction of what I guessed was his kitchen.

'I'm not sure I should have come, sorry.'

'No, I understand why you did. And I really don't think you're lying, or delusional. And I'm sorry about your family.'

I wondered if he was thinking about sex or what we were doing the last time I was here, but when I met his eyes I saw that he wasn't. He was genuinely sympathetic. I also trusted that he wasn't going to go and tell anyone or have anyone sent after me. But. . .

What if it wasn't him?

'Is there anything you can do?' I asked.

'No,' he said in an apologetic tone. 'Not within the confines

199

of the law and. . . my job. You can't just go investigating a senior colleague.'

'No, I get it.' I nodded. 'Sorry for. . . um, crashing your Sunday.'

I stood up.

So did he.

He took me by the arm and gave me a hug. It took me by surprise. For his skinny frame he had a powerful grasp.

'If you want to come and talk more about it, that's fine,' he said.

He knew I wouldn't.

My face was buried in his chest. 'OK.'

I knew I wouldn't.

I left thinking, What if it wasn't him?

What if it wasn't him?

Chapter Twenty-Five

Everything was bathed in a low green light, in the dream.

I always knew when I was in dreams. As a child I'd even been able to wake myself up from them at will. I used to shut my eyes tight, hiding from the monster searching for me in a deserted supermarket, convince myself I was going to open them to see my darkened room, and more often than not I did.

I never forgot them either. Years later I could recall specific dreams.

Lucid dreaming, they called it.

In the dream, I was following her through the corridors of a house, but the house went on for ever. On each door was a house number: 128, 129, 130, 131, 132. . .

Up stairs, red hair, up more stairs, looking back at me, footsteps coming up behind me—

I started running, after her, away from them.

The men with the *blades like this*.

Up and up, no more doors.

They were going to kill me because I should be dead.

Green light.

A door that I turned into, rattling the handle, but when it flew open there was a five-year-old girl with half a head sitting on the lap of a man with a comb-over, blood running from the open brain on to a hand rubbing a thigh and rubbing a thigh—

I'm here to ask you a few questions, if that's all right with you?

There were pieces of glass under my feet. Pieces of glass embedded in the child's hands.

I wanted to reach out and push the pieces of her head back together, wipe off all the blood and take her with me. I wanted to go back and hear what she had had to say that day when I'd walked out.

Kiki, look!

But I ran, again, and the footsteps getting closer, two pairs of them.

'Go *away*!' I screamed back down the stairs, stumbling, thinking that I was going to die the same way as them, the way I'd been supposed to die. . .

Another door. Locked.

19.

The girl running ahead of me wasn't Seiko, I realized.

Red hair, into a room—

It was Caroline.

Room 25. Inside, breathing hard, shaking, locking the door because there was a key and the footsteps disappeared. I waited, sure that they were going to try and hack their way through, but there was only silence.

Don't die.

I wasn't dying now. Not today.

I turned and she was in my room. Except it wasn't my room; it was my old room, in my parents' house. There was an old pile of art books in the corner. I don't know why I noticed because she was standing in the middle of the room.

Caroline.

This is what made him love.

Green light.

There was a Klimt poster on the wall. I used to Blu-Tack the base down and hide a small bag of weed behind it when I was in England. In Japan I didn't need it.

She was standing in the middle of the room, watching me with those blue eyes, lascivious in their intelligence. Breathing through her slightly parted lips, she smiled a little. She walked towards me before I walked towards her, back and back against the door, where she took my wrists and held them above my head and kissed me and a surge of energy rose in my chest.

I wrenched my hands out of her grip and pushed her back and back on to the bed, running my fingers through her red hair, her body lithe and hard under mine. In the green light she looked like a nymph painted by Waterhouse, pale and firm and heaving with desire.

'Ohhhh. . .'

In the dream, I knew what her voice sounded like. Like a sigh.

In the dream, I tore the pencil skirt off that body, *my* body, pressed my lips against her skin, until she rose up on her knees and put her hand between my legs and *fuck*, I was so wet, and she slid her fingers inside me and there was this weird buzzing sound as she was looking down at me, this weird buzzing sound and this was only a dream. . .

I knew this was only in the dream.

I closed my eyes on her parted lips and red metallic hair falling across her face and her fingers rubbing against my cunt and opened them and Mark's flat was buzzing.

My head was clouded with dreamscape and I got up, half walking and half staggering into the living room to answer the intercom.

'He. . . ahem – hello?'

'Where the fuck have you been?'

It was Alexei's voice, low and urgent.

They must have followed me here from Noel's.

I let them in, because there was no point in trying to keep them out.

Muttering, 'Fuck sake. . .' I walked back through to the bedroom to pull on a T-shirt and skirt, trying to think myself out of still being so visibly flustered and aroused. I straightened the crumpled duvet and took a quick look at myself in the mirror before they knocked at the door.

As I opened it they both shoved their way inside.

'Sure, come in,' I said, closing the door behind them.

'Did you think we wouldn't find you?' Alexei spat at me, pacing with rage. His hair was slicked back, giving his face a rabid canine appearance.

'No, not at all.' My voice was blank and cracked with tiredness. 'But I had to move suddenly and I thought you'd eventually call me anyway. You still owe me a passport after all.'

'Don't. . . get smart with me, you fucking *bitch*! What was all that shit we hear over the recorder? You try to run and hide, yes? We need you to get recorder from Noel's office, you just forget about that?'

'No, I didn't forget. Someone I didn't want to found out where I lived and then I had to move.' I folded my arms, infuriating him with my calm. 'Is this about something else you need me to do or did you just want to give me a telling-off in the middle of the night?'

With a snarl, Alexei whirled around and grabbed me by the throat, dragged me to my knees and screamed into my face, '*Fuck you!* You know I could *kill* you, bitch. I will *rip your fucking head off*! You do what *we* say; you are *mine*! When we do not need you any more I WILL FUCK YOU UP, you *fucking whore*, I'll make you suck my *fucking dick* because *you do what we say*! You *understand*!'

I couldn't breathe.

Jamming my tear-streaked face into his crotch: '*You fucking understand?* I will tell you what to do tomorrow, and *you will fucking listen*! You *understand*?'

Isaak was silent.

'You *fucking* whore.'

Alexei dropped me, threw me to the floor like a mannequin, and then the two of them left.

I hadn't even had the sense to plead for my life, I'd been so taken by surprise.

Shaking, I scrabbled back in the direction of the door to check it was closed and locked, but they wouldn't be coming back tonight. They wouldn't need to. They'd made their point. The longer I sat there trying to stop myself from counting and fighting for breath the more my throat began to hurt, and I stood up on unsteady legs to go and get a glass of water.

I took the glass into the bathroom to wash my face and had to look away from my red and puffy-eyed reflection.

Sitting down on the bed and rocking backwards and forwards, I smoked a cigarette, frantically inhaling the smoke into my lungs as though it was fresh air. One dagger was under my pillow and the other was in the bag of money.

I was going to have to kill them all and that was the moment I decided.

Chapter Twenty-Six

There was a voicemail from Alexei the following morning that I didn't listen to. I changed into my suit and the persona of Detective Naoko Mishima and headed straight out to meet Mark, who was driving us to Feltham once more to talk to Leo. Feeling pessimistic and disheartened, I didn't speak much in the car.

There was a faint ring of bruises around my neck but they were covered by a yellow chiffon scarf that didn't suit me.

'Kenneth Gordon was raised in Kent,' Mark told me, doing the talking for the both of us. 'No children; he has, er. . . sperm count problems. Married for thirty-five years to the same woman, Madeline Gordon, but she was hit by early onset dementia at the age of forty-six. She's fifty-one now and had some in-house care. But a few years ago she had to be moved into a home. It's pretty sad.'

'How do you find all this out?' I asked, unsure whether to feel sympathy for the man I already felt as if I knew, but who might be the wrong man. . .

Sick wife who needs round-the-clock medical attention. And what if it wasn't him?

What if I killed him and it wasn't him?

'I'm trying to find out if he's ever worked as an informant or if he's ever sold info to anyone I know,' Mark said, ignoring my question. 'If he has, it's only a matter of time before I find out. There're only so many people an officer of his rank would talk to. I mean, there're only so many people I know who could *afford* him. Nic would be one, but he uses someone else.'

'Sounds common,' I remarked with a dark smile.

'I'd tell you how common, but you'd never call the police again.'

'I wouldn't anyway.'

'They have their time and place.'

'Do you think Leo will talk to us?'

A pause. 'No. But it's worth a try. Maybe appeal to his conscience if he has one.'

'Do you think he will talk to us if I tell him the truth?'

'Well, there's a time and place for that too.'

Mark left his car in the visitors' parking and walked us through the same doors as last time. The same warden looked me up and down and the same one took us through to the interrogation room while trying to see down my shirt.

'You should try wearing that to work.' Mark snorted as we sat down to wait for Leo. 'Must be the air of professional corporate woman. Look at these guys: they're just *gagging*, no pun intended, to lie down and have some girl walk up and down their backs and whip them.'

My dream about Caroline from the night before sprang to mind and I had to look at the floor. It was unnatural, surely, to find another human being so fascinating when you had never even spoken to them.

'Have you ever met Noel's wife?' I asked as we waited in the tiny claustrophobic room, instantly wishing I hadn't.

To my gratitude, Mark didn't react with scorn. He barely reacted at all.

'Caroline? A few times. Have you?'

'I've only seen her, twice, in passing.' I blushed.

'She's one of the quickest people I've ever met. Fast, serious and extremely, *extremely* appealing. You know what I mean, if you've seen her.'

It was nice of him to indulge me with this trivia. 'Is she nice?'

'Yeah. Wouldn't want to ever get on the wrong side of her, but she's nice.' He glanced at me, and then continued. 'Noel feels overmatched, but then he's right. If life were a Regency costume drama she would have been married off into her own class and they both know it, but that's not how love works, is it?'

I swallowed, unsure as to whether the knowledge was making me feel worse or better.

Mark nudged me. 'You're not the only person who's ever had to look at a marriage from the outside, you know. For a while you're not sure whether you want to replace the other person or become them. But it's not their identity, it's their memories you want. Yeah?'

I exhaled audibly. 'You sound like you have some experience here.'

'Well—'

Footsteps, the door opened, and Leo Ambreen-King entered with a warden holding two cups of tea. I never did get to hear what's Mark's experience was because Leo sat down and glared, and I became choked up and panicked.

The warden loitered for a moment until Mark sipped his tea and said, 'Thanks,' indicating that, yes, he should definitely leave us alone.

'No comment,' Leo said, as soon as the warden had left.

'We haven't yet asked you a question.' Mark sat back in his chair, amiable.

'No. Comment.'

'Who did you call after the last time we spoke to you?'

Eyes to the table. 'No comment.'

'You must have called someone. He tried to kill her.'

It was as if he forgot his script. Leo looked up, stricken, unable to keep his fear from his young eyes. He unfolded his arms, which dropped to his sides.

'What?'

Mark indicated his head at me. 'The man you called, the one who paid you to kill Nate Williams, he tried to have her murdered when you alerted him that two people had come to see you. He knew she was on to him, you see.'

I could hardly believe what Mark was saying.

Leo was gazing at me, open-mouthed.

Mark raised his eyebrows, encouraging me to elaborate.

I took a breath. 'The boy you killed, Nate Williams, he saw the faces of the men who murdered my entire family. He was the only one who did. I know someone paid you to do it, no matter what you say, and I know he was a police officer. He may have given you a false name but he's really called Kenneth Gordon and he has a shit comb-over and you know who I mean, *right*?'

Leo looked between us, face wide, a living exclamation mark. 'Who the fuck are you? You crazy!'

'You fucking *listen* to me!' I snapped, taking the drawing out of my pocket and sliding it across the table at him. '*This* is him, isn't it! He's said he'll sort you out when you leave, with money and a job or whatever shit he's promised you, but he won't. Know why he won't? Because he's a liar. He's a liar and he had you kill a *boy*! This piece of shit tried to have me hacked to death after you spoke to him – now *admit it*! Fucking *admit it*!'

Cringing. 'You ain't police?'

I wanted to climb over the table and punch him in the face, pummel him into the floor. 'Oh, have a gold star! Well fucking done!'

'Look.' Mark stood up, one hand on my shoulder as if to hold me to the ground. 'Let's all just calm down for a moment, OK?'

'I can tell 'em!' Leo glowered, baring his teeth. 'I can tell 'em you ain't the police, *Inspector*.'

I sat down. 'Go on. I bet they'll believe the word of an illiterate child-killer over us.'

'Who the – what the fuck are you asking me?'

'I—'

'Leo, we know you've been promised money from DCI Kenneth Gordon,' Mark interrupted me, which was probably for the best. 'DCI Kenneth Gordon is responsible for the deaths of her parents, her sister, almost her own death. . . after you told him we'd come to see you. We're just asking you to stop lying. He's not going to keep his promises to you. You must know that. What obligation does he have to someone like you? You're nothing. You are nobody to someone like him. His association with you is a piss-stain and you won't ever see him again. You will never see anything of what he's promised you, not one thing. You know that, right, Leo?'

Leo seemed very small suddenly, shrinking down in his chair and shielding himself with his forearms and trying to duck his face beneath the collar of his uniform shirt.

I wondered what kind of life he led in here. Was he the sort of boy who had learnt by way of the cigarette burns down his back that the only way to assert your authority was with increasingly brutal acts of violence? Would he talk to me, take me seriously, if he knew I was capable of hurting him? Because that was the only language he understood?

He must have known that whatever he had been promised was a fantasy, but he probably wanted to believe it, even now. It was the only way his crime could be justified. Without the reward, another kid was dead and he wouldn't even be able to enjoy any benefits from it.

'I don't know what the fuck you talking about,' he said, raising a hand to his mouth and curling it into a fist.

I was still standing.

I put both hands on the table and leant forwards a little, speaking quietly. 'Leo, I'm going to find DCI Kenneth Gordon and bring him to justice with or without your help. You just need to think very carefully about whether you want to be on my good side or my bad side when that happens.'

He looked me up and down.

I was barely blinking. 'If you're on my good side, I have a reward for you that's better than anything that he promised you, because I'm going to reward you with your life. You'll get to leave behind your sorry fucking episode as collaborator with the scum who killed my family, and live whatever piece-of-shit life an *insect* like you can make for yourself.'

My hands were shaking a little and I tried not to let it creep into my voice.

'If you don't tell me the truth right now, and end up on my bad side, I'm going to find DCI Gordon, cut out his insides and *decorate* him with them like a fucking *Christmas tree*, and then. . . one day. . . maybe when you get out of here but maybe before, I'll find you and do exactly the same to you. They won't even know if you're a boy or a girl by the time I'm done with you.' I had moved so far across the table we were almost face to face. 'Now you seem to think you're a pretty good liar, so look at my face. Do you think I'm *fucking* lying?'

Mark didn't say anything else.

Leo stood up, never taking his eyes off me. 'You. . . You fucking crazy. . .'

I kicked the leg of the table and the sudden noise made everyone flinch. 'He *paid* you, Leo! Admit it, he fucking paid you!'

Leo backed away against the wall, turned and started banging on the door of the interrogation room.

'I wanna go back!' he shouted, still looking at me as though I was about to attack him. 'Hey! Oi! I wanna back now! Oi, lemme out!'

I wanted to cross the room, grab him by the back of his collar and smash his face into the closed door until he confirmed to us what we both knew. I wanted to be able to *make* him tell us what we needed to know. I wanted to hurt him so much, with a heavy violent need right in my gut, that it scared me a little.

Taking deep breaths, I forced myself to sit back down, and exchanged a look with Mark.

I am sitting on a mountaintop.

Leo continued hammering on the door with both fists.

I can hear the wind in the trees.

But I wanted to smash his face into the door until there was nothing left.

I couldn't read what Mark might have been thinking.

'Lemme out! Oi! OI! LEMME OUT! FUCKING LET ME OUT!'

Chapter Twenty-Seven

'I don't drink,' I said when Mark offered me a whiskey in his kitchen after driving me back, waving away the bottle on sight.

'You should,' he replied, pouring himself one. 'I think you'd make a fabulous angry drunk.'

'You think I have repressed anger issues?'

'Girl, I *know* you have repressed anger issues. I've seen them in action. In fact, calling them repressed is a bit of an exaggeration. You make a shotgun in the face look repressed.'

His tone was good-natured but he must have been saying it for a reason.

'You think I went too far,' I said, hoisting myself up to sit on the worktop next to the cooker and taking off my jacket, but not the chiffon scarf.

He took a sip of whiskey and thought. 'I think we could have got further by making him feel worthless rather than scared, but you were in the zone. It was a bold move and it could have worked. I wouldn't regret it too much.'

I didn't. I wished I could have gone further. So much further.

'You'd be a natural at my type of work,' Mark said with a wink. 'Don't let that go to your head too much.'

'Can't we just torture it out of him?' I asked, looking him right in the eye. 'I mean, can't *you* just torture it out of him?'

'If he wasn't incarcerated, but—'

'No, not Leo. Gordon.'

It seemed like a simple proposition, but I didn't expect Mark to react with such sensitivity to the idea. He sipped his whiskey and took a breath.

'I wouldn't advise it, no,' he said.

'Why?'

He put his glass down on the work surface and turned to face me. 'Because if I said to you, "Did you kill these people?" you'd say no, wouldn't you? Because you'd know you hadn't.'

'Well. . . yes.'

'Now imagine I kept asking you, with the intention of getting an admission, "Did you kill these people?" and all the while I was flaying pieces of skin off your back. Do you think you'd keep telling me the truth? Or would you just tell me what I wanted to hear, so it would be over and I could just kill you?'

For a second, I tried to imagine him flaying someone alive and wondered if he ever had, but just as quickly I pushed all the mental images away in disgust. Even though he was working for me, even though I heard the little hints and offhand comments, I couldn't picture him actually torturing someone.

My lip curled a little. 'No. No, I guess I'd just tell you what you wanted to hear.'

'You can't torture an admission out of someone. You can torture information out of someone because information is there to be checked and confirmed but otherwise. . . hell, torture him for punishment, Seven, not for an answer. At least then it's fun.' He grinned. 'And more importantly it's worthwhile, of course.'

I tried to estimate the number of people he might have killed and tortured but gave up.

'Are you wondering how many people I've killed?' he asked, eyes sliding sideways at me.

For the first time since I'd met him, I saw something in his face that scared me: a kind of repulsive elation. For a moment, I thought he was the Devil himself. Maybe it was a similar expression that my grandmother had seen in me that had made her feel so uneasy? Well, that and what had happened with the bastard cat. But that had been an accident, obviously. At least I think it had been.

'No.'

'Yeah, you were, but I don't know now. I used to keep count but it reaches a point where you just can't, because it's your day job. Would you keep count of how many papers you delivered or braces you fitted?' He looked at the ceiling. 'I'm pretty sure it's into triple figures though. . . It would have to be, I've been doing this a long time.'

I'd never before been able to guess at his age. His features could be placed at twenty, thirty or even forty, in different lights.

'How long?'

He just smiled at me, and finished his whiskey. 'I'll see if I can get anything else out of the police, see if I can get an informer on the informer. What are you going to do?'

I noticed that he asked this with a pointed look at the chiffon scarf.

Without thinking, I swallowed and it hurt. 'I don't know.

Work. Take my mind off it.'

'If anything weird is going on, or. . . something happens, please call me.'

'Yeah, of course.' I smiled. 'Do you still have that basic info sheet on Gordon?'

'Yeah.'

'Can I have it?'

A knowing expression, and then he went to retrieve it from his bag. 'Yeah.'

It wasn't said out loud but it might as well have been because we both knew what he was thinking, and it was that, once again, I wasn't as good a liar as I thought I was.

In a state of boredom and slight curiosity, I decided to look through the flat when Mark had left, thinking that I might find some clue as to. . . to what, I didn't know. It might have been just any old clue as to *him*. I thought more and more about Darsi's signs and symptoms of the psychopath and tried to work out if Mark was one. Or, more importantly, if I was.

You'd be a natural at my type of work.

There wasn't much lying around. Just the few bits of food in the fridge, some dark men's clothes in the wardrobe, TV, remote controls. . . But what I was really interested in was the locked chest of drawers in the living room. I guessed that Mark must have the keys because I couldn't find them anywhere. I turned the place inside out looking for them until I eventually sat down on the floor in front of the drawers with a packet of biscuits and one of my daggers, furiously inserting it into the locks and attempting to destroy them with brute force.

'Fucking. . . Come on, you bitch!'

I took the dagger out and kicked the piece of furniture. I slid the blade into the small opening between the drawer and the chest and tried to crowbar it open but that didn't work either. I was sweating by the time I threw the dagger to the floor, snapping, 'Fuck!'

Sitting down again, I ate a couple of biscuits while eyeing up the drawers as if they were my mortal enemy. I'd smash them up if it weren't for Mark noticing. It was absurd really. I didn't even know what was in them but suddenly I had to find out. *I had to find out!*

Fuck it, I'd buy him a new chest of drawers if I needed to.

The dagger was too big so I left the flat, knocked on the door of the person living three floors below and borrowed a screwdriver. There was no one in the flat directly below, which made me wonder if Mark owned that too, for convenience.

I returned with the screwdriver, inserted it into the lock and slammed the palm of my hand into the handle. It jammed. I wrenched it from one side to the other, moving my feet into a fighting stance.

Another twenty minutes and something moved.

Strands of my hair were stuck to my face.

'Yes! Yes. . . Come on!'

I dropped the screwdriver and wrenched open the top drawer.

Nothing.

Just DVDs.

I collapsed to the floor, feeling as if I'd just swum a mile. This was crazy. If I could have looked at myself I'd think this was fucking crazy.

Just DVDs.

Struggling to my feet, I looked again. The DVDs were all blank but for dates written across the front in green marker. But there weren't *just* DVDs, I realized; there were camcorder videos too. Everything was dated. The earliest was from the early 2000s.

I took a handful of the DVDs from a year ago and put one into the DVD player attached to the colossal widescreen TV.

I sat cross-legged on the floor with the remote and pressed Play.

Maybe they were sex tapes?

There was a shot of a darkened ground, maybe stone, maybe metal. It was hard to tell for the dust. The space was windowless and airless and I could see a foot that was maybe Mark's; then the camera was set upon a flat surface facing outwards. Mark grinned into it, adjusted the light and said something inaudible before the sound was turned on.

Mark backed away and revealed the rest of the tabletop and a man, naked as far as I could tell, seated, tied to a chair at the end of it. He looked much the same as any other man, without clothes or any identifying features or items. It was just a man, a man with longish brown hair, stubble, eyes wide with terror and breathing through his teeth, saying what I guessed might have been, 'Please!' in Russian. His voice was high-pitched and nasal with fear.

There were no windows, no natural light, just a harsh flare coming from somewhere off screen.

I looked down at the date on the cover in my lap.

'09/01/10'.

Mark was saying something in Russian, his arms folded. He made a slight indication to the camera and waved. The man's eyes followed him and for a second looked directly at me.

A brisk shout and Mark punched him in the face; he took his chin, forced his eyes back upwards, towards the face of the person the man knew was going to be his killer. He pleaded for his life again, I assumed, or denied whatever it was Mark thought he had done.

But torture wasn't done for an admission; it was done as a punishment. . .

Mark took off his shirt, revealing a chest and torso of tattoos, arms of tattoos. . . He wrenched the man's head back by his hair, pointed into the camera again and he had the same smile on his face: the one that had frightened me earlier. He punched the man in the face again, and again. When a tooth came loose he pulled it out and held it up to the camera while the man spat blood down his chest.

Something in Russian again, something gleeful and animated.

I'd only ever seen Mark talk. I'd never imagined this, even when he'd told me.

There was blood on his hands, on the backs of his hands. He disappeared behind the camera and came back with a knife.

Incoherent wheezing through the broken teeth.

Mark shouting something in Russian and laughing. Pulling the man's head back again and showing him the knife, holding it right in front of his eyes.

I made as if to pause it or switch it off but I didn't. I couldn't. I had to make it to the end.

He dragged the man's head back and forth in short jerking movements, all the while telling him something, screaming it into his ear until he must have said all he had to say, because then he slit his throat.

The jet of crimson partially hit Mark and for a second the man simply hung in mid-air, as his hands clawed at the space in front of him, before sagging down in the chair, head slumping forwards.

Mark looked back towards the camera, knife held upwards by his side, moving in and out of the glare of light.

Everything went black.

He must edit them, I thought. He must actually go back and edit them to some sort of dramatic effect before storing them away, in this place that no one knew he owned. I doubted it would even be in his name.

I took the DVD out and put it back in its case. I didn't feel sick. My response was more external than internal. Inside I felt nothing but my skin was crawling with what felt like electrical current, or burning, as if I was covered in something corrosive like bleach.

Lighting a cigarette, I took out another DVD, one labelled '07/12/08'.

This one was from a handheld camera, maybe a phone. Mark had his arm around the man's throat in front of a mirror. It looked like a public bathroom. Mark looked younger, or at least he had a different haircut.

The man was wearing a suit.

He spoke English.

He said, 'Please. . .'

Mark laughed.

The man said, 'Please!' again. He was English.

'You know I'm going to kill you,' Mark said in a high

sing-song voice, like a nursery rhyme. 'Then I'm going to kill your wife. . . Then I'm going to kill your daughter.'

A shiver went down my spine at the childlike tune.

'No, no! Please!'

Mark slit his throat too.

Had he been lying when he said that he'd lost count? He had kept a record of every single one. I stood up and counted sixty-four DVDs and camcorder videos, and they couldn't be all of them. Maybe he'd lost count because there had been too many before he began filming them? He must have started young. He might have been as young as me, or maybe even younger.

There was no hint of remorse or complication in what he did. In his mind, he saw himself in the right. To him, I could imagine that the rest of the world seemed to be the ones who were doing things wrong.

I put the DVDs back in the drawer and listened to Alexei's voicemail. There was no way to lock the chest of drawers again, but I reckoned it would be a while before Mark felt the need to check on them. And besides, I would be gone by then.

'We will call you from outside the Underground later tonight. You will have the recorder for us then.'

I finished the cigarette and went to bed, but didn't sleep.

Chapter Twenty-Eight

I'd be gone, I decided. Soon. Somehow.

When I went into the Underground that evening I took the bag of money and a change of clothes. I was on edge, not meeting anyone's eyes, sure someone was following me. The daggers were always with me now, concealed upon me under my clothes, in my boots or under my jacket. While I was working – in the sexy school uniform today, I put them in one of the lockers with everything else. None of the other girls looked at me.

Daisy wasn't so easy to mollify.

She stomped into the dressing room behind me and snapped, 'Where the bloody hell have you been?'

I started at the direct address, whirling around. 'Fuck, Daisy. You want to wear a bell or something?'

She frowned. 'Someone's got a stick up their arse. Why are you so jumpy?'

'Nothing, just. . . Nothing.' I pushed the bag even further into the tiny locker and slammed the door, hoping that she wouldn't pay too much attention to it.

She liked to play stupid, Daisy. In fact, she kinda liked it. She liked people thinking she was stupid enough to not understand\the things they spoke about in front of her; it made her feel powerful. One of her favourite expressions to use amongst a group of men, that I guessed was from a TV show or movie that I'd never watched, was, 'Well, I don't know much about the pound sterling. But I do love fluffy kittens.' It was said in a mocking posh voice and they always took her seriously, laughed at her, too dense to realize that she was laughing at them.

Her hair was pulled up into a severe ponytail, making the suspicion on her face even more obvious. 'Where have you been lately?'

'Nowhere. Just taking some time off.'

'I called by your place and you weren't there.'

'I was sleeping over with someone.' I took the key out of the locker and put it in my bra. 'So how's things with you?'

She stared at me. 'You're being really weird, you know that?'

'Sorry, I'm just tired.'

A glance at the locker. 'Well, got a load of Americans in tonight. Love it. Fucking *lunatic* tippers, eh? Monobrow's about too if you wanna go see him or. . . you know, if you wanna go see him. He's in the purple room with some old guys and Coralie.'

'Thanks,' I said, changing into my costume, but keeping the scarf around my neck firmly in place.

She watched me for a moment, waiting for me to say something else, but I didn't so she left. It was so hard lying to her. It made me act as if she was someone I barely even knew.

Walking across the club floor I tried to clear my mind with the music and lights, the chatter and laughs, the drinks and naked skin. I stood to the side of the stage, looking out over the tables and bar. Daisy had added some character to the place in the last week or so by putting skulls everywhere: glittering Damien Hirst skulls and clear glass skulls and Mexican painted skulls and skulls wearing gas masks. I liked it and I guessed Noel and Ronnie approved too.

One of the Irish girls was onstage giving a burlesque show, with blonde pigtails and flaming batons.

Content that everyone seemed occupied, I went upstairs to Noel's office and checked the door. It was unlocked and no one was inside. I retrieved the old recorder from behind the printer, put it down into my underwear and went back downstairs.

It seemed like so long ago now, that time when I'd planted it, when I'd thought I was being so clever.

I considered going into the purple room, one of the four private rooms, to talk to Noel, but I was no match for Coralie and I didn't want to invite the comparison. A quick scan of the crowd told me that Mark wasn't here. It was taking all of my self-control to resist watching the rest of the DVDs and recordings in the chest of drawers, fascinated by the alien side of him that I hadn't yet witnessed.

Smiling, I sat myself down between two Americans who were talking loudly about the CIA. They seemed to like me listening, pouring them drinks. I guessed it must make them feel as if they were educating a child.

After a while, when I saw Coralie appear on the club floor and make her way to the dressing rooms, looking flushed, I got up from my seat and attempted to waylay Noel on his way up to the office.

He appeared in the doorway and for a second our eyes met.

Neither of us said anything, but he took a packet of cigarettes out of his pocket and indicated his head at the fire door, where I couldn't follow him if I wasn't on my break. I gave him a small wave as he stepped outside.

No wedding ring.

Bored of the Americans, I returned to the dressing rooms to put the recorder in my bag, only to find Daisy loitering uncomfortably close to my locker.

'Is something going on with you?'

'No – hell, no. What gave you that idea?' I moved past her to the locker to get my coat, afraid that she would see inside but unable to make a move without drawing attention to it. 'Noel seems quiet. You spoken to him at all?'

'I think it's over, you know, his *marriage* thing.' Her eyes never left my locker as I took out my coat, trying to obscure the bag as much as possible. 'I mean for real, rather than her just leaving again.'

I took out my daggers, sheathed, and put them in my handbag with as much nonchalance as I could muster. The recorder would have to stay where it was.

If Daisy was right and Caroline had gone, then I couldn't help but think it must have been something to do with me. While his wife and I had inhabited separate worlds it must have been easy for Noel to kid himself that what we were doing had nothing to do with his marriage. But after she'd passed me in the corridor something had changed. That look, in the corridor. . . I'd mistaken it for superiority but maybe it wasn't? Maybe it had been a confirmation?

'He's an alcoholic,' Daisy said, taking a file from her own

locker and scraping at her nails. 'He thinks I haven't noticed because it's just him and he always drinks, but he doesn't drink like normal people. He drinks like he doesn't want to live. You must have noticed, right? I mean, you spend more time with him than me.'

'No, I really don't.' I shrugged. 'Alcohol isn't his problem, his *problem* is the problem. Alcohol is just a. . . symptom.'

'And what's his problem then?'

'That he doesn't want to live sometimes.' I tried to minimize the statement. 'That's all.'

'That's not all. Something's going on here with work as well, but he won't tell me what. I've fucking needled him from every bloody which way and he still won't say anything, which means it must be pretty screwed up. Has he said anything to you about it?'

I didn't buy her small talk for a second. This was her method of interrogation.

'Hm, he said he was getting Nic to sort out some stuff for him but he didn't say what.' I figured that she wasn't the only one who could interrogate. 'Has Nic mentioned anything?'

She frowned. 'No. He's been out a lot though. Like, every day and sometimes all night too. I fucking hate his flat on my own at night. I think it's haunted. Mark does too. Sometimes I have this nightmare that something's creeping round the bed with really long fingers.'

I laughed.

She waved a pill box at me. 'Wanna go get a bit fucked? Ronnie's coming.'

I considered it for a moment, but then shook my head. 'No, I think I'll just head home.'

'Where you staying?'

'Kentish Town.'

I smiled, but as I passed her to leave I knew I wasn't fooling her. She leant against the row of lockers and watched me until I was gone.

She knew something.

When I got outside I put my hand in my pocket and it was empty. I didn't think anything of it until I'd called Alexei and dropped the recorder with the driver a couple of streets away. It was then that I checked all my pockets again and I knew for sure that she knew something, because Nic's drawing was gone.

Chapter Twenty-Nine

She'd pickpocketed me! I almost couldn't believe it. The little bitch must have actually pickpocketed me. Or else she had somehow got into the locker, which was a much more worrying prospect.

I couldn't go back and confront her, so I let it go. I had no idea what conclusions she'd draw from it, or whether she'd even correctly identify the sketch as Nic's. But at least it was nothing to do with Noel and the Russians.

A day went by. Two days.

Daisy didn't come into work.

I wanted someone to call me, *anyone*, to tell me something new about DCI Kenneth Gordon. If I was going to disappear, he'd be the person I'd care most about leaving behind. But I didn't have a choice. I sat on the floor at the foot of my bed and drove myself half crazy with thinking, but I didn't have a choice. *I didn't have a choice.* I couldn't leave, not without him, because once I left I'd never be able to come back.

Until now it had seemed a distant obstacle, but the closer this day had come the larger it had risen in front of me and now here I was, a victim of failed perception.

I took out my mobile and called Noel, but hung up before

it started ringing.

Another few minutes of fidgeting with it in my lap and I called him again.

I hung up.

I scrolled through my address book and hovered over 'Mark' but I couldn't tell him. He'd be more loyal to Noel and Ronnie than he was to me. There was only so much I could expect him to do. Daisy wouldn't understand. Too much had happened. She'd tell Noel because it was the right thing to do, because I couldn't. . . Even thinking of Seiko did nothing to calm me. Even if I did find her again, how would I be able to face her after everything I'd done? She'd be able to tell; she'd see that I'd changed. The killing and the lying would have painted something invisible across my features that only she would be able to see.

But I had to leave.

All roads here pointed to dead. I was surrounded by people, suffocating with people, but no one who could help.

Don't die.

Then my phone rang and it wasn't any of them.

My hands started shaking the second I recognized his voice.

I whispered, as though I wasn't alone, 'How did you get my number?'

'You left it, remember? First time you were here.'

'Oh.' I had a vague recollection of Mark leaving some numbers but I hadn't known my mobile had been one of them. 'Um. . . Hi.'

Leo Ambreen-King was also speaking quietly. His phone call sounded public; I could hear the movement and activity going on down the line. 'I get a call out sometimes and. . .

Did you really mean what you said? You can sort me out?'

I could barely stop my words from running into each other. 'Yes! Yes, I will. I promise. I give you my word.'

'Really? You got that kind of money?'

'Yes, really.'

'I was thinking about what you said. . . and about your parents and stuff. I didn't know it was anything to do with anything like that. I didn't know there was a kid involved, I mean a little kid. . . I wouldn't have done it I'd known it was some shit like that.'

'I believe you.'

'And I'm really sorry about your family and. . . stuff.'

'Thanks.'

'And you promise you'll sort me out?'

'I promise. You have my number. I promise!'

He lowered his voice even more, so that it was almost hard for me to hear him. 'That picture you showed me was this guy who. . . I thought he was police. He talked like police. *You* didn't. He, er. . . found me through a mate who said I could do some work for him and he offered me a load of nice shit, money, a flat. . . It's not like I had a future where I was, it wasn't like I was gonna go to college or any of that, so I thought. . . I thought he would sort me out, so he asked me to shoot this kid who I didn't even know and he told me this kid was a thief and that this kid had done some real bad things so. . . I did it. I didn't ask him what this kid had done, really. He wouldn't have told me anyway.'

My eyes had filled with tears. I couldn't speak.

'There was something else though,' Leo said, talking faster and faster, as if he had been waiting to say this for years. 'He thought for a little bit that I was gonna have to kill someone else, just one more person, this older guy. Like. . . twenty or something. But in the end I didn't have to; he never asked, and then I was nicked so it didn't make a difference anyway.'

Jensen McNamara, I thought. I wondered if it was my lies that had saved his life.

'Why. . .? Why did you phone to tell me this?' I asked, biting my lip in an effort to control myself.

'I thought. . . Well, it was what your mate said, your partner or whatever. I thought, he's not gonna do anything he promised, is he? He's not gonna sort me out. Someone like me doesn't mean shit to someone like him.' He sighed. 'You guys really shit me up, but you're real people and everything you told me kinda made sense. You ain't one of *them*.'

I forced the words out around the lump in my throat. '. . . Thank you.'

'And. . . the kid that I. . .'

'Nate Williams.'

'Yeah.' His voice became strained. 'Look, I didn't just do it cos I was offered money or whatever. He told me this kid, Nate Williams, had done real bad things. I thought. . . I was doing in some criminal, you know. I'm not a bad person, I swear I ain't.'

'It's OK, I know.' It was all I could offer him. 'Thank you, Leo. Thank you so much for calling me, I can't even say how much it means. . .'

'That's fine. I gotta go, but I'm gonna call again.'

'Right, OK. Leo, thanks—'

The line went dead and I pressed the phone against my forehead.

233

'I was right.' I banged the phone against my skull and started laughing as I repeated the words over and over again. 'I was *right*.'

By the time Alexei called and told me they were picking me up for a drive-by, I felt calmer. I'd been psyching myself up for that call at least.

I wouldn't need both until the evening, but one dagger was strapped between my shoulder blades underneath my jumper with my homemade harness. I knew almost exactly what I was going to do. If my plan didn't work, I wouldn't live to regret it anyway. They'd made their stance on doing away with me and taking back my indulgent share of the money pretty clear when Alexei had been shaking me by my throat.

This time I sat in the middle of the car, wedged between Alexei and Isaak, while the driver wore sunglasses in the front, even though it wasn't sunny enough to warrant them.

I memorized the name of the street we stopped on.

'Over there.' Alexei pointed in a vague direction, towards some semi-detached houses.

'Who lives there?'

'Neville Hallam. We heard him being discussed on your recorder.'

I recognized the name, but only a little. 'And?'

'There is a back door through that gate, where the cat is. But you think you can simply walk through the front, yes?'

I gave Alexei the most scornful of glances after I'd managed to identify which house he was talking about. 'Well he's a man, so *I* can, yes. You can't. You won't be able to come in with me, you'll attract too much attention. It's a nice idea, but you know it can't actually work, right?'

'You will make it work.'

'Alexei.'

The driver's voice from the front surprised me. It was firmer than usual, a definite slap-down, and Alexei reddened.

'She is right,' the driver said. 'We have no reason to deviate from the strategy that worked last time, least of all for your need to control. What do you think she will do, Alexei? She will not be armed sufficiently to restrain the family and then turn on you.'

His English wasn't as good as Isaak's but better than Alexei's.

It irked me being discussed in the third person but that wasn't what prompted me to speak.

'The family?' I repeated, looking at the house with the cat rolling around on the driveway and the neat row of plants and the bicycle tracks down the front lawn.

'Two children: the daughter is a toddler and the boy a teenager. The older boy may not be there but the mother will be.' Isaak's expression didn't change for a moment when he talked about children, but I saw Alexei purse his lips a little.

My theory about him having a family of his own was confirmed, which meant that he had something to lose. I wished that I knew enough to attack him through them rather than attacking him directly. It would be easier. It made me think of Mark's terrifying sing-song voice. . .

'And what do you expect me do with them?' I snapped.

'Whatever you need to do.'

I looked between them. 'Seriously?'

235

'Think of it as a test of loyalty,' Isaak said, his hollow white cheeks appearing even more sunken than usual.

'What, killing a kid? A two-year-old!'

'We never said you'd *have* to kill them,' Alexei chimed in. 'Just that you will have to deal with them. They will be there.'

Isaak got something out of his pocket and held it near my face.

It was a passport. The excitement leapt into my face before I remembered to remain stoic.

'If all goes well,' he said, enunciating every word, 'you get to take this home.'

Out of the corner of my eye, I saw the driver nod.

I thought back to what had happened with Issa and felt the colour drain from my face. I doubted I'd be able to talk my way into the house with the promise of sex as I had last time. I could talk my way past any man, but not a woman.

'OK, what time do you want to do it?' I asked the driver.

'Nine.' Alexei glared at me for having addressed someone else.

'Do you know how hard it's going to be, getting into a *family* house at night? They won't just let anyone in, you know. They have children.'

'Are you saying you will not be of any help?' he sneered.

'No.' I sighed. 'No, I'm not saying that. It's just going to be harder than last time, that's all.'

I searched for Nic's car but couldn't find it. He may have been parked nearer the house. I knew he had a silver Audi from all the times I'd seen him pick Daisy up, but maybe he wouldn't be using his personal car for a stakeout?

'Fine.' Alexei sat up straighter, trying to brush past the

driver's putdown. 'We will go in, but after you have taken care of Neville Hallam and the. . . others. We will give you some time to do what you need to do, then we will enter through the back door, where you will let us in out of view of the road.'

'OK, fine. Permission to bring my bag, like last time?' I looked down and noticed that Alexei had a white band of skin around his ring finger, where he had removed a wedding ring.

'We will search you, so do not think of trying anything clever. All weapons are to be kept in the bag until you are inside. No guns.'

'That's ridiculous, even the pathetic thing you gave me with one round in it will be better than *no* gun!'

The driver raised his hand. 'The Derringer is fine.'

For a moment I thought Alexei was going to cry. He sank a little lower in his seat and was silent, chewing his gum furiously. I guessed they might have had an argument amongst themselves before coming to pick me up. The atmosphere between the three of them was simmering and it didn't seem to be anything to do with me.

Isaak put my passport back in his pocket.

The driver started the car and reversed out of our space, turning around a little way down the road.

I stayed as low as I could, out of sight of the windows, but I hadn't seen any sign of Nic. I just hoped he hadn't seen any sign of me.

Chapter Thirty

I typed the name of the street into the GPS on my phone and caught the underground from Mark's flat when the Russians had left me alone. It took me about forty-five minutes to get there and during the entire journey I was praying: Let Nic be there. It all depended on being able to find Nic. If I couldn't find him then I was severely lacking any sort of back-up plan.

It took me a while to find the house; the houses on suburban roads like this were all too similar. But the cat was still wandering about the driveway and the lawn still had tyre tracks across it.

I stopped outside Neville Hallam's house and couldn't see any sign of a silver Audi parked in the road. Crouching down to pet the cat, I tried to spot Nic in the front windows of any of the surrounding cars.

The little black and white ball of fluff wound itself around my fingers.

'Come on, where the fuck are you?'

I stood up and carried on down the street, in the opposite direction to where we had parked earlier, and that was when I saw it. Nic wasn't parked in the road. A silver Audi was parked in someone else's driveway, almost obscured from view by a garden hedge, but not quite.

Taking a deep breath, I made my way over, rehearsing my story.

I'd gone through all the questions he was likely to ask me and I had an answer for them all. But still, there was no way of being certain.

I knew he must have already spotted me when I'd paused outside Neville Hallam's house. When I was close enough to see the shadow of a figure through the windscreen I gave him a small wave. When I was close enough to see his face Nic got out of the car, looking left and right down the road. He was wearing dark jeans and a hoodie that didn't suit him. He also looked as though he hadn't slept properly for days.

'Er. . . what are you doing here?' he said, not bothering to conceal his annoyance or surprise.

'I need to talk to you. It's urgent.'

Standing behind his open door, guarded. 'How did you know I was here?'

'Noel told me.'

'Why would he tell you?'

I blushed, or at least I tried to look as though I was blushing. 'We're pretty close, you know. I don't know if Mark would have mentioned it but. . . Noel tells me things. He said you were watching Neville's house because of what happened last time.'

Nic glanced up and down the road, looking deeply unhappy with the idea of speaking to me about this. 'Look, Seven. . . It is Seven, right? Get in. You'll draw attention.'

I did as he said, and opened the passenger door.

'In the back,' he said, sounding paranoid, probably thinking I'd been followed.

I got into the back seat and Nic did the same, rubbing his eyes. On the floor there were a couple of sandwich wrappers and several empty cans of Red Bull. I picked up a pile of crumpled newspapers from under me and shoved them into the back of the seat in front.

'Thanks for the drawing, by the way,' I said, checking on my phone that I still had a good few hours left to get back to the flat. 'It really helped.'

'Er, you're welcome. What's urgent?'

I glanced over my shoulder for dramatic effect. 'This house you're watching is going to be robbed tonight.'

His eyes narrowed and I started to sweat.

'OK, you've got to understand that I'm quite surprised here so. . . one, how the fuck do you know about that? And two, how do you know it's gonna be tonight? Also just. . . how the fuck do you know about that?'

I wanted to sit on my hands to stop them from trembling and giving me away, but the best I could do was clench them together tight. 'I was working in the club last night and I heard a group of Russian men, youngish guys, talking about it. They thought no one could understand them because they were all speaking in Russian but I know Russian, I learnt it when my dad said I had to learn another language. I already had an advantage what with speaking two different languages fluently anyway—'

'OK, OK, I get it, you know Russian.' He cut me off, gesturing for me to hurry it up. 'What did they say? Did you get their names?'

'Um, no. Sorry. I think one of them was called Alexei – maybe. They were laughing because they were talking about robbing Noel and Ronnie while in their own club and neither of them would know. But they definitely said it was tomorrow night. . . Well, they said it was going to be tonight.' I was doing my best to come across as young and as nervous as possible. 'I knew you were going to be here because Noel told me you'd be watching.'

Nic stroked the stubble on his chin, unconvinced. 'You and Noel are close?'

I nodded. 'I know he's married and. . . I'm not proud of it but he does talk to me. He talks to me about a lot of things. I know they lost a load of money recently and that it was stolen and someone died.'

'It's OK, I'm not judging you.' Nic pulled a face he must have thought was reassuring. 'I've been there and done the *married* thing and it didn't work out very well for me.'

'You were married?'

'No! *Fuck* no!' He laughed, ruffling his overgrown hair. 'Daisy would crack up if she heard that. . . No, I wasn't married, I, er. . . got involved with this woman and she was married and it was. . . a bit fucked up. So, no, I'm not judging you, don't worry. I'm just asking questions.'

I knew I was thinking about Caroline too much, but she sprang into my mind again unbidden. 'Did her husband find out?'

He might have seen the guilt on my face. That might have been what caused him to share such an intimate detail. I wondered just how much of my shame was visible to the world.

'Yes, he did. I suppose they always do, in the end. Like I said, it was fucked up. . .' For a moment he trailed off, staring ahead into space, but then he shook himself out of it. 'So, why come to me? Why not Noel, if you guys are so close?'

'Of course I couldn't just go to Noel.' I imitated being offended. 'His wife has just left him and he's already turned into a borderline alcoholic over this. I couldn't exactly take this shit to him and stress him out even more. Also, I figured it's not like there's anything he'd be able to do that you wouldn't be doing already.'

Nic ran a hand over his face again and gave himself a small slap, blinking hard. 'Right. OK. . . How many were there in the club? These Russians.'

'Three.' I frowned, picking at my nails. 'Look, I also didn't want Noel to do something stupid and get hurt. That's why I didn't go to him. I don't want them to hurt him.'

He gave me a smile. 'That's fine; I wouldn't have mentioned it myself. Best not to with these things, until they're over. People get stupid and think they can go all maverick. Thanks for telling me.'

'Look, I know he has kids. The guy who lives here, Neville Hallam. . . I wanna go warn them.'

Nic shook his head. 'Absolutely not.'

'But they have to know!'

'You know the saying what they don't know, won't hurt them?'

'That's bullshit! They have *kids* – you can't just let them be oblivious!'

'Nothing is going to happen to their kids, Seven. How shit at my job do you think I am?' He raised his eyebrows at me. 'I'm not just here to look after the money, you know. I'm here to look after them too. If it was a choice between their lives and the money, obviously we'd choose them. You know

Noel, he's not a monster. . . and neither am I.'

I couldn't imagine Nic doing things like Mark, like I'd seen in the videos. But then I hadn't been able to imagine Mark doing them either, until I'd seen it with my own eyes.

'Sorry. I'll go now. That's all I wanted to tell you.' I let myself out of the car and paused, shivering in the open air. 'Um. . . don't tell Noel I was here, if that's OK. He won't like that I didn't tell him and that I came to you. I mean. . . he'd be really pissed.'

'Don't worry. As far as I'm concerned, you weren't here.' Nic smiled at me awkwardly. 'Thanks for this.'

'No problem.' I sighed. 'I want to believe you, about caring about them more than the money, but. . . you're right, I know Noel, and if he really cared about them and their kids more than the money, he'd be looking after it himself, in *his* flat, or at the club or something. He wouldn't have let it go into a family house after the last guy died.'

Nic knew I was right. He couldn't argue with me.

'No harm is going to come to anyone in that house,' he said.

'Right. . .'

I shut the door and walked down the driveway and on to the road, past Neville Hallam's house and back in the direction of the tube station.

When I was far enough away from Nic I stopped and leant against a wall to let myself gasp for breath, overwhelmed with relief. He'd believed me. Thank God, he'd believed me. Nic Caruana wasn't stupid, but he was tired, and there was no reason for him to think I would be lying. I was just a girl, after all. Just a girl.

Chapter Thirty-One

Everything looked different at night. Even though I'd seen the street and the house twice I had trouble finding it from where the driver parked around a far corner. It was a ten-minute walk but it took nearer fifteen I was so disoriented. I knew Nic would see me as soon as I got close and was conscious of every movement: whether I was walking too purposefully, looked too confident or too poised. . . I had to look scared.

I *was* scared.

'You're fine, you're fine, you're fine, you're fine,' I said to myself as I walked. 'You're not going to die. You're not going to die. You're not. You're fine, you're gonna be fine. You're not going to die.'

I glanced in the direction of Nic's car as soon as I recognized the house.

'Fuck. . . You're not going to die. You're *not*.'

I jogged up and across their lawn, not looking in the direction of the silver Audi. I only stopped muttering to myself when I approached their door and, after standing there for a minute or so, rang their doorbell.

Nic would be watching me, wondering what the fuck I was doing.

What the fuck *was* I doing here? How had I got myself into this utter fucking mess? A joke. A joke about a password and now here I was. Well done, I thought. Well fucking done, Seven.

I didn't expect Neville's wife to answer the door, but she did, with the chain on. I smiled at her. I saw the relief that crossed her face at the realization that I was a girl. Just a girl. She had a sweet face, with the sort of warm features a mother should have. Her dirty blonde hair was pulled up into a ponytail.

'Hi, Mrs Hallam, is Mr Hallam in?'

'He's on the phone. Sorry, who are you?'

'It's about work, Mrs Hallam. It's very urgent. I'm Noel Braben's PA.'

'Neville's boss?'

'Yeah.'

She looked over her shoulder back into the house and then back to me, frowning. 'It's nine o'clock.'

'I know. It's really urgent. Not something he could have talked about over the phone.' I shrugged, making myself seem small, harmless. 'I really don't mind if you want me to stay here until he's free.'

'. . . OK. What's your name?'

'Daisy.'

'Daisy. OK, wait here.'

The door shut.

I waited, forcing myself not to look back at the car, nor catch Nic's eyes. Neville would be more likely to recognize Daisy's name than mine. She helped them more with the infamous 'books', after all. Give it a few years and she would probably be running the Underground herself. I took a step back and looked up the front wall of the house, at the bedroom windows. One light was on. Probably the teenager.

If this didn't work we were all going to die, I thought.

The door opened again.

Neville appeared, looked me up and down and said, 'You're not Daisy.'

He wasn't a tall guy but he had a military look about him. Military discharge maybe. Crew cut, couple of tattoos, a silver tooth, sensitive eyes.

'I know, but you have to listen to me.' I put a hand against the door in case he tried to slam it. 'Your house is going to be raided in about ten minutes. You need to get everyone upstairs now and keep them quiet and out of sight, otherwise you're all going to die. You get it?'

I'd confirmed his worst-case scenario. With barely a hint of fear he pushed me off his doorstep so that he could move forwards and look up and down the road.

'Who are you?' he asked. 'Why would Noel send you?'

'Do you really think he'd come himself? Don't worry, I can deal with this, I really can, but I need you to get your family upstairs now! Where's the money?'

'I'm not telling you! Fuck off, you think I can't protect my own family?'

'No.' I ran up to the door and forced it open as he tried to shut it on me. 'No, I don't because I know these people: they will kill all of you. You think they'll spare your kids? Your daughter, how old is she? Two? Well, they'll kill her first just for the hell of it. They *like* that sort of thing.'

'Don't. . .!' He pointed a finger at me. 'Don't talk about my girl like that!'

'Look, Noel sent me because I know how to deal with them, OK? I'm kinda. . . I'm kinda undercover, OK? I might have to take the money and then bring it back but I can get them out of your house without them hurting anyone. I promise.' I glanced over my shoulder. '*Please* hide everyone upstairs. You must have known there was some risk of this happening, right? Look. . .' I jabbed my thumb out into the night. 'Look, I know Nic Caruana is parked right over there and he'll get involved if it comes to it. But if he comes over here it's probably because someone's dead, so let's not encourage that.'

'Caruana?'

I nodded.

He wanted to question me, I could tell. He wanted to ask why a tiny little girl was undercover with people who wanted to kill him. But he didn't, he shouted to his wife and left the door open so I could follow him inside. I stood there rooted to the doormat and leaning against the back of the door, while the inevitable argument ensued in the living room to my left, out of sight.

'Upstairs,' he barked at her. 'Now. Upstairs. Take Courts with you.'

'But. . . Why? Who is *she*?'

'It's *work*. Please just. . . do as I fucking say, OK?'

The little girl started crying.

I ran my hands over my face and willed her to be quiet. I was sure I'd used up all my time already.

There was a poem on the wall, written in embroidery, that looked as though it had been written by an elderly relative: '*If*

I should die before I wake, I pray the Lord my soul to take.'

'Neville.' His wife's voice had become low and sharp.

'Look, Caz, just fucking *go*! This is fucking serious, love! Like, life or death serious. Now get Courtney upstairs and shut her up!'

Neville's wife walked past me on her way to the stairs, red-faced and wishing death on me with her eyes. The girl was still crying.

Neville followed her into the hallway and shouted upwards, 'Tyler! Help your mum now! Now!' He turned to me. 'So exactly what's going to happen here?'

'You're going to hide upstairs and two or maybe three men are going to come through the back door. . . very soon. I'll tell them you're all restrained in one of the bedrooms upstairs. Then we'll take the money and I'll bring it back to Noel tomorrow. Where is the money? . . . It's not in a bedroom, is it?'

'No, it's. . .' He stopped.

I spread my hands. 'You can either tell me now or have someone kill you for the answer when they get in here.'

'I have a gun,' he said. 'Upstairs, in case this happened.'

'Good for you.'

'The money is behind the fireplace in there. It's not a fireplace, there's a panel that comes out.'

I raised my eyebrows. 'Wow, at least you didn't pick somewhere too predictable.'

'If I hear anyone coming up those stairs who doesn't sound as if they have your little bird feet I'll blow them to fuck.'

I nodded, trying to hurry him along. 'OK, OK, right. But *please* stay quiet.'

Finally, he made his way up the stairs. I checked the living room first before walking forwards past the kitchen and into a dusty utility room, with a washing machine and a pile of shoes and an open door to a second toilet.

I rested my hand on the back-door key, hanging out of its lock, and turned it.

There was no bag this time. I hadn't even brought my gun with the single shot, choosing instead to leave it with Alexei, and it was too dangerous to bring my dagger. Being armed was too conspicuous and likely to be more a hindrance to my believability than a help. I couldn't let Nic see that I was armed.

He would be on the move by now, maybe watching from outside, but I had no idea when he'd choose to intervene.

I walked back through to the hallway and sat on the bottom stair, away from any windows. Rocking a little, I tried to stay calm and not visualize every way this could go wrong. But there were so many ways. Too many.

'Fuck,' I muttered to myself as I heard the back door open. 'OK, go.'

Standing up, I met the two of them in the hall. Alexei looked distinctly less pleased to be here than Isaak, whom I had never seen so elated.

'Where is it?' Isaak asked.

'Behind the fireplace.'

'And where are the family?'

'I've tied them up in the bedroom upstairs.'

'Right.'

Isaak started up the stairs and I took his arm. 'Wait! The money's behind the fireplace in there.'

'I know. We are not just here for the money.'

'No. . . Wait!' I pulled him back again, getting shrill. 'They're not even going to see you! I told you, I tied them up, why involve them?'

'Because we don't trust you.' He smiled and pulled his arm out of my grip. 'This isn't just about the money. I want to see if you are as loyal as you always say you are.'

'No, don't! Come on, they're just kids!' I scrambled up the stairs after him. 'Alexei, look! You've got kids, right? You don't have to – Wait! No!'

Someone fired a shot. I guessed it was Neville because the ceiling above my head chipped and I started down the stairs just as Isaak began yelling. Alexei grabbed me by the back of the neck and screamed at me, 'What did you do? What the fuck did you do?'

'He fucking shot me! He. . . Fuck!'

Isaak was running down the stairs when Neville shot him in the back and his chest exploded outwards towards us. His body flopped down on to the banister and juddered the rest of the way down, with his head at an awkward angle and twitching.

Alexei dragged me into the living room, gun out, close to my head.

Neville shouted, 'Get out here, you fucking coward!'

I looked towards the barrel held against my eye and almost threw up.

'You fucking bitch! You *fucking* bitch!'

I was facing the window, waiting to see Neville appear in the doorway. If Alexei didn't shoot me then Neville would, by accident. And where the fuck was Nic?

There was silence outside the room.

Muffled noises of skin scraping carpet, of Isaak slowly dying.

'Come in here or I shoot her!' Alexei snapped. 'I blow her fucking brains out!'

Silence.

Neville said, 'OK. OK.'

'Put your gun down where I see. . . where I can see!' Alexei pulled me backwards, and I could feel his heart pounding against my spine.

Neville dropped his gun to the floor where we could both see it.

Alexei glared at it for a while, breathing into my ear through his teeth. 'OK. Now you come.'

'Promise you won't hurt my family!'

'If you do not come, I kill your whole family!'

I wondered if it hurt to be shot in the head. Was it how it looked in the movies? Instantaneous? Did you feel any pain as it went in? Even for a second, before it hit whatever nerves or cluster of blood vessels were responsible for making you register that kind of thing? Or did you linger, watching out of a useless skull for a few minutes before you went?

Neville appeared in the doorway, hands first, hands in the air.

'Move!' Alexei gestured to his right.

Neville took a few steps to his left. He didn't look scared.

Alexei laughed and pushed me towards Neville.

I turned and froze, waited.

'Now, I kill you!' Alexei said, waiting for a moment as if to let the statement sink into me.

Neville hadn't looked scared. . .

There was a shot, silenced and muffled. Alexei crumpled to the ground clutching his ankle. The gun fell from his hand and I kicked it away instead of picking it up but it didn't matter because I looked to my left and Nic was standing in the living-room doorway with his gun trained on Alexei.

'Fuck! Fuck! FUUUUCK!'

There was blood on Alexei's hands, which I realized was pulsing from his ankle. He writhed, curled into a ball, cursed, spat, started screaming in Russian. . .

Neville ducked past the both of us and tore back up the stairs towards his family, glancing at me with barely concealed rage.

Nic was standing there looking at me, waiting for some kind of reaction and suddenly I remembered what I had to do.

Without exerting much effort, I burst into tears.

'I'm sorry, I. . . I'm sorry, I just had to. . . I had to warn them!' I hid my face in my hands, keeling over slightly. 'I'm sorry. . . I'm sorry!'

'Hey, it's fine.' Nic reached out to me with one hand and touched my shoulder, while keeping the gun on Alexei. 'It's OK.'

'I'm sorry, I didn't mean for this! I. . . I'm sorry.'

'I know, it's OK.'

Looking up at Alexei through my hands, I saw that he had started laughing. He was still holding his ankle, but now he was laughing up at the ceiling, manically, as if he no longer knew we were there.

Nic took his hand off my shoulder and stood over him. 'Who are you working for then?'

Alexei just continued laughing.

'Who are you working for?' Nic asked again.

Alexei didn't stop laughing, but he looked past Nic straight at me.

I thought for a second that he was going to say something, but he didn't.

He fumbled for the gun that he had strapped under a trouser leg and Nic shot him again through the side of the face. It fell out of his palm when he flattened to the red-spattered carpet in a collage of his own brain tissue. It was my gun with one shot that I'd left with him in the car.

Nic shook his head. 'Who the fuck carries a Derringer any more?'

They were both dead.

I stared at Alexei's lifeless body.

They were both dead.

It was over.

Nic reached out and tentatively touched my shoulder again. I didn't expect he was the sort to give out hugs willingly. 'It's OK. Really, it's OK, I know you were only trying to do the right thing. You were only trying to help them. This wasn't your fault.'

I nodded at him, but he was wrong. It was my fault. I'd almost had an entire family killed. I'd killed others. It was no one's fault but mine. For a moment I wanted to tell him all of it but of course I didn't, because there wouldn't be any point now other than to ease my conscience – what little of it remained.

Alexei and Isaak were probably going to end up in an unmarked grave, wherever Nic and Mark hid people once they were dead and had become objects.

I wondered what Alexei's family would think, whether they would ever know what had happened to him.

Nic picked up the Derringer and put it in his pocket.

'One for the collection,' he muttered.

I wanted to ask for it back but I couldn't, so I watched him take my gun away. On my way out I paused by Isaak's body at the bottom of the stairs. Looking back, I saw Nic crouched by Alexei, going through his pockets looking for identification or other clues.

While he had his back to me, I swiftly crouched and took my passport out of Isaak's pocket. With it clutched in my hand like a rosary, I went and sat in Nic's car and had a panic attack hidden behind my hands.

I was alive. I didn't die.

I counted to seven.

Chapter Thirty-Two

I'd kissed her before. In fact, we'd kissed a few times, but it never seemed to change anything between us. Things never got awkward.

One thing I never told Mark about, because I hadn't thought it was relevant at the time and I almost didn't remember it, was the night I went around to Seiko's house. I hadn't planned to. It was late but I hadn't wanted to stay inside.

On my way to the kitchen for a drink I stopped, listened for a moment and then sat down on the stairs. My parents were talking at the kitchen table again, where they always sat for their big and serious adult conversations. But that wasn't why I stopped. I wasn't interested in their conversations. I stopped because I could hear my father crying.

I'd never heard him cry before.

It is one of the deepest forms of betrayal: when you finally witness one of your parents cry. Adults didn't cry, I believed while growing up. I didn't even think adults *could* cry. That was why I forced myself to stop crying by the age of thirteen. It was something to grow out of.

Hearing Dad crying, even though I had no idea what it was over, hurt me as much as if he had slapped me round the face.

'I wish that. . .'

That was all I heard of what Dad said.

'I wish that. . .'

I couldn't quite hear what my mother was saying, so I turned and made my way back upstairs. Feeling unsafe, I packed an overnight bag and left the house without saying goodbye to either of them.

I was too young to make the connection, but shortly after that we moved to London for the last time.

While walking through Toshima-ku I texted Seiko to let her know that I was on my way. I couldn't stay at home with that atmosphere creeping through the rooms, knowing that my father was crying downstairs.

The draping overhead cables that criss-crossed above my head looked like spider webs in the glare of the street-lamps.

Seiko let me in and hugged me, as she always insisted on doing even though I detested hugs.

'Where are your parents?' I asked, following her through to their TV room where she was watching something with Arnold Schwarzenegger in it.

'Having dinner with their work friends in Shibuya. They said they would be back after I'd gone to sleep. What's wrong?'

'Nothing, it was just. . . My dad's really upset about something and it freaked me out a bit.' I sat down beside her on the hard floor in front of the sofa and chairs.

The house was humid. It was the rainy season but I'd managed to get here without being drenched, an umbrella hanging from the crook of my arm.

'You think it's about money?'

'No,' I said, too quickly. 'No. What makes you say that?'

She shrugged.

At fifteen we were too young to know how money worked. To us it was this fantastical thing that had made the parents of kids we knew at school have fights. The father of a boy in the year below us had hung himself last year and everyone said it was over money. There were rumours that it had been written in the note he'd left behind for his wife to find. After that, money had taken on connotations of evil to us. Too much of it or too little of it made people fight and kill themselves. You had to have just the right amount of money or things became bad. At that age I had no concept of the things my older self would do for money.

'No.' I crossed my arms. 'It's not about money. Definitely not. I'd know.'

'I don't think so. Your dad is a good person. My mum says that people who worry too much about money rather than what they can do for others are people who don't care about anything else. She says they only care about themselves. It's a failing of character. Or something. I don't know. . .' She put her arm around me and smiled. 'I'm sure your dad will be fine.'

'Have you ever seen your parents cry?'

'My mum once, after my great-grandmother died. Her mum's mum. But she stopped pretty quickly. She thought it was dis-respectful to a person's life if you sat there and cried about them for too long. I was really young though. I've never seen her cry again.'

I laughed. 'My mum cried for weeks when her mum died. I didn't mind so much. But you know. . . in London everyone cries all the time. Not the men, but the women cry all the time. It's tiring. Isn't there some better way to express yourself?'

'Not everyone can be an artist.'

'I'm not a good artist. Anyone can be a bad artist.'

We watched the movie for a while without saying anything.

I can't remember who touched whom first. We were already touching anyway. Whoever escalated things was irrelevant, because it happened every time. All I remember clearly is my forehead being close to hers, touching hers, and I could see flecks of mascara caught in her eyelashes and the brilliant smudged yellow and green eyeshadow. When I was kissing her I felt nothing outside of me, nothing around us. Just her.

'Kiki,' she said, faces still touching. 'Have you ever done it with a girl?'

I couldn't lie. I had, once before. About a year ago when I'd been too scared to so much as brush skin with Seiko, another girl I didn't know as well, Chiaki, had taught me some things when she'd caught me watching her a little too often. She had pink bits in her hair and was a year older than me and I'd thought she was so cool. It had been easier to learn with someone I cared about less. I looked at it in an almost clinical fashion at the time. These were things that I had to learn in order to be good enough when it came to doing it for real, in a way that meant something.

Chiaki had a boyfriend. I think he probably knew.

I nodded, in answer to Seiko's question, but then I panicked. Would she view it as some kind of betrayal?

But I needn't have worried. She just smiled at me and said, 'I haven't.'

'It's easy, I think.' I snorted with nervous laughter. 'Easier than boys.'

We were kissing again. I held her face. She gripped my hair. I moved my thumb back and forth and round her nipple until it hardened and she made a tiny whimper against me. Breathing heavily, she took both of my hands and pushed me back and down until the back of my head lay upon the ground and she was holding me down with a strength and a need I hadn't expected of her.

Pulling my vest up to my neck, she ran her lips across my stomach and the base of my ribs. Raising herself to press her mouth to mine again, I felt her hand slide along my leg to the inside of my thigh underneath my skirt to between my legs.

I swallowed and shut my eyes as she rubbed me through the fabric of my tights. It wasn't that hot but I was already sweating, small electric pulses shooting up through my abdomen.

'Is this OK?' she asked.

'Yes!'

Writhing against the floor, I grasped her hand and interlinked my fingers through hers, pressing her fingertips and palm against me as I arched my hips a little.

I opened my eyes and Seiko was watching our hands, fascinated. I shut them again and grasped at any part of her body I could reach. I'd touched her before, loads of times, but never like this. Her body felt completely different now that I had total access to it. I'd never noticed how deep the curve was where her waist met her hips before. Her collarbone was sharp. I pushed my fingers into her mouth and she sucked.

When I met her eyes she giggled and blushed.

I started laughing as well, even though I could hardly breathe, almost delirious with arousal. I took my fingers out of her mouth, pulled my skirt up and pushed my hand into my underwear.

Biting her lip, Seiko followed my lead and I started panting at her hand resting on top of mine, bringing me to orgasm—

I was about to cry out when we both heard voices outside the window and then the front door. Pulling my skirt down, we scrambled back into stiff seating positions. By the time her parents came in we were watching the Arnold Schwarzenegger movie without touching, sitting a bit too far away from each other and bit too artificially posed, but they didn't notice. They had no reason to.

The movie was too quiet or maybe my senses were just dulled from the shock.

I was being offered jasmine tea and I came to enough to nod and say thanks.

Seiko was so damn good at acting naturally that, as I looked at her, I wondered whether what had just happened had been some sort of hallucination. But she caught my eyes for a second and I knew that it wasn't.

I stayed in her bed that night, as I did every night I stayed there. It wasn't as if there was anything to suspect, with two girls who had been friends and sleeping in each other's beds since kindergarten.

We didn't really talk about it then, as it was happening. I guess we both felt too inexperienced to articulate the complexity of the things that needed to be said. Looking back, I wish I'd had the guts to say everything to her I'd wanted to.

Chapter Thirty-Three

I had Nic drop me a couple of streets away from Mark's spare flat, so that he wouldn't see where I was living, and walked the rest of the way as if I were in a trance. My mind was blank. There was nothing in me except a concrete thudding of emotion.

I supposed I didn't have much time until someone tried to find me, so I packed as soon as I let myself in. I laid my passport on the bed, away from everything else, so that it didn't get lost amongst my few possessions.

When that was done I made the mistake of laying my head down for a moment, and when I opened my eyes the day's early hours had passed. *Shit*. I got up and rubbed my eyes, touching the strap of my overnight bag. I lifted it and glanced at the door, but put it down again. There was still something I had to do. I stood frozen in the centre of the bedroom and, still blinking sleep out of my eyes, called a number from the landline. I hung up, and then called again.

Seiko answered the phone immediately the second time, in Japanese. I knew it was never far from her hand. The sound of her voice choked me, made me have to sit down on the floor beside my bed and listen instead of talk. I felt as though if I opened my mouth my soul would come rushing out.

'Hello?'

I breathed, but couldn't speak. It was as if I was on the phone to a version of my younger self, peering down a wormhole, back past all the hideous things I'd done.

'Hello?'

She was patient and tenacious, Seiko. It would take her a while to hang up.

'. . . Hello?' she said again, with no trace of frustration.

I was hurting my own face, pressing the phone against it with such ferocity.

There was a long silence.

I panicked suddenly that she might hang up and tried to say something of worth.

But she got there first.

'. . . Kiki?'

My exhale was audible down the line. Addressing me by my name made it harder to say anything back. People had always called me Kiki, here and there: Noel, girls at work, but it had always meant more coming from her.

'Kiki, is that you?'

I breathed, and breathed, and breathed, and spoke.

'How. . . did you know?'

'You're the only person I've ever met who can tolerate silence for that long.'

I felt sick.

'How are you?' she asked.

There was no reproach, no hysteria, no questions, nothing about how I'd not stayed in touch or the years we hadn't spoken and the letters I promised I'd write. My parents would never have been this calm if I hadn't contacted them for this long.

'I'm in London,' I said, biting my lips.

'I thought so. That's not answering my question though. How have you been?'

'I'm. . .' I smiled to myself. 'Honestly, I've been better. I prefer it where you are, you know?'

'You should come and visit more.'

'I would if I could. I'm saving up.'

'Can't your parents come back once in a while? How are they?'

It had been that long. I couldn't believe she hadn't been the first person I'd called after I found them. Maybe I'd felt embarrassed? I wasn't sure. . .

'Um, they were in an accident,' I said, unable to give her anything but the stock story. 'They all were actually. Kinda just me here now.'

There was a pause. Seiko wasn't the type to come out with a knee-jerk condolence. I was grateful, having heard enough perfunctory apologies to last me a lifetime. Why did people do that anyway? It's not as if they'd been the ones to do it.

'How do you feel?' she asked.

I was relieved at the question. 'Nothing yet, I've not even cried over them. Is that weird?'

'I don't think so.'

'I think. . . I miss Dad more. Is *that* weird?'

'It doesn't sound weird to me. I imagine it's what most of us feel, maybe missing one person more than the other, but they just don't say it.' She laughed. 'You never had that problem, with not saying things. They were good people.'

'Mum tried. . . maybe a little bit too hard, but she tried.'

'Are you painting?'

I was tempted to lie. It seemed pathetic that I wasn't painting. A defeat.

'No, I haven't done anything like that in a while. Life has been a bit too. . . real.'

The last time I'd seen her had been the day I left for England for what, although I didn't know it, would be the last time. She didn't come to the airport; I hadn't wanted her to. But then the letters had petered out and then the phone calls and then the emails and then that was it. I had no interest in social media and neither did she. But these were all excuses really, to mask what I really thought: that we had both been glad I'd left. It had saved us both the disappointment and heartache of realizing that Japan was a dead end. There had been nowhere to go, no future that would have satisfied me: pretending to be friends when it had become too painful to even consider wanting to be her friend.

'Have you changed much?'

I assumed she meant physically, but I wanted to say yes, I'd changed a lot. I wasn't anyone she would know or recognize any more.

'No, I'm always going to look fourteen, I think. What about you? You don't sound different. . .'

'I'm not different. I'm never different with you. It's been a long time but I don't think I'll ever forget how to be myself with you.'

'So you're not yourself all the time?'

'Yes, but I'm a different version of myself with everyone. I don't think I have a personality. I think I'm just a reflection of pieces of other people I'm with at the time. Don't you think so?'

I had a long think. 'No. I'm always the same. I don't think I find other people interesting enough to let them affect me so much.'

Seiko giggled.

I couldn't help smiling at the sound.

'Oh, Seven, you're so bad.'

I realized that without her here my sarcasm had lost its humour. With no one to laugh and counter it with optimism, my dissociative and dismissive tendencies had actually become a noticeable part of my personality. I found people more diffi-cult now than I had ever found them. Seiko I had never found difficult.

'Are you seeing. . . anyone?' I didn't bother trying to make it sound like I didn't care.

'Not really. A bit, but. . . No, not really. Are you going to come back?'

My voice became strained. 'I don't know.'

'So you mean no?'

'I mean I don't know.'

'You only say you don't know when you mean no.' A small laugh. 'You would never admit to not knowing anything. But. . . it's OK, if you don't want to come back. I suppose your mind could easily have changed since the last time you emailed. You know, you always said you hated it there. . .'

'I really don't know. I mean. . . I *really* don't know if I'm going to come back. It's complicated, you know.'

She didn't speak for a while.

'Is it because of me?'

I hated myself. 'No! God, no! Of course it's not you. Why would you think I didn't want to see you?'

'Because until now I didn't even think you wanted to *speak* to me.' It was unlike her to snap. 'I'm sorry. It's just been a long time and. . . I thought we would always talk. Even if it was just talking. I love talking to you. I thought we would always talk.'

If I had been there I would have hugged her and stroked her hair. She loved me stroking her hair. It calmed her down and she became still and quiet and I'd never felt closer to anyone than I had to her when I was doing that.

I could feel the tears welling up in my throat. 'I thought that too. . . It's my fault.'

'It's not just your fault.'

'No, it is. You know when you asked if I'd changed? Well, I have. . . quite a lot. I've done some really. . . really terrible things. Really bad. I was so stupid; you wouldn't believe I could be so stupid! I don't think these things would have happened if you were here, you know.' I sniffed. 'I stopped talking because I was ashamed. . . I didn't think you'd like me now. I thought you'd hate this person.'

'I'd never hate you!'

'No, you don't know—'

'What could you have done that's so bad?'

'Oh, Jesus. . .' I snorted. 'How long do you have?'

'I have all day and all night, if you want.'

She meant it too. But I didn't have all night and she could tell from my hesitation.

'It's OK,' she said. 'You don't have to talk for that long.'

'I'd like to. I just can't. I've kinda got to go soon actually.'

266

'OK.'

I love you, I wanted to say. *I love you. I fucking love you.*

'It was really nice to hear your voice,' I said, biting my lip.

'You too. If you. . . If you do come back, please come and see me. Promise me that you'll never come back without seeing me.'

Her voice was small and faraway. I wondered if she was about to cry as well.

'I promise. I wish I could see you. We should video call or something.'

We would never video call. It sounded ridiculous even as I suggested it. We both hated talking to machines too much.

'Bye.'

I held her on the line for a few more seconds. '. . . Bye.'

I didn't have the will to hang up, so she did. I put the phone down beside me on the floor and started to cry a little. That was another reason I'd stopped talking to her: I knew I made her feel as if she wasn't good enough, and I hated that. I hated that *I* wasn't good enough. I hated that I'd become the sort of person who would disappoint her. I hated that I'd never be brave enough to tell her what I wanted, or ask her what she wanted, and every time I spoke to her I knew that any slim chance I'd had to make either of us happy was gone.

And now I had to go and kill a man.

I stood up eventually and slung my bag over my shoulder. Some of my clothes were still here, some things that I couldn't easily carry along with my money and weapons, but every other trace of me, aside from the unlocked chest of drawers, was gone.

With tears still pricking at my eyes, I left.

I wasn't planning ever to come back.

Chapter Thirty-Four

The care home I found, after stashing my bag in my locker at the Underground and napping for a couple of hours on a row of chairs pushed together in the dressing room, looked expensive. Somewhere in there, behind the rows of flowers and over-friendly signs, was Madeline Gordon. I could have gone straight to her husband but some morbid fascination made me stop by.

I couldn't go in; it was unlikely Kenneth Gordon would stop by at the exact time I'd chosen, but I stood for a while outside and eyed up the building anyway. I wasn't sure what early-onset dementia was. I could only assume it was like normal dementia, but one that hit a person younger. Maybe that made it OK? I thought, if she's at a point where she doesn't recognize him anyway, did that make what I was about to do so bad?

Feeling this uneasy wasn't something I'd been prepared for. They didn't have any children. What if, without him, she wouldn't have anyone to visit her? What if the money ran out and she had to be moved elsewhere? She could end up in some shoddy council house with a carer who turned up once a day if she was lucky, a carer who maybe wouldn't really care. . . It wasn't her fault her husband was such a scumbag.

But there weren't any two ways about it. It wasn't as if he'd left any family members of mine left alive to visit me if I ever ended up in a hospital or care home. If anyone should feel guilty about the consequences of his death it should be Kenneth Gordon. He was the one who was responsible for it, after all.

With a newfound resolve, I left the care home and took the underground to the station nearest to Kenneth Gordon's home address. Even though I was resigned to waiting for at least three or four hours, I guessed that I wouldn't have much time. If Nic said anything to Mark about me being at the Hallams' house the night before it wouldn't take a huge leap of deduction for them to put two and two together. Then the walls would start closing in. . .

It took me almost an hour to find the house, which was small, terraced and unassuming. I left it and took a walk around the area until I found a nearby pub, where I sat in the corner with the same drink until four o'clock came and went. In the bag strapped across my chest were my two daggers, a roll of tape and some money. Nothing more. It was all I needed.

I felt sick.

I thought of the last time I'd left my parents' flat and walked to Jensen McNamara's.

I thought of sitting in the Relatives' Room considering killing myself.

And then the man who walked in and asked me questions. . .

Something had always been wrong. I'd known it.

It had taken three years to confirm it, but I'd been right. I'd always known it was he.

Those black fucking lunatic eyes. . .

I almost considered drinking I was so scared, scared to my very bones, but I didn't. I waited until four-thirty and then walked back to Kenneth Gordon's house, where I sat on the kerb with a good view of his door and the road he'd be walking down if he were coming from the tube station.

It took a long time, so long that I thought he wasn't going to appear and that maybe I'd got the wrong house, but he appeared just before six o'clock. I watched, so still I couldn't breathe, until I was sure it was he. People look so different in photos than they do in motion, with their different clothes and walks and heights. But this was he. He was bald, but it was he.

He huffed as he walked, bright red with a dark patch of sweat down the back of his shirt, until he entered his house.

I didn't want to follow him. I could just go get my stuff and go to the airport. I didn't need to think about any of this ever again.

Instead, I stood up and went over to the house. There was a kid on a bike some way down the road but no one close enough to notice me. While standing outside his front door I took one of my daggers from my bag and held it behind my back.

I cleared my mind and rang the doorbell. I hoped, when it came to it, that I'd be able to move, that my nerve wouldn't fail me and leave me rooted to the spot.

Footsteps.

The door opened.

He recognized me instantly but it didn't matter because I kicked him as hard as I could in the balls, making him drop to his knees before I roundhouse-kicked him in the chest and sent him on to his back.

I came inside and shut the door.

By the time I turned around again he had, somehow, managed to overcome the pain and stop grabbing at his crotch long enough to sit up. I went to slam the handle of my dagger into his head but as I swung down he punched me in the face so hard that I lost my footing and fell against the wall. He snarled and launched himself upwards but I turned the dagger round and jabbed it into the top of his arm.

He crumpled again, howling and screaming until a blunt impact to the skull with the dagger's handle almost knocked him out cold. The blow sedated him enough for me to pause for breath and take the tape out of my bag.

My left eye was pounding like a motherfucker and threatening to shut.

I surveyed him. He was rolling from side to side; blood was trickling out of his arm and spreading across his shirt. He was too heavy to drag into another room so I'd have to question him here. It wasn't ideal but it would have to do.

I put on some rubber gloves I found in the kitchen and stood on his chest to tape his mouth, ankles and wrists. I stashed the gloves in my bag, figuring I'd drop them in a bin on the way back to the Underground or the airport.

There wasn't much in the house, I observed as I went from room to room to check for any other occupants. There was a single bed in the bedroom, but with a photo of his wife next to it. I went to pick it up but didn't. It felt disrespectful. She had short curly hair and smiled like someone who was still happy despite having had a difficult life. There were marks of strain all over her face and in her eyes.

I felt guilty and went back downstairs.

Putting the dagger down, I had a go at dragging him into

the kitchen, just because it was the nearest available space, but he was too heavy and I had to drop him.

I sighed and sat across his stomach, giving him a slap. 'Hey!'

There wasn't much response.

I worried that I'd hit him too hard and ran through to the kitchen, only just remembering to turn the tap on and off with a tea towel, to get some water to dash across his face.

That woke him up.

He opened his eyes and focused and rolled around a bit, conscious, so I put the cup and the tea towel back and then stood over him. He became still and glared at me with an intensity that almost made me shudder.

'Right,' I said, unsure now of what I could say to him. 'You know who I am, don't you?'

Slowly, he nodded.

'Obviously I'm going to kill you. You must have got that by now because of the whole. . . tying-you-up-and-having-a-knife thing. So, er. . . just get used to that idea fast, and then I have a proposition for you. Now, I know your arm hurts but it's not that deep; you're not going to bleed to death. But the thing is, if I take that tape off your mouth and you start shouting I'm going to have to knock you out again, and again, and again, and it's going to get way more painful for you. So if I take this tape off, can you save yourself the trouble and just shut the fuck up the first time?'

He didn't protest. I took that as compliance.

I leant down and ripped the tape from his mouth.

Luckily for him, he remained silent, but he was still staring. His stare was corrosive. I wanted to make him stop, but not as much as I wanted to appear in control of this situation.

I knelt down and sat across his stomach again, resting the dagger across my knees.

'A couple of years ago you had some guys with machetes. . . Hell, one of them was probably the same guy you sent to finish me off, right? After Leo called you? Anyway, you sent some guys with machetes to our flat and—'

I stopped. Suddenly, and for the first time in my life, it was hard to talk about it.

Clearing my throat, I made myself carry on. 'You had Sohei Ishida and Helena Ishida and their five-year-old daughter murdered. . . for some reason. And I want to know what that reason was.'

Silence. He was breathing through his nose, bleeding silently, staring silently.

'Look, you're going to die anyway! If you tell me why then I'll kill you really quickly, you'll hardly even notice, which is a fuck-load more than you deserve. But if you don't tell me I'll just torture it out of you and, seriously. . . I have a lot of pent-up anger to vent.'

He just sneered at me, still without any sound, with a slight curl of the lip.

I'd never seen so much hatred in someone's face.

'Was it because of your wife? Something to do with money?'

'Don't talk about her. *Don't!*' he spluttered.

'Oh, what, because it's a *sensitive subject*? Unlike you killing my whole fucking family?' I stood up and stamped on his chest, hard. 'Fuck you! Fuck you! *Fuck*, why did you do it?'

He didn't even stutter. 'Because you're here now, I know that you're fully aware there is nothing you wouldn't do for someone you love. She needed me. Maddie needed me to do what I did. I did it all for her.'

'Then why?' I blinked back the tears. 'Why? Was my dad some fucking gangster? Was it a hit?'

He shook his head. It didn't look like a confirmation; it was more like he couldn't be fucked to talk to me. It was a shake of the head that said, 'Just get it over with.'

'Why, you fucking. . .' I rammed the dagger under his chin. 'TELL ME!'

He sighed, like someone who wasn't remotely scared. 'Oh, just kill me.'

I was about to, but that was what he wanted me to do. He wanted to incense me into killing him quickly.

Hesitating, I leant against the wall instead. 'No. No, I'm not going to *just* kill you.'

'I'm an atheist, so I don't think I have to bank points with anybody by confessing my sins before I die.'

'That's bullshit. What do you have to lose now anyway?'

A smirk. 'Nothing.'

It was spite. He wasn't going to tell me out of spite. He'd enjoy that, I realized.

I looked at the dagger in my hands, then back up at him. 'I'll kill your wife.'

'No, you won't.'

'How do you know?'

'You're not a monster.'

Now it was my turn to smile. 'Of course I am. You made me one.'

A couple of people walked past outside and I stiffened. His eyes followed the sound and for a moment I thought he would cry for help but he didn't.

I brought his attention back to me. 'But I won't kill your wife for nothing. If you tell me why you had my family killed I'll leave Madeline alone. It's not her fault; she's blameless. A bit like my sister was. But if you don't tell me anything then I will kill her. I'm not saying I'll enjoy it, but hey, I won't exactly have anything left to lose either.'

I'd expected this to be more frenzied, but we were both calm. I was getting the impression he might have some grudging respect for me.

'You might kill her anyway. How do I know you haven't already?'

'You know I haven't.'

'You'll torture me whether I tell you what you want to know or not.'

I mulled it over, remembering what Mark had said about torture. 'I'd want to, obviously, but. . . it would be a waste of time. I don't think it would be as fun in reality as what I've thought about in my head. All the same, I bet you wish you'd had me killed when you had the chance.'

He smiled. 'Yeah, I do. . . now you mention it and I'm tied up like a fucking turkey, yeah, yeah I do.'

'So?'

'I knew this was going to happen sometime.'

'What? You knew I was coming?'

'Not you specifically but. . . someone. Someone was always going to do this. I've been expecting it for years. That's what happens if you shaft enough people enough times.' He shifted his weight from side to side, grimacing. 'Obviously, looking around here, you can tell I didn't keep any of the money for myself. It was never about *just* getting

275

money. Care homes, proper ones, don't come cheap.'

I stood totally still, scared of distracting him.

'Your father wasn't a gangster, he just. . . saw something once. He saw something he shouldn't have and he testified against someone he shouldn't have and instead of going into Witness Protection straight away as he was advised, he wanted to simply move country. . . as if it were that simple, as if no one would follow him if it involved buying a plane ticket. But then he did go into Witness Protection eventually, or a protection of sorts.' He looked smug. 'I'm surprised you didn't know.'

There was a deep pain in my chest. 'What did he see?'

'Run-of-the-mill murder. His real mistake was being too stupid to back away from testifying.'

'It's not stupid, it's brave. It's exactly the sort of thing he would have done,' I muttered.

'Would you rather he be brave and dead or a coward and alive?'

I looked away, unable to retort.

'And what. . .?' I took my hand away from my mouth, trying to compose myself. 'You told them where he was? You've done it with other people? Is that what. . .? Do you do that for money? Sell out witnesses in Witness Protection to whoever is looking for them?'

'You'd have done the same thing if you were in my place. I'd be prepared to bet my life that you've fucked over people for much less than your loved one's health, *girl*.' He laughed darkly. 'Not that I have my life to bet any more.'

I didn't even have the excuse that I had fucked over people for someone I loved and cared about. Could he tell? Could he tell just by looking at me and talking to me that even compared to him I was morally fucking bankrupt?

'Who were the people you sold us out to?'

He shrugged as best he could. 'I didn't ask.'

'And you came in to question me.' My lip trembled a little. 'Do you usually do that?'

'No, but I had to check you hadn't seen anything.'

'And Leo. . .'

'Piece of shit.'

'Fuck.' I chewed at one of my nails, getting more and more worked up. 'You're not even sorry, are you?'

'What's the point in being sorry?'

'Because I'm going to kill your wife,' I said.

His eyes widened in the half-second before I swooped down upon him and held his mouth shut, stifling his exclamation.

In the moment when our faces were close I repeated myself in a sing-song voice, 'I'm going to kill your wife.'

I plunged the dagger through his neck. As he died, gurgling, oxygen trying to enter and leave his lungs and meeting nothing but a wall of metal and blood, I kept my face inches from his. I felt his body heave and shake and give out underneath me. I stood up, pulled the blade out and leapt back to avoid the jet of crimson that sprayed the length of his torso.

Then he was gone.

In that moment I kinda understood why Mark liked to film his jobs. I wished that I could have seen my face. He was gone. My family were still gone. I expected to feel something like happiness, but physically I just felt dizzy and ill: a sensation similar to the one I recalled from the only time I'd been drunk. Emotionally, I felt nothing.

I took my dagger into the kitchen and washed it, pulling my dark cardigan over my hands to touch things.

The sun was still up. It wouldn't take long for the corpse to begin to smell and rot.

I tried to think of something cool to say to him on the way out, but the sight of his body made me nauseous so I left in silence. I couldn't even work out if it had been worth it. I wished that Mark were here so I could ask him about it but there was no one left for me to talk to now.

Chapter Thirty-Five

I was on the tube on my way to the Underground when I was struck by a paralyzing thought: I hadn't packed my passport. It wouldn't be at the club in my bag. It would still be on my bed in Mark's flat, where I'd probably fallen asleep on it before I decided to call Seiko and become distracted.

I banged a fist into my leg, resisting the urge to snap, 'Shit!' out loud. How could I have been so fucking stupid? I looked around me at the other passengers, as if they could offer me a solution. But there was only an old Indian woman and a man in paint-stained dungarees. I was going to have to go back.

Muttering to myself under my breath, I stormed out of the carriage at the next stop and changed direction.

I didn't think enough time had passed for anyone to have fully understood what had happened yet, I thought. . . I hoped. It wasn't as if I had a choice in going back, but I wanted to be at an airport that evening and the end of the day was creeping up on me; like a rapist at a deserted train station it was creeping up on me.

It was still uncomfortably hot and beads of sweat were running down my face by the time I reached Mark's building. My phone had rung once: it was Daisy but I ignored it. It rang again and it was Mark but I ignored that too. I took the lift up and, with a deep breath, let myself back in.

There won't be anyone there, I kept telling myself. There won't be anyone waiting for me. I'd just get my passport and—

But there were people waiting for me.

I guess I deserved it: to die because of my own stupidity. I hesitated, with the door half open, and wondered if I could run. But it would only make things worse, so I came further inside and shut the door behind me.

The driver, I recognized. The other man, I didn't.

There was no point in being tense or ready for a fight so I sat down instead. I crossed the room in silence and sat on the sofa with my hands in my lap and my bag on the floor.

I sighed. 'So. . . I guess you're here to tell me off.'

The taller man, the one I didn't know, wasn't exactly handsome. More. . . compelling. He had strangely shaped lips, pale skin and neat dark hair. His suit jacket looked expensive and the heat didn't seem to be affecting him. Everything about him was meticulously placed and I could tell from how he held himself that this was the man in charge.

'Seven,' he said, in a soft Russian accent that wrong-footed me. 'It is *Seven*?'

'Well. . . yeah.'

'I know your full name but if you want to be called Seven then I will address you as such. You have met Mr Yakimov.' He held a hand out to the driver, who was still wearing sunglasses and said nothing.

'Um, yes.' I wasn't sure what he was aiming for with the pleasantries but it was definitely making me feel worse. My insides were knotted and I was finding it hard to sit still.

'Look, if you're going to kill me then you might as well get it over with. I just don't cope very well with suspense and it's been a bit of a weird day.'

Maybe it didn't really matter if I died now? I'd done what I wanted to do; I'd killed the man who'd killed my parents and sister. Did it matter that much if I stayed alive, just existing out of an attachment to routine?

The man indicated for the driver to sit down opposite me, but continued standing.

'Do you know who I am?' he asked, like some celebrity.

'No.' I figured it would be appropriate to know the name of the person killing me. 'Who are you?'

'My name is Roman Katz. Alexei and Isaak, and this good man here, work for me. Well, they did work for me, until you put on your show. It was very clever, you bringing Nic Caruana. What did you tell him to make him help you?'

They both listened with attentive expressions.

I stammered, becoming more and more short of breath. 'Um, well I knew he was watching the house so I. . . I, er. . . went to him and said that I'd overhead some guys talking in the club about raiding a house. I made out that I wanted to warn them. . . so that when he saw me going in he'd think it was just me. So he came in after me.'

Katz smiled at Yakimov. 'It is very clever, yes?'

Yakimov didn't seem quite as amused as his boss. He said something in Russian, sounding irritated.

Katz waved away his protest. 'You are from Japan?'

My leg started jigging up and down. 'Yeah, originally.'

'I love Japan. I went there twice and everyone is so polite and. . . what is the word? Never mind. Everyone is so polite. I like how you bow. I like. . . er. . . hierarchy. I would not get seen by a guard at a train station because I looked like a westerner and the Japanese queue up behind me refusing to be served until I am. Wonderful. And the food is wonderful!'

'I'm glad you enjoyed yourself.'

The more he talked to me as though we were lunch-dating, the more he terrified me. I decided I would not cry in front of him. No matter how scared I was, I would not cry.

'You'd better hurry up,' I said, sitting on my hands. 'If you hang about too long this guy called Mark Chester might walk in and you really don't want to meet him.'

Something in Katz's face changed. 'Mark. . . Chester?'

'Yeah, this is his place.'

'Mark Chester's apartment?'

'One of them, I suppose. I get the impression he has a few. Why? Do you know him?'

Katz glanced at Yakimov. 'Yes, I know him. I don't know this place. I don't know him. . . closely, but I. . . You're living in one of Mark Chester's apartments? Why?'

I was struck by the crazy idea that name-dropping Mark might save my life. 'He was helping me with a job actually, tracking someone down. I just came from there.'

Katz stood up and took a few steps towards me. He looked down and searched my face, and reached down and slowly turned my head to the side. His hands were freezing and his touch like leaves. He ran a finger over my neck, hesitated and then turned my face into the light and examined my swollen eye. He stepped back, smiling.

'Blood,' he said, going back to his position on the arm of

the sofa and eyeing my bag. 'You are quite the mystery, no? Where did you come from?'

'I just killed someone actually.'

'Who?'

'No one you know.'

Another glance was exchanged between the two of them.

'I'm sorry about Alexei and Isaak,' I said, not feeling remorseful at all but thinking it was a tactful thing to say. 'They were going to kill me anyway so. . . I'm sorry, they were probably related to you guys, right?'

'They were related, but not to me.' Katz's expression was disdainful. 'It is only now I find out about you. They were stupid, reckless. They should have seen what was going to happen; they did not think about the consequences.'

Yakimov snapped something in Russian again, gesticulating. Katz raised his voice and stood up to reply and cut him off. I shrank a little lower.

'You have some choices to make, Seven,' Katz said, turning to me again with no trace of anger left in his voice. 'I can shoot you, right now, in the head. . . right there.' He pointed at me, two fingers extended, thumb in the air. 'It will be quick.'

I swallowed. Here it was. 'OK. What's the other option?'

'You bring your money and your. . . fake passport and your clever brain inside that pretty face of yours and you come and work for me.'

Yakimov put his head in his hands.

I watched Katz's face, which remained still, for any sign of a joke. It must be a joke. He was trying to lull me into a false sense of security and then shoot me.

'I'm. . . sorry? What?'

283

'I would like you to come and work for me. One of you would be worth two of Alexei and Isaak, after all. You could think of it as a compensation, you working for me.'

My mouth fell open as I racked my brains for the sinister subtext, but I couldn't find one in his tone or in his demeanour. 'You want me to come and work for you? After all this. . . you're offering me a job?'

'I am offering you *their* jobs. You have a face no one would accuse of anything and you think. . . forgive me, but you think like a man. I mean this as a compliment. Killing you would be of no use to me. I take no delight in killing for fun; this is not a game. I like people with brains working for me and I think you are perfect.'

A slideshow of a new future moved behind my eyes. I had no doubt that Roman Katz was a charming and opportunistic psychopath, like the rest of them, but what did I have to lose really?

'Are you serious?'

'I am never not serious. My wife uses an American way of speaking when she says I have a *sense of humour bypass.*' He chuckled but Yakimov was now glaring at him. 'Her American is far superior to mine.'

'What would you want me to do?'

'Anything I want.' His smile was dead; everything about him looked dead. 'But you would be paid a lot. More than you are now. More than you can expect anywhere else.'

I tried to choose my words carefully for once in my life. 'And what if I say no? Is that not one of my choices?'

'You could say no, but why would you?'

'I'd like to go home.'

'To Japan?'

I nodded.

'It is understandable. Are your parents there? Your boy-friend or something?'

'My parents are dead and. . . But there are people there.'

Katz folded his arms and shrugged. 'OK, so you have a love there. But what would you do? Love does not put food on your table or buy you a nice house. . . nice car. What would you do for a living? The same job you do here? You would dress up that great mind and go take your clothes off for rich men again? Would you be satisfied with that?'

I reddened. 'Maybe not, but the only reason I did all of this was so I could go home, and if I have a choice then I should at least try. Otherwise this would have all been for nothing and I don't think I could live with that. . . assuming you let me live, of course.'

Yakimov sneered at me and said, 'Not if I had my way.'

'*Silence!*' Katz whirled upwards and drew a gun from inside his jacket, jamming it against Yakimov's head and spitting, 'I have heard enough from you with your *insubordination*! Shut the fuck up or I make a third job for someone to fill! You *never* fucking question me again!'

Yakimov had both hands above his head, breathing hard, eyes to the floor. 'I apologize.'

I wished I hadn't chosen to start the debate about going home. It might come across as pushing my luck. I picked at my nails until the atmosphere subsided and Katz put the gun away.

He shrugged. 'If you want to go, you can go. That was a third choice.'

I didn't believe him. 'You wouldn't just let me go. What's the catch?'

'There is no catch, not for me. I just know that you will be back.' He sounded so damn certain as he stood up and handed me a business card. 'When you change your mind, which you will, you will go to this restaurant, ask for a seat in the upstairs bar and ask for a glass of port. Then I will come and see you, and we will talk.'

I took the card and my hand shook. His fingers lingered on mine for a while.

'And you think I'll definitely come back then?' I said, my voice catching in my throat.

'It's what you're good for.' He saw right into me, right through me. 'You know it.'

Chapter Thirty-Six

As I walked I couldn't stop looking behind me, peering inside buildings and through the windows of passing cars, but as far as I could tell no one was following me. Katz had seen something, the same thing that Mark had, the psychopathy that Darsi Howiantz had talked about. It made me feel disgusting inside, that he might have looked into me and seen something cold and unfeeling that he wanted to exploit.

Noel called. I wanted to ignore it but if I ignored it I'd never have another chance to speak to him. I wondered if he already knew everything, or whether I'd be afforded one more conversation untarnished by betrayal and violence and deception.

I answered the phone, halting in the middle of the street and letting groups of tourists walk around me in the dying light.

My passport was in my pocket. I felt broken inside.

'Hey, what are you doing?' He had that voice on, the one he always put on with me when he was tired and horny. 'Come over.'

I hated how much I wanted to see him again; hated how weak it made me. I took the phone away from my ear for a moment to think. There wouldn't be a flight at this time of night anyway. I could either sleep at Noel's or sleep in an airport.

'Hello? Are you there? Seven?'

'Hey, sorry.' I put the phone back to my ear and wiped sweat from my forehead. 'One condition.'

'Anything, my lady.'

I put on such a coquettish voice that I physically cringed. 'You switch your phone off and focus all your attention on me. . . I miss you.'

'Done! Make haste!'

It's what I'm good for. The hand holding my phone dropped to my side with a despondent and audible thump after I hung up. *It's what I'm good for.*

We didn't talk much until the following morning, when Noel seemed happier than I'd seen him in weeks, in his relaxed and sweaty post-sex state. It was only in the heat that the make-up I'd used to cover my black eye had started to run and he suddenly sat up on his elbows and frowned.

'Are you OK, baby? You have a. . . thing?'

I went to touch my eye but it was still tender. 'Oh, it's nothing, I just hit my face on a table.'

'You're the least clumsy person I know.' His expression darkened. 'Did someone hit you?'

'Of course not.' I rolled my eyes. 'Who would hit me?'

'Hm. . .'

The wedding ring was gone. He must have seen me check because he became quiet and took a few seconds to think about his words.

'We're getting divorced,' he said.

I was too surprised to say anything tactful. 'Oh.'

'She hasn't just left, she. . .'

'She really asked for a divorce?'

'No.' He grinned. 'Actually I asked. Thanks for the assumption.'

'Shit, sorry. What changed? I mean. . . you don't have to talk about it if you don't—'

'She made me feel like a child, in every way really. She was smarter than me, more mature. It wasn't even her fault she made me feel like that, it was actually me that was just. . . too insecure to deal with it. I always expected her to come to her senses and leave eventually so, like an idiot, I started trying to give her reasons to.' He snorted. 'I suppose a psychologist would probably say I was trying to feel in control of the situation. I just wanted to feel that, when she left me, it would be for something really shit and horrible I'd done instead of looking at me one day and realizing I'm. . . nowhere near fucking good enough for her.'

I sat up on my elbows also and rubbed his arm.

'But I feel OK,' he said, nodding. 'I didn't ask for a divorce to. . . finally *make* her leave me, I asked because I couldn't keep doing this fucking tragic dance any more. She's here, she's not, she's here, she's not. . . It was rough. . . for both of us. She would never ask though. She's too kind.'

So it wasn't because of me. It wasn't because of what happened going into the lift. That confirmation brought me a little relief.

'What about work?' I asked, lying back down again.

'Oh, Nic called with some good news.' He turned on to his side to face me. 'Some good news. He hasn't got it totally sorted but. . . I don't think we're going to be seeing much trouble any more. He's great, so fucking worth the money. You ever met him?'

'No,' I lied. 'Never. I've seen him pick Daisy up a few times.'

'He's a funny guy. Really. . . weird. Him and Daisy are a really fucking weird couple of people.'

'Yeah, I think Daisy's been to a few too many acid raves in her life.'

He laughed, childlike. 'Remember that time she came running in and said that John Lennon had been shot?'

'Haha, yeah, fuck that was funny. . . And you said—'

'Yeah, I said *that was a long time ago, Daisy*.' He shook his head. 'And then she said it must have been Elton John cos she heard it on the radio, but there was nothing. I still don't know what the fuck she thought she heard, sometimes I think she's just fucking. . . *hallucinating*.'

I let the smile linger and then fade from my face.

'Do you want a coffee?' I asked, glancing at his clock.

It was nine-thirty, at least three hours before Noel liked to get up.

'Yeah, if you're up.' He rolled over and shut his eyes, flushed and oblivious.

I got out of bed and put on my underwear to go and put the kettle on. Then I went into the bathroom and locked the door. Once inside I stood and stopped myself from hyperventilating. It was almost too much to be near him, thinking that at any moment he would get a call or there would be a knock at the door. . . I had slept, but not well. I never slept well any more. That was my punishment.

Shaking myself out, I pushed myself into action and I opened his bathroom cabinet to see a line of pill boxes.

There were mood stabilizers, anti-depressants, contraceptives and sleeping pills. I took out a few more sleeping pills than the recommended dose and took them with me into the kitchen, checking Noel was still in bed. It wouldn't be enough to harm him, just knock him out for a while. He'd probably feel nauseous when he awoke but that was it.

I mashed them up in one of the fancy pestle and mortars that I'd never found any other use for in Noel's overly glamorous kitchen.

When the kettle stopped boiling I mixed them into his coffee, gave it a few minutes to calm down and then brought it back through to the bedroom.

'Hey, you not having anything?' He sat up against the headboard to take the mug from me and instantly gulped down half of it.

'You know I don't drink anything you have.'

'You're so straight-edge.' He raised his eyebrows at me and almost entirely finished the coffee.

I got back into bed, cuddled up to him and waited, tense and watching the clock.

Noel looked down at me and gave me a nudge.

'You're lovely,' he said, with genuine warmth. 'I know you're like super tough and that's what you want people to think of you and everything. But I think you're lovely.'

I hugged him tighter. I couldn't say anything.

You're a piece of shit, I thought, hating myself. You're the worst kind of person.

I lay there for what felt like years, willing him to fall asleep, when he finally put the mug down by the side of the bed and lay down next to me.

'You still tired?' I asked, my voice so quiet it barely rippled the silence.

'Hm. . .' He rubbed his eyes but didn't open them. 'Thought coffee was meant to. . . Hm.'

That was the last thing I heard him say to me.

I waited for ten more minutes before sitting up and out of his embrace.

Tears welled up in my eyes as I turned away and sat on the edge of the bed putting my clothes back on. I checked for the umpteenth time that I still had my passport and stood up. I looked back once, from the bedroom doorway, and he was peaceful. I'd never had to see his fury or his hatred in person. At least the last memory I had would be a good one.

I went into the kitchen and couldn't find any paper so I sat at the table and wrote a letter on the back of a brown A4 envelope.

Dear Noel,

This is a confession.

I wanted you to know that I have betrayed and stolen from you and even killed, and for that I will never forgive myself. I never wanted things to go this far. I hope you can believe that I never ever would have hurt you.

I'm sorry. I couldn't be more sorry.

Seven

Then I started crying, on my own in the middle of his silent and pristine flat. I wanted to go back and look at him, one last time, but I couldn't bring myself to do it. I stood up, hot tears running down my face and into my hands and on to the brown A4 envelope with my confession on it. When I thought I'd finally stopped I just cried some more; the sort of crying that made it hard to breathe or even think, the sort of crying that felt like a coma I was never going to wake up from.

Nothing, not the money or my flight or my passport, could make me feel hope or relief. It wasn't worth it, I realized. It didn't feel worth it now that I'd fucked over one of the only people I knew alive that had cared for me properly; cared for me in a way that was almost pure and untarnished and true.

Hunched over my knees, I sobbed until I felt I didn't have the strength to walk.

But I knew I had to walk so, weak and trembling, I left.

Chapter Thirty-Seven

I left the taxi and crossed the street towards the Underground, my convictions gone. I wanted to hand myself in, give up, but I'd come too far now. I couldn't spend the rest of my life thinking about Noel, because I was going home, because Seiko would know I was thinking about someone else.

The back door was unlocked, which was surprising. I assumed that Daisy had forgotten to lock up properly the night before and let myself in.

I went straight into the dressing rooms and put on one of Coralie's fur-rimmed parkas that she always left overnight. There wasn't any extra cash in the dressing tables; just make-up, make-up remover and pieces of cheap costume jewellery. I took a string of fake pearls, for the hell of it.

My reflection was a state, pale and dishevelled and scared, so I covered the cuts and bruises as best I could with the stupid chiffon scarf and brushed my hair. My eyes were blank. I'd never seen them so clear.

Everything I needed was standing out to me, as if in high definition. My breathing was shallow and fast, but I wasn't trembling any more.

'Move,' I said aloud to myself. 'Money. Get the money.'

I fumbled with the key to my locker and felt for my passport in my pocket for the third time. It was still there. I opened the locker and the bag of money wasn't in it. I slammed the door shut and opened it again, in case it had reappeared. But it hadn't. Of course it hadn't. It was gone.

'Fuck!' I kicked out, starting to panic. *'Fuck!'*

Daisy. It had to have been fucking Daisy. . .

I stormed into the main club and found Daisy's key behind the bar. My throat was aching so I drank some water straight from the tap. The cash float was already in the till and I pocketed that, but it wasn't nearly enough. I wondered if I had the time to try and break into the secure box in Ronnie's office where the profits were dropped.

'So what are you doing?'

I looked up and Daisy was standing the other side of the club floor, in the doorway leading to the stairwell. I should have known. The lights had been turned on and the cash float was in.

My bag was by her feet, just inside the doorway.

Silence.

'. . . You're early,' I said.

'No, it's eleven. I'm late.'

It had taken me longer to leave Noel's than I'd thought.

I shut the till. 'Look, it's not—'

'It's not what it looks like?' She took a step towards me, eyes narrowed.

'No, it is. It is what it looks like but I've got to go, OK?' I walked slowly to the end of the bar with an eye on the bag and then the exit steps.

'No, not OK. Why? Where's Noel? Why do you have the

national *deficit* in your locker and why did you have one of Nic's sketches in your fucking pocket? What's going on?' She took a gun from behind her back and pointed it at me. 'Hey! Stop moving!'

I froze and put both hands up above my head. 'So. . . Nic's letting you carry now?'

'No, hearing someone sneaking around this early I thought we'd been broken into so I took Ron's. What the fuck did you think I was going to do?' She indicated her head at me, with this hard look on her face. 'So, what's going on?'

'Look. . .' My hands dropped to my sides. All I could think about was getting out. 'I did some really stupid things. I'm not proud of it. It makes me feel like shit but I *had* to do them and now. . . if I don't go then they. . . not just them, fucking *everyone*. . . they're going to come after me and I don't have my bag or my wallet or *anything*, OK, I just have that bag! So I came here.'

The gun didn't relax for a second.

'Come on, Daisy,' I said, swallowing. 'We're friends, right? I don't really have many. . . Why would I lie to you?'

'I don't know. What do you mean by. . .?' An expression of realization and horror came over her face. 'It was you. It was you, wasn't it? You were the one setting up these raids, you were. . . *Fuck!* You! Fuck, Noel was even talking to me about suspecting *Ronnie* of being up to something and all the time it was fucking *you*!'

She knew more than I thought. Apparently I wasn't the only person Noel was close to.

'It's not like that!'

'Oh really, well how the fuck was it?'

296

She took a few more steps towards me, until she was pretty close. I didn't know how good a shot she was, but with a boyfriend like Nic Caruana I doubted she was going to miss me from where she was standing.

'How was it, fucking everyone over?' she snapped.

I was shocked by how her reaction, her disappointment, gutted me.

'You don't understand, I didn't have a fucking choice!' I cried. 'You think I was doing it for fun? You think I would have done it if these Russians weren't going to just kill me if I said no? If I said I didn't want to help them any more? What was I *meant* to do, Daisy?'

'You could have told someone, you idiot bitch! You could have told Noel, or Ronnie, or you could have told me! That's how friends fucking *work* – you tell them things! I could have helped you, I could have. . . *Nic* could have done something, or Mark! Isn't that obvious?'

It felt obvious, the way she said it. But none of them could have helped me really, not when it was all my fault, not when I'd been the one to start all of this in a moment of stupid immature opportunism.

I didn't have anything to say.

'I'm. . .'

'If you say you're sorry I'll shoot you.' She shook her head. 'Jesus. . . All this time and Noel was doing his fucking head in, drinking and drinking and it was you. It was fucking *you*. *Fuck!*'

'I fucked up, OK,' I said, spreading my hands. 'If you don't want to hear me say sorry, then that's it. I never wanted to hurt anyone. I never would have hurt Noel or Ron. . . ever.'

297

She ran a hand through her hair and glanced back at the bag. 'You know I've got to tell them, right?'

'Daisy. . . I've got to go.'

'You're not going.'

I looked at the steps. 'I've got to go.'

'Don't be fucking dense.'

I took a step. 'Look—'

'STOP!' she screamed.

I swiped an open bottle of whiskey from the bar and threw it at her.

Daisy fired a shot into the ceiling as she blocked it and it landed at her feet. I knew I wouldn't make it to the door or the bag so I ran for the gun instead, catching her around the waist and sending us both crashing to the floor into the pool of whiskey.

She was much stronger than I'd anticipated and I paid for the misjudgement. My face hit the ground as she grabbed a fistful of my hair and slammed my head down. She stood up, kicked me in the ribs and pointed the gun as I sat up on to my knees, stunned.

'*Bitch*,' she hissed, flicking her hair out of her eyes.

I got up, slowly, having twisted my ankle on the way down.

'Fine,' I said, exhausted and in fresh agony. 'Fine.'

'Fuck, Seven, why? *Why* did you fucking do all this? I mean, this is. . . whack.'

'If you're going to shoot me, Daisy, then go right on ahead.' I sighed, resigned, just waiting for her to call Ronnie and make it all end. 'You know, all I wanted to do was go home. I thought if I did this. . . I could go home. That's why I did everything, OK? That's why I killed people, that's why I did what the Russians told me, that's why I did this for money, that's why. . . I didn't *choose* to work here, you know! It's not like I even wanted to do this and get passed from guy to guy like a fucking second-hand book!'

'Well, I know life hasn't exactly taken you out for fucking dinner and made an honest lady of you but—'

'Yeah, no shit! Come back to me when you've had *everything* taken from you! You lose your whole fucking family and you don't know why, you come and work here where losers come to throw money at you and all the time you *still* don't know why your family were hacked to death by a couple of thugs with machetes! Come back to me and tell me how *unfair* life is when that happens to you!'

I brushed whiskey off the coat.

'Well, go on,' I said, tired of fighting with her, tired of the whole fucking situation. I was starting to feel lightheaded. 'Call Ronnie. I'm right here. It might even be a relief, to be honest.'

'He'll off you, you know. Like, *really* off you.'

Oddly, the knowledge didn't scare me. 'Yep.'

'You stole their money.'

'I know. Believe it or not, that's not even the worst thing I had to do to convince them not to kill me. Like I said, I'm not proud.' I felt sick. 'But I'm alive, or I *was*. I don't even know if that was a better option now but, you know, you just choose to stay alive at the time. It seemed a better idea, or maybe it was just a. . . habit.'

Tears sprang to my eyes.

If I wasn't mistaken Daisy looked glassy-eyed too.

'You know. . . I didn't think anyone would get hurt. . . and so many people have died.' My voice kept breaking. 'And I can't bring them back. And Noel. . . Fuck, I can't even *say* how much I want to make it so this never happened! But it has. . . and it's all my fault. But I just wanted to get out of here. That's all I wanted. I just wanted to go home.'

She sniffed, and slowly lowered the gun.

I wiped my eyes, embarrassed.

'What are you doing?'

'Just. . .' she said, looking at the floor. 'Just fucking go.'

I wasn't sure if I'd misheard her.

'What?'

'Go.'

'But—'

'Seriously, just go.' She crouched and slid the gun across the floor to me. 'Just make it look. . . convincing, and I won't even have to lie that much.'

'What do you mean?'

'I mean, Noel and Ron will *know* I was here, they'll *know* I will have seen you so. . . it can't just look like I told you to scram, can it? If you do this, I'll call an ambulance and then it'll look. . . like this didn't happen.'

I picked up the gun and stared at her. 'You want to. . .? You want me to—'

'Look, don't get overexcited, OK?' She walked away, picked up the bag and slid it across the ground at me. 'Just shoot me somewhere that's not. . . too important. I'm right-handed, if that makes a shred of fucking difference.'

I picked up the bag and slung it over my shoulder.

Daisy raised her eyebrows. 'Get a move on then.'

Glancing at the steps behind me, 'Daisy, I. . .'

'Don't say thank you, it's. . . I don't know why, it doesn't feel *appropriate*.'

I nodded. 'OK.'

'Just get it over and done with.' She shut her eyes tight, her fists clenched by her sides and grimacing. 'Go on! Don't tell me when!'

'OK.'

'If you come back, *I'll* do you in. For real.'

'OK.'

I pointed the gun at her and aimed for an arm, nauseous at the thought of missing my target with her slight and bony frame. She didn't look tough enough to withstand a bullet, with her blonde side-ponytail and little striped dress. It was like shooting a hummingbird.

My body hurt. Everything hurt. I took a breath, keeping both eyes open. I didn't fully understand why she was doing this, but I could question it later.

After a couple more seconds, I shot her.

The bullet clipped her left shoulder.

I didn't see what happened next. I didn't even see her hit the floor because I ran.

Chapter Thirty-Eight

Outside of movies and literature there's no such thing as foreshadowing. When terrible things are about to happen there's no foreboding background music or claps of thunder to let us know to prepare ourselves. Everything remains trivial and routine up until the moment it isn't.

I woke up and found myself staring at a half-finished painting of. . . something. There were bits of a face, amidst all that colour, but I didn't have a feeling of it yet. I was hoping that the longer I worked on it the more familiar it would become until I began to care more about the outcome, instead of just going through the motions.

People were the same. Sometimes I invested the work with a simulation of emotion in the vague hope that I would begin to care about the outcome, but I never did. I went through the motions with people too.

It was nearing midday and I felt drunk on sleep.

I righted myself and pulled on a skirt and vest top to go and get some breakfast.

My sister was watching a cartoon in the living room, with a forgotten copy of *The Very Hungry Caterpillar* in her hands.

In the kitchen I found Mum making coffee.

'Afternoon!' she said, raising her eyebrows. 'Sleep well?'

I didn't know at what age my mother succumbed to stress and stopped being beautiful. Maybe in the last couple of years, when the money ran out and we moved back to England for the last time. She was always tired now. I couldn't see any time in the future where she wouldn't be tired, not when nothing seemed to make her happy.

'Actually no, all I could hear was the real-time episode of EastEnders downstairs. As far as I could tell he was shouting at a girl who was actually called Mercedes. Shouldn't you or Dad bang on the floor or something?' I toasted some bread and yawned. 'Or send an angry note?'

'We don't engage crazy people, darling.'

'Must really suck being so angry all the time.' I buttered my toast and took it back into my bedroom.

'Kiki!' my sister called to me on my way past but I just smiled at her and carried on.

It wasn't so much a bedroom as a glorified cupboard. There was just enough room for my bed and an easel, with newspaper covering the floor. Not much else. Sometimes I fantasized about setting the place on fire, just to make something happen.

My phone buzzed and I picked it up to see a text from a guy who lived just across the estate.

WHAT U DOING? COME OVER.

Romantic.

It wasn't as if there was anything else to do, other than lie here and think or wait for the idiot downstairs to start shouting again.

I took a decadent amount of time over my make-up, brushed my hair and shouted to my mum, 'I'm going out!'

'Kiki, look!'

'Maybe later.' I waved at my sister and smiled. 'I'll come play with you later, OK?'

I didn't even see Mum on the way out, but I passed my father on the stairs, carrying a shopping bag. He gave me a hug and asked me where I was going.

'Oh, nowhere, just a friend's house.'

'OK, sweetheart. Come back for lunch please.'

'I'll only be a couple of hours.'

He looked tired. He wasn't much taller than me and when we hugged I could rest my head on his shoulder.

'I love you, sweetheart.'

'Love you too.'

I don't know why I didn't look back at him as I said it. There is no such thing as foreshadowing. If there were I would have looked back so I could have seen him one last time, or stopped to play with my sister or say a proper goodbye to my mother. But I did none of those things. I just carried on down the stairwell, avoiding the banister.

Outside I could see the Williams boys from a couple of floors down playing football.

I could hear the guy who lived below us doing pull-ups in his hallway.

It was overcast. I almost couldn't be bothered to go. I didn't even really like Jensen that much. For a second I took out my phone and toyed with the idea of sending a text saying I was busy, but figured that two hours of mediocre entertainment would be more interesting than staying at home.

I put my phone back in the pocket of my skirt and as I left the building I walked into the path of a speeding car, which slammed on the brakes as it halted just beside me.

'Hey, are you fucking blind!' I shouted through the windscreen as I stormed away across the road.

I hoped that no one would get out of the car and follow me.

'Don't engage crazy people,' I murmured to myself.

Epilogue

Narita Airport had been quiet – humid and very quiet. I got a bottle of green tea out of the vending machine and waited in the deserted Arrivals area to text Seiko and ask where she was living now. I didn't tell her that I was here, just posed the question. Most of my other numbers had been deleted, and once the text was sent I turned the phone off, planning to buy a new one as soon as possible.

I wanted to step outside and breathe the familiar air but I went straight underground on to the Narita Express instead, settling for watching the brown and green fields pass outside the window. It had been nerve-racking waiting for my bag to appear on the baggage carousel, but it had reached me without any trouble. Now it was nestled between my feet.

I arrived at Ikebukuro and bought myself a rail pass with the money I'd exchanged at the airport, and stepped outside to turn my phone on again. I'd missed the smell of food here. Even the fast food being sold from vendors was better than the majority of food in London.

Everyone dressed better.

No one was looking at me. Not a soul.

I'd forgotten how refreshing it was to be in a place where

you didn't look so different, where you could just blend in without hassle or stares.

Seiko had texted back.

She was living in Kashiwa, which was about fifty minutes away by metro. She also asked me if I was thinking about visiting.

I realized now that she had replied, now that I had somewhere to go, I was losing my nerve. I wasn't sure I wanted to see her again, if I could stand it. What if she was seeing some guy now, whom she was happy with? Who was I to crash that? Was I just going to hang around at the periphery of her life and hope we could recreate something like before?

I moved into the aggressive sunlight and looked up at the buildings, creeping up, layer upon layer of dormant daytime neon. It was so quiet. Even the busiest streets here were so quiet and calm. No wonder we all lived longer.

Not wanting to do anything drastic that day, I caught a train to Toshima-ku and walked around until I found a local guesthouse with a spare room. There were a couple of Italians talking in the front room but I went upstairs and hid myself away behind my wooden screen. I took off my shoes, relishing the feel of my feet on the bamboo floor, and unpacked my sofa bed to sleep.

My phone was off. What was happening in England wasn't my business any more, not my problem.

I slept.

The jet lag must have affected me more than I thought because I didn't wake for over twelve hours. It was nearing six in the morning when I regained consciousness. I blinked and sat up, noticing that I was still in my clothes. I also hadn't dreamed for the first time in weeks.

I sat down next to my bag and did my make-up in a hand-mirror, before dressing in a skirt and Slayer T-shirt to leave.

The streets were quiet. No pavements. I passed a fruit and vegetable market on my left and said good morning to the owner. Toshima-ku looked like a toy village next to any London borough, but I loved it. I'd missed the sense of being lost among these small unnamed streets.

I stopped at a vending machine and got myself a water and halted again at a market stall to buy a savoury doughnut, before entering the station.

On my way over to Kashiwa I had a long time to think about what I wanted to do. But there was no action plan. I think, looking back, all I wanted to do was see. Once I'd seen, I'd know what to do. The obvious path would reveal itself and I'd follow it, but I needed to see her.

I ate the doughnut on the way to Seiko's house and stopped when it came into view. I walked back and forth past it a few times to make sure it was the right flat, in a square white and grey building. When I was certain it was hers I paced to the end of the street and waited, just out of sight, for a while. She would have to leave or go to work at one point.

There were no cars here. No breeze. I shut my eyes and just enjoyed the sensation of the sun on my face and the tranquillity in the air.

I am sitting on a mountaintop.

I could hear the words in Seiko's voice, like the first time she'd taught me.

The nerves in my stomach felt like termites, eating me away.

All I had to do was see her.

Then everything would become clear. . .

It might have been half an hour, not much more, but there was movement down the road. The door opened and a boy came out, wearing a blazer and yellow skinny jeans. He had a thin face and fluffy hair and he paused to hold the door open and the girl that came out after him was Seiko. I could tell, even from a little way away.

She was thinner, as if she exercised now, with shorter hair and sophisticated adult clothes.

The boy kissed her, they talked, she looked at her watch and the two of them walked towards the station, hand in hand. I wished that I could see more of her face, but I could tell from how she was walking that she seemed happy, relaxed, content.

I wasn't sure what I was feeling, but I tried to smile as I watched her go, even though I simultaneously felt like crying.

If she had been alone I still wouldn't have called out.

What I was meant to do had become abundantly clear.

I didn't hate London, I realized as I watched the land-scape pass outside the window. Not as much as I'd thought I hated it. London hadn't spat me out yet. Neither had Tokyo, in fairness, but Tokyo didn't want me; not the me I had become.

At least here I'd have to face it, I'd be forced to think of it every day. I'd see the memories in the buildings and roads and stations and maybe, just maybe, one day, I'd see a familiar face for real and they wouldn't look at me with anything like relief or forgiveness.

I caught a taxi to the outskirts of Chelsea and walked into the restaurant with a name I couldn't pronounce, because the sounds didn't exist in either of my languages. I caught my reflection in the mirror above their bar and I had only a hint of a two-day tan.

I'd paid for the taxi with almost the last of the money I kept for myself. Not that I'd been left with vast amounts in the first place, but most of what I did bring back I put in a bubble-wrap envelope and left inside the door of Madeline Hallam's care home, along with a very precise letter about whom to spend it on. It wasn't as if they'd treat the money suspiciously. To them it would be a simple charitable donation, maybe by one of Mrs Hallam's relatives or a relative of her recently deceased husband.

It wasn't her fault, after all, I'd thought.

I'd only needed the money to get home.

The host met me with the polite but slightly patronizing smile they always save for the parties of one. The surroundings were opulent: all golds and reds. It smelt of spices. There were only a few scattered tables: couples and businessmen taking late lunches.

Don't die.

'Table for one, miss?'

I supposed I didn't look mature enough to be called 'ma'am'.

'No, a seat in the upstairs bar, please. And I'd like a port.'

He looked at me as though I'd slapped him with his own menu and I knew I'd found the right place.

'Are you sure?' he asked, his eyebrows contorting frantically as if they were live animals.

'Yeah, I'll wait here, don't worry.'

'May I ask your name?'

I sat down by the entrance and dropped my bag.

Any remorse I felt was displaced by necessity, as it was every time.

'Tell Roman Katz that Seven is here,' I said, smiling, 'and I want to talk to him about his offer.'

BB 5/14
BW 1/18